THE ONLY SALOON IN TOWN

Center Point
Large Print

Also by Reavis Z. Wortham and available from Center Point Large Print:

The Journey South

THE ONLY SALOON IN TOWN

A Cap Whitlatch Western

Reavis Z. Wortham

CENTER POINT LARGE PRINT
THORNDIKE, MAINE

This Center Point Large Print edition
is published in the year 2025 by arrangement with
Kensington Publishing Corp.

Copyright © 2024 by Reavis Wortham.

All rights reserved.

This book is a work of fiction. Names, characters,
businesses, organizations, places, events, and incidents
either are the product of the author's imagination or are
used fictitiously. Any resemblance to actual persons,
living or dead, events, or locales is entirely coincidental.

The text of this Large Print edition is unabridged.
In other aspects, this book may vary
from the original edition.
Printed in the United States of America
on permanent paper sourced using
environmentally responsible foresting methods.
Set in 16-point Times New Roman type.

ISBN: 979-8-89164-395-6

The Library of Congress has cataloged this record
under Library of Congress Control Number: 2024944858

THE ONLY SALOON IN TOWN

CHAPTER 1

As the sun settled behind the low hills behind them, a band of twenty rough, unwashed men appeared on a rise overlooking the heat-blasted adobe village of Jarilla. Fifty miles north of El Paso and anchored by a water well in a sunblasted courtyard, it was more a gathering of squatty buildings in a sea of sage and creosote scrub than anything else.

The bearded German calling himself Deitrich Pletz was the true definition of a savage with filthy, greasy hair hanging to his shoulders. Dressed in a mix of oft-patched clothes and stained buckskins, the man with no morals grunted a humorless laugh and cut rheumy eyes toward Henry Schaefer. Though he spoke English, his accent was thick with the fatherland he'd left at age fifteen.

"I see a lot of money in zis— cesspool."

Schaefer thumbed the pistol on his belt. "All of 'em?"

"What we can."

"Don't see many men."

"They're like Apaches in this part of the territory. Some cut their hair to their shoulders, so from a distance you can't tell 'em from their women."

Fast to shoot, but sometimes a slow thinker,

Schaefer rubbed his big hooked nose as he considered their comments. His salt-and-pepper beard harbored a number of living critters, and on occasion, one would crawl out on the end of that large protuberance originating from between his eyes and take the sun.

"I can tell up close, though, though it won't make much matter. We'll just sort 'em out when we're finished." Schaefer's eyes narrowed. "I doubt there are many guns."

"A handful, but it wouldn't make any difference if there was." Pletz spat a stream of brown tobacco juice at a skinny dog that sidled away with its head turned, a submissive grin on its lips. He twisted in his saddle to address his pack of wolflike men, brothers to the carnivorous four-legged beasts of the plains. "Don't stop. We keep on riding through, but make a head count."

Twenty men of similar constitution and consideration scattered and drifted down the slope to the village. The inhabitants vanished like smoke at the first sight of the heavily armed riders. Here the hem of a dress fluttered through a door and vanished. There a child's face appeared in an open window before unseen hands yanked them back before closing the wooden shutters.

Chickens squawked and ran from underneath their horses' hooves as the army of mounted men poured down hardpack spaces between buildings and wove around like drifting waters.

They passed the well and a trough full of clear water glistening in a hollowed-out cottonwood log. Needing the water but not inclined to stop, Pletz waved a grime-encrusted hand toward the opposite edge of the village. Blood had dried around his nails, much like the others.

To his right, two middle-aged Mexican men stepped out of a windowless building to watch them pass. Painted letters on the adobe above the door said, CANTINA. A single, twisted mesquite post out front was the only place to tie a mount of any kind. Chewed on top by restless animals, the sides were polished smooth from decades of hands and reins.

The pair watching them pass had hair to their shoulders, piquing Pletz's interest. He absently rested a hand on the butt of a Colt snug in a holster on his right hip. The scratched and scarred stock of a battered Winchester rode in the scabbard on his saddle.

He frowned at the weapons in their hands. One gripped a well-oiled revolver that looked fairly new, and the other cradled a worn but apparently serviceable lever action rifle in his arms. Their presence was an intentional challenge to the men. Though they were vastly outnumbered, the villagers glared at the riders, but neither of them made eye contact with either of the gang's leaders.

Never changing his mount's pace, Pletz rode past them with a nod. The younger of the

Mexicans nodded back, but the one holding the rifle appeared to be counting the men on horseback. These men looked too intelligent and prepared for him, and the gang's leader felt the heat rise in his face.

He hated for people to act smarter than him, or more uppity, like they were better than men who made a living with guns. Maybe they recognized him for who he was, but if not, they sure understood *what* they were, and squaring off with the unknown showed uncommon bravery, or phenomenally stupid cockiness.

Pletz could have gotten a job in some store back east when he first set foot in South Carolina. It would have been a step backward in his mind, working menial jobs back in his hometown of Hamburg. Even as a youngster, he wanted more, and was tough enough to take what he wanted.

He'd honed his moneymaking skills through a variety of schemes and plain robbery, avoiding hunger but living in hovels. The most he'd ever pocketed was when he robbed and murdered a jeweler on his way home one night. The man scuffled and Pletz broke his skinny neck.

After that, he found killing came easy to him, especially for money, and embarked on a months-long spree of murder robberies until the Hamburg police started going house to house in an effort to find the responsible criminal. When they got too close, he bought a ticket to northwest France and located the port of Le Havre, an embarkation port for emigrants from Alsace, Switzerland, and Normandy. He purchased passage to America with blood money, sailing down the Seine River, through the English Channel, and the Rhineland states.

Once in Charleston, it didn't take him long to acquire operating cash. With his experience, all he had to do was find a dark alley and cut a businessman's throat for what was in his pockets. That gave him enough for a room and food. The next night Pletz dragged another well-heeled city man into a different alley and again left a body behind.

For the next week, his coin purse swelled until he had enough money to strike out west. He wanted open spaces, no law, and had a fire in his belly to take other people's money and lives. Blood became his grail and it led to gold in his saddlebags, and even more in a Texas bank in the fast-growing town of Angel Fire.

The bank was essential for someone who lived on horseback but needed a place to store funds until the time came when he could leave such work and go back east to find a more civilized way of life.

He found what he was looking for out there, and especially in small Indian villages, and Mexican settlements like Jarilla where Schaefer stared straight ahead as they passed the cantina, eyes fixed on some unknown object. "They don't look too tough to me."

"Compared to us, nobody's tough." Pletz shifted his chew and scratched at some of the irritating livestock living in his beard. "I ain't much in the mood for working today. I'd like to lay up in the shade for a while and count our wares. What we have needs to dry anyways. They're beginning to smell pretty high and they won't be worth a thin silver dime if they rot. Let's find somewhere to camp for the night."

"And then we'll see what happens?" Schaefer raised an eyebrow.

"Unless we run across some Apache camp in the next couple of miles, you know what'll happen back here at daybreak."

Schaefer's hand went to the razor-sharp butcher knife in his belt. It was a habit he bowed to a dozen times per day. The minute they met at a buffalo camp a hundred miles north, Pletz was impressed by the man's ability to sharpen a knife and the speed in which he could skin a buffalo.

They hadn't gone another hundred yards from the village when Pletz changed his mind and reined up. He turned his horse back toward the little settlement. Facing his men who showed no surprise at the sudden reversal, he grinned, leaned over, and spat.

"Hell, I don't see no reason to wait. We keep seeing Indian sign, and I'd rather sleep back there behind them walls than out on a blanket again tonight. Maybe a thick pallet would feel good."

A sudden energy ran through them all. Pletz felt it and glorified in the feeling he inspired and controlled. These were killers, all. The dregs of uncivilized society and like a pack of cur dogs that would do his bidding or, at the drop of a hat, turn on each other at a moment's weakness, and that included Pletz and Schaefer, two of the most vicious white men to ever ride west of the Mississippi.

The others placed hands on the butts of their pistols and knives, and some drew long guns from their scabbards. Laughter, thick and phlegmy, came from more than one throat and, feeling the change in their riders' demeanor, the horses perked their ears and shuffled their hooves.

Pletz rode back through the pack of renegade killers. "Let's go to work!" He spurred his horse in the flanks and shouted a statement in his native language. *"Es ist Zeit für die Kopfhaut!"*

It didn't matter that his words were unintelligible to the mixed group of killers from many walks of life and races. With a grunt, the roan underneath him dug in and broke into a hard run. Thunder followed behind as he charged back into the village and directly toward the two men who still hadn't moved. Their expressions of concern changed to terrified determination when the guns they held rose. They fired at the same time.

Bullets whizzed at the oncoming charge, and a war whoop erupted from one of the men behind Pletz. One chunk of lead fired by the villagers found flesh. A rider grunted and cursed, and the sound of a falling body followed. Pletz snatched a Colt from a red sash around his waist. It was easier to use at a hard run, and more accurate.

The first bullet missed the man holding the Winchester, but his second shot caught the villager in the side, spinning him around. The rifle flipped into the air, and he fell back against the wall behind them.

A volley of gunshots peppered the man holding the revolver, plucking at his clothing. His face twisted in pain, and he fell and was still. Pletz's horse slid to a stop at the corpse's feet, and he dismounted as smooth as any Texas cowboy bulldogging a calf. Still holding the smoking pistol, Pletz hit the cantina's partially closed door with his shoulder and charged inside.

He paused in the dim light at the sight of a bartender behind the plank counter who raised both hands. "*No, por favor!*"

Because the bartender's chopped black hair came halfway down his neck, Pletz shot him in the chest. He dropped behind the bar with a rattle of bottles and broken glass. The only customer bolted out the back door, and the bloodthirsty German threw a shot in that direction that did nothing more than blast a splinter from the thick doorframe.

"Fast as a rat!"

The rattle of gunfire came from outside, telling him his men were at work. Screams and shouts filled the air as he stuck the now empty revolver back into the sash and drew a second, looking for another target. The room was empty, the silence broken by liquid glugging from a bottle somewhere near where the bartender fell.

He relaxed and stepped around behind the bar, stepped over the body, and reached for a bottle of what he figured was tequila. He pulled the cork and smelled the contents. Smiling at the oily odor of agave, he tilted it and took a long, deep swallow around the chew of tobacco in his cheek. Screams and gunshots registered from the outside.

While he was keeping one cautious eye on the door, a flicker of movement caught his attention. It was then he saw a young woman crouched against a stack of casks and wooden boxes in the corner near where the customer disappeared. Face half-hidden by the young woman's long, blue-black hair.

Pletz tilted his sweat-stained hat back to reveal a pale forehead. "Well, *hello!*"

She held up both hands in fear. The hard lines around her mouth were deep from fear. "*No tengo dinero, pero puedes tomar lo que quieras!*"

Fluent in Spanish, Pletz grinned at the translation in his mind when she said there was no money. "Oh, girl. What you have is money, all right, and I'll take whatever I want with your say-so or not."

The Colt in his hand barked. The slug caught the woman high in the chest, and she collapsed with a look of surprise and a deep sigh. Laying the smoking pistol on the bar, he took another swallow of tequila.

"Damn. That's good."

Gunfire outside rose and fell, devolving into a few scattered shots. He spat out the wad of cotton boll twist and took another long swallow, swishing the oily liquid around the few yellow teeth left in his mouth before spitting it out. A shape appeared in the door, and he snatched up the revolver.

Realizing it was Schaefer, he stuck it back behind the wide strip of red material that held it in place. "One went out the back when I came in."

Schaefer held up a bloody scalp in one hand and a knife in the other. "Probably this one. What're you drinking?"

"Mescal." Pletz thumped the jug down on the wide planks where men had leaned and enjoyed drinks in peace. "Help yourself."

Drawing his own long, skinny knife from behind the sash, the scalphunter came out from behind the bar and leaned down and went to work on the woman. He wrapped her long hair in his fingers and ran the edge of the blade around the crown of her head. With one foot in the middle of her back, he yanked hard and the scalp popped free.

Schaefer pitched his trophy on the bar, picked up the container Pletz sat down, and took a long drink. Scattered gunfire popped for a few more seconds, and then all was quiet.

Pletz rose and held up the long black hair and gave it a shake. "Mexican hair looks just like Apache. Look how thick this is. I might keep this one for myself for a saddle ornament."

"You say that every time, but then get to thinking it's worth a hundred bucks and you change your mind." Schaefer looked over the bar and saw the bartender's body. "You gonna take that one too?"

"It's kinda short."

"You know them Apaches will cut their hair when they're grieving. It'll sell."

"You're right. All they can do is say no to paying for it."

Familiar voices came through the open door. Two rose in argument, and Pletz laid the bartender's scalp beside that of the woman's long locks. He went to the door. "If any of you sonsabitches touch them two there that I killed, I'll stretch your hair on one of my frames. Go finish cleaning up this damned town so we can get some rest tonight and won't have to worry about any you missed."

17

"There's half a dozen kids we did for." The voice belonged to the youngest of the band, Leroy Booth. Once a buffalo soldier, he'd killed his sergeant after an argument and disappeared one night.

Pletz and his men came upon him in a cold camp in a New Mexico arroyo with a pair of Apache scalps lying nearby. When they pressed him for information, Booth said he intended to find somewhere to sell them for the bounty. The young man was ecstatic when he realized he'd fallen in with a group scouring the territory for the same thing.

The plaza was littered with bodies lying still in death. Pletz addressed Booth, who was stuffing fresh cartridges in his pistol. "They already dead, them kids?"

"Sure 'nuff."

"Take 'em."

Booth turned away to finish his work, and Pletz leaned on the doorframe and studied the conquered village now silent except for the screaming of a wounded burro. One of his bearded men cut the animal's throat with a knife, silencing it. Small hooves kicked for a moment before they stilled.

He glanced down at the two men he'd murdered and sighed at the realization that their hair was shorter than what the bartender wore. It would be hard to convince the Texas officials they were

Indian, though some of the Pimas sometimes cut their hair short for religious ceremonies, or when a family member was killed.

"This business is getting harder and harder." Pletz went back inside and leaned on the doorframe where he could watch the plaza.

"Yeah." Booth followed and trailed around to the shelves where he began setting a variety of crock containers and bottles out for the boys who would soon be in and thirsty. "But I 'magine we have a thousand dollars' worth of hair each by now."

Pletz studied the village glowing in the twilight. What could burn was on fire, and he frowned. "Don't you idiots think we could have stayed here tonight? Them fires'll draw in whoever will see 'em."

Booth shrugged. "I didn't start them. You know how the boys are when they get stirred up."

The rumble of running hooves made them look up to see a man named Sandoval racing down the short street. "Riders coming!"

"How many?"

"Twice our count. I think it might be territorial rangers."

Like Texas Rangers and rurales down south of the Rio Grande in Mexico, the hard-riding band of New Mexico volunteers were tasked with cleaning up bandits and Indians. Range hardened and iron tough, they were barely better than those they chased, and more than one crossed the thin gray line between right and wrong whenever the situation demanded it.

However, they were damned good at what they did. No one in their right mind stood up to them, and even the desert-hardened Apaches avoided them at all costs.

Pletz spat. "Dammit! I bet they been trailing us. I've had a feeling, and it wasn't Indians like I thought. Get your horses!"

He darted back inside, scooped up his scalps, and rushed back out to see Schaefer vaulting into the saddle. Pletz fired twice in the air, "Let's ride!"

Wild eyed and bloody, his men assembled in the plaza, whooping with success. The sky was on fire, blazing with color as the sun fell behind the buildings and boiling smoke. It backlit their hats and shoulders with a rim of light that gave them an otherworldly appearance.

They mounted up, flashing bloody scalps they stuffed into bags hanging from their saddles. Schaefer handed Pletz his reins, and he mounted up to lead the whooping barbarians out of town at a dead run in the opposite direction, intending to lose the rangers in the gathering darkness.

Schaefer spurred up beside Pletz and shouted into the wind. "Where to?"

"Head east. We cross into Texas and they won't follow."

"We need to sell these scalps. Why don't we make a run for Chihuahua?"

"That's where they're expecting us to go. That swallow of mescal got me to going, and now I have a powerful thirst. I say we ride to Angel Fire. That's closer. I need to pick up something there and then we'll go."

Schaefer nodded and allowed his horse to drift back. Pletz listened to the men riding behind him and thought about all the money they carried in hair, and what he had in the bank there in Angel Fire. He was a firm believer in banks, though they often got robbed.

It was better than burying money. Back in Germany, he had an old uncle who buried several jars of coins between two strangely shaped trees in the woods near where they lived. A fire swept through, taking out all the trees, and he got down sick in the bed for two years. When he was finally healthy enough to go get the money and relocate it, the land had changed so much he never found the jars. For all the family knew, they were still there.

For Pletz, the era of scalphunting was coming to an end. The number of renegade Indians had dropped so much that they were reduced to killing Mexican villagers instead of taking Apache and Comanche scalps. It was time to take off his wolf's clothing and become something else.

He grinned to himself. Maybe he could shuck those boys, clean up, and return to his roots as a German businessman in Fredericksburg. If that town settled by his people was still growing like he'd heard, he could soon use his own intelligence and the cash in the Angel Fire safe and outsmart everyone there. Before long, he could own that piece of central Texas.

All he needed to do was find a way to distance himself from the others and stay alive.

CHAPTER 2

"Taking a train would have been better than riding these nags all this way." My boyhood friend, Gil Vanderburg, tilted his hat back and wiped at the rivulets of sweat coursing down his temples. He rode slumped in the saddle under a hot, late summer sun, riding as comfortable as if he was in a rocking chair, though he usually sat lighter in the saddle.

We were tired of traveling and kept our mounts at a walk following a game trail leading west through an ocean of buffalo grass. I hoped we were coming up on a watering hole with a place to camp for the night, because the past two sleeps were dry camps without a fire.

I'd been watching the land and saw it was changing slightly, with a few more rolls and water cuts than we'd been passing. The breezy Llano Estacado surrounded us without a tree in sight. Some folks back home in Fredericksburg think the plains are flat as a skillet, but like an ocean, they rise and roll well beyond the horizon, occasionally broken up by a creek or gully like the one before us.

"There's no train to Angel Fire, yet."

I threw a cautious look behind us. Along the way we'd come across signs of people traveling with unshod horses. I suspected there might be a large Comanche war party about. Before we left town, I'd heard talk of renegade bands who were robbing and murdering in the area.

Gil always had a better idea, and they were usually not quite wrong, but seldom the way he'd seen them. "To take a train, we'd still have to ride up to Fort Worth, and that's the long way. Pay the fare for us and the horses, and still get back to court too late. Dad wants us to pick up Wilford Haynes and get him back to jail in time for his trial."

My dad was the county sheriff of Gillespie County and let Wilford out of jail long enough for him to help his family to get their crop in, with the promise that he'd come back when they were done and finish serving his time for stealing a pig from Old Man Johnston. Our town was small enough that everyone knew each other, and the Haynes family was barely surviving with their only son in jail for pig theft, and for knocking Johnston in the head to boot.

Wilford said he didn't do it, but old Miss Rhodie swore she saw him going by her cabin with the piglet in a sack the night it disappeared, and Dad had to run him in for the assault more than the theft itself, because in his opinion, stealing a piglet wasn't much of a crime. Hell, a sow usually ate two or three of the litter the minute they hit the ground.

Dad thought a lot of Wilford and put value in his promise to return. He'd known the family for years and they were solid, God-fearing farmers who minded their own business and tended to raise kids the way they were brought up, by following the law.

But fear took hold of the young man, and he lit out like a scalded cat. Dad put out a paper on him, and after a few months we got word that he was in jail in a hardscrabble, fast-growing town on the edge of Comancheria called Angel Fire. He deputized me and Gil a few months earlier, and when the old man told us to go pick Wilford up, we did it.

Comancheria was a huge section of land ranging from not far west of San Antonio almost to Santa Fe, south of there to Mexico, and up into Colorado. Controlled by the various Comanche tribes who liked nothing more than to kill anyone on their land, it was a good place to get your hair lifted and more than one unfortunate person found that to be true.

The cavalry'd taken most of the starch out of those bands determined to kill every white man they saw, but as is life, younger men always wanted more, and were harder to corral by either their elders, or the army.

Even the buffalo hunters out there showed some smarts and from time to time gathered together for safety when the Indians got stirred up. Armed with big .50 caliber Sharps that could throw a chunk of lead for a mile, those old boys made a living killing things and were *still* spooked when the savages painted their faces, bodies, and horses for the war trail.

Most of the Comanches who were raiding, we'd heard, came not from the territories to the north, but were from much farther south. Comanches were broken up into different bands who chose their own leaders and led their lives as they saw fit, until someone with spirit led them on revenge raids, which is what was going on right then. They were madder than usual because more and more people were traveling through what they called their country, and even establishing ranches out in the most inhospitable parts of Texas.

Unlike most Texans, I understood how they felt. If I owned such a big chunk of country and outsiders moved in to take over, or to cut roads where none had been, I'd'a been mad too. My dad explained it to me once that rang clear as a bell.

"We have our farm here. What would you do if other people from Ireland, let's say, came in and built houses, settled where the cornfield and garden are, killed our stock for the hides, and even said they were going to move in with us? I know what I'd do. I'd load up everything that could shoot and run them off. That's what the

Indians are doing, but they'll lose because there are too many of us.

"Now don't get me wrong. The Comanches took this land from the tribes that were here first, and those Old People did the same long ago. The Tonkawas, Karankawas, Apaches, and the Tano-Tiguas have been fighting and killing each other before we showed up." He looked at me that day and sighed. "We took Texas from the Mexicans and now the Comanches, but one day someone else'll likely come in and do the same to our descendants. It's the way of the world."

Fifteen years later, after that talk in front of our Fredericksburg house, me and Gil were a hundred miles west of town. We'd been on edge ever since we hit the plains, our heads swiveling like owls, looking for war parties that could pop up over those low swells like prairie dogs.

Gil used his only hand to wipe his hat band dry. "Instead of riding all the way out here to pick up a pig stealer, I'druther be back in town with Esther. She said the weather was gonna change soon and she was thinking about killing a couple of pullets to make chicken and dumplin's."

"You're gonna need to punch a new hole in your belt if she keeps feeding you so good."

"I'm like an old deer. You know them young bucks are slender with a flat belly, but an old seven- or eight-year-old will have a sagging belly. I'm looking forward to sagging someday myself." He patted his flat stomach. "If we can get back out of this territory with our hair."

To make things worse in that part of Texas, Charles Goodnight and his friend Oliver Loving had been driving cattle through Comanche territory for years as the folks in Kansas started turning back herds because of Texas fever, otherwise known as tick fever. Folks in Denver still needed beef, though, and those two tough old ranchers blazed a trail north several years earlier, but it grated on the Indians to the point they fanned out to kill every person they found.

We finally came in sight of two cottonwood trees jutting up by themselves in the distance, telling us there was water and possibly a good camping spot nearby. The narrow game trail we followed crossed a wider track winding through the grass and leading in that direction, a sure indication of water. The sun was thinking about going down, and we wanted to rest the horses after a long day in the heat.

I pointed. "That's what I've been hoping for."

"I've been hoping to come across a saloon." Sometimes Gil looked at the darker side of things. "That's probably just a seep."

"We can dig it out, then. At least we'll be down in that draw with a little shade and not likely to skyline ourselves. We can have a fire too, for a hot meal. Let's give 'er a look."

I was right about the trees. A deep, almost

dry cut slashed the rocky ground, running from northwest to the southeast. Centuries of rain and floods carved the gash through the land and undercut a steep bank, gouging out a deep pool that held water year-round. It was so clear I saw little minnows finning beside drowned limbs on the bottom.

We studied the damp ground around the water hole, looking for fresh human signs. There were only hoofprints from deer or antelope, and dozens of paw prints from the smaller critters that came in to drink in the mornings, or evenings.

At that time of the day, birds swooped in to drink before going to roost. Unseen animals rustled in the grass and leaves from the trees that had already shed their leaves due to the heat. Tiny frogs hopped and minnows darted away from the bank, along with water spiders that raced across the still surface.

Gil swung down and groaned as he stretched his spine. Despite his missing left arm from the elbow down, he was a powerfully built man who last weighed on a cotton scale at 190 pounds. Compensating for the missing limb, his right arm was thick and defined from much use. "That water looks so good I might go swimming."

"You beat all. You're the only person I've ever heard of who wants to swim in Comanche territory. That's a water hole I intend to drink from, and I don't need your stink in it."

"Didn't say I would. Said I'd like to." His buckskin gelding lowered his nose to the water, blew to clear the surface, and sniffed. Satisfied with the smell, he drank while Gil studied the clear water with an expression telling me he just might wade in after all.

My steeldust mare sucked up water in great volume, and I noted the dust caked on her hair, held there from days of sweat and lather. I dropped the reins. I'd trained her to stand ground tied, and never worried that she'd run off.

Kneeling, I took off my hat and dipped a hand into the water and drank too. "I say we make camp here tonight."

"Sounds good to me. I bet this buckskin'll be happy when I take his saddle off. He probably needs a good roll."

Our peace and satisfaction didn't last long. Before the mare got her fill, her head jerked up from the creek when a bullet whizzed past and struck a cottonwood tree only two feet away, gouging out a chunk of bark. I twisted on one knee, using the steep bank for cover, and the Russian .44 jumped into my hand without thought.

Squatting only a few feet away, Gil matched my actions and drew his own pistol. In that short two seconds, Comanche war whoops filled the air, along with more gunfire coming from behind us. Bullets snapped and cut through the grass, clipping twigs on a small willow on the opposite side. Snorting from the noise, my mare rolled her eyes but stayed where she was.

Thumb-cocking the revolver was second nature as I dropped back and sideways, falling with one shoulder against the rocky bank and looking through the thick grass that provided two feet of extra cover. Not as well trained as my horse, Gil's buckskin thundered past, reins flapping and snapping like whips, the heavy stirrups and his hooves missing my head by only inches as it leaped up the bank and disappeared.

"I hate that knothead!" Gil rose slightly to see through the grass at the same time a painted warrior flung himself over the bank with a whoop. The Comanche tried to take Gil down with sheer momentum, but despite missing one arm, Gil twisted away and avoided a slash from a knife. Gil backhanded the brave with his pistol and when the man staggered back with a broken jaw, he shot him point-blank in the face.

Blood and gore sprayed across the grass; guns cracked nearby. Puffs of smoke rose from concealed warriors in the grass who fired at Gil's shape. He ducked out of sight against the steep bank. They missed, but the gunsmoke told me where at least two of them were hiding. I threw three shots each at where I thought they'd be, and Gil's pistol barked twice.

He cursed his horse as a horse made by the

very devil himself. "After we kill all these young bucks, I'm gonna be walking."

I broke the revolver open and ejected the spent shells with my thumb, measuring the distance between where I huddled and the Spencer pump shotgun in its scabbard on the mare. Right at that moment, I wanted that scattergun more than anything in the world.

"You're more confident than I am that we're gonna get out of this." I stuffed six more rounds into the cylinder and snapped it shut.

Muffled footsteps and the flap and rustle of buckskin gave me just enough time to react, thumbing the pistol's hammer from half cock to fully back as a warrior bare from the waist up rushed my position with a war club in his fist. His eyes were wide with excitement, and he whooped, hoping to frighten me, and for the sheer joy of murder. Comanches loved a good fight, and war was almost a religion to them.

Thinking he'd be the first to count coup by knocking me in the head with that rawhide club made from a large round rock lashed with leather strips to a stout handle, he was in too much of a hurry. Instead of caving in my skull, he missed, and I threw him off, drawing the big bowie knife riding in a sheath at the small of my back.

He knocked my gun hand to the side, but I slashed with the razor-sharp blade, making him jump back. He came in swinging again, and I used the knife arm to block it, firing the Russian .44 point-blank into his chest. His momentum carried the already dead man past me, and he landed with a dusty thud at my feet.

Gil was firing steady less than ten feet away. I barely had time to cock the revolver again when another warrior popped up in the tall grass. He would have had me, but I'd moved a couple of feet. Intent on where I was a moment earlier, he was half a second behind in finding me. His head snapped in my direction as he was coming over the bank, and he overcorrected.

The bowlegged man's feet slipped, and I punched a hole in his stomach with the .44 at the same time Gil fired. His muzzle blast made me think *I'd* been shot, but there was no time to stop and take stock. Staggering sideways, the warrior was tough as boot leather and somehow recovered from the shock of being hit twice. He yanked a knife from his belt and set his feet to charge when my Russian fired again and he was down.

Though the bowie knife was in my hand, I had no intention of getting into a cutting fight with a man who'd practiced slashing and stabbing from the time he was big enough to walk.

Gil's pistol cracked twice more as an arrow hissed somewhere between us and skipped through the grass on the opposite side of the creek. I've been shot at with guns more times than I'd care to admit, but the sound of a flying arrow always gave me the willies.

The shooting stopped, and Gil took advantage of the lull. "You see 'em?" His voice was calm for our situation.

"Just the ones who were headed for me."

"Two others down over here. I need to reload."

"Go ahead on."

He'd been shooting at the same time I was busy killing men. There'd been a lot of shots around us, and it was all I could do to concentrate on those closing in on us. Reloading for Gil took time, since he had only one arm. I'd cut the other one off to save his life several months earlier. He'd already learned to handle life with a single hand, though certain simple chores slowed him down, like opening and closing the buttons on his pants.

He pushed the ejector rod and shoved the hot hulls from his Colt's cylinder. Tucking it under his left armpit, he thumbed shells from the loops on his belt, palmed them, and like a crooked dice player switching a pair of bones, worked the fresh bullets around in his fingers to stuff one after another into the empty chambers.

It was quiet, and that told me our attackers were working their way closer. They sure weren't going to quit after one little exchange. There was no need to charge right into the barrels of our guns, so they did one of the things they were good at, snaking through the grass. Gil snapped his cylinder back into place, and, taking a chance, I jumped to my feet and rushed around behind the mare and my shotgun.

I had a Henry rifle on the other side and slid it free also, since his was gone with the buckskin. "Here!"

He holstered the pistol down and caught the rifle in midair. There was no need to Malachai a round into the chamber, for a weapon like that was useless. He thumbed the hammer back and used the stump of his left arm to steady the long gun.

No one shot at me, so I grabbed the saddlebags that held extra shells and food. Darting back to the bank, I holstered the pistol and listened. Four men taken out of their war party wasn't something Gil Comanches would tolerate. They might leave to avoid more bad medicine, but on the other hand, I figured they were mad as hornets and determined to take our hair.

When I was a kid growing up, I found I had a knack for working my way along the ground like a snake. Once I even crawled up on a feeding doe to within five feet, though the time I tried to sneak up to a flock of turkeys, one old guard hen saw me and they flushed.

Never one to sit back and wait for trouble to come to me, I did exactly what the war party would do themselves. "Here I go." I took my hat off and laid it on the ground. "Watch out, one of 'em's likely go around and come in from the other side."

Seeing my intentions, Gil laid the Henry close by and drew his pistol again. It would be easier to fire the handgun than the rifle in close quarters.

Crawling like a lizard, I scrambled over the bank and, staying on my belly, swung out in a wide semicircle. The smart thing to do would be to get away from where they thought we'd be holed up, and I figured to come around and we could catch them in a crossfire.

It had worked up in the Oklahoma territories some months back when a war party had us in a similar situation, with our backs against the Red River. That day I crept around behind them and backshot as many as I could before they knew I was there. I hoped it would work again.

My main problem was movement in the grass. When I worked around those others in the territories, I mostly used brush for cover. Anyone standing or sitting on horseback could see it part and flatten as I crawled through it, and to make me even more nervous, there was always the chance of meeting a diamondback rattler nose to nose.

With the shotgun in my hands and the revolver slid back over my hip, I moved slow and steady to get out from between them and Gil. A hawk cried somewhere in the distance, and I felt the sun hammering down on my bare head.

Other than the hawk, it was quiet. There was no more shooting, and I hoped it meant they were gone. Maybe I was wrong and we'd hurt 'em enough that they'd already lost their stomach for fighting.

Or then again, one could have already come up behind Gil and cut his throat.

CHAPTER 3

Pistol in hand and the Henry ready, Gil hugged the grassy bank and kept watch on the sheer drop a couple of feet overhead. From his position, a charging Comanche would have to rise or stand upright to see where he was taking shelter, giving him the angle for a shot.

If they came down the dry draw from either direction, or approached from the almost flat side opposite the creek's pool, he'd see them with enough time to react. Sweat trickled from his temples as the sun settled and the cottonwood's shade crept closer.

Cap had been gone for a while, and with no gunshots, or even sounds, Gil wondered if they'd already killed him. No. Not Cap. He wouldn't go under without shooting everything he could lay eyes on. Like an old grizzly bear, Cap was always better left alone, as that band of Comanches was about to find out.

Cap was the most competent man he'd ever known, and he operated under one code: to do what was right while keeping his word. If Cap said something, you'd better believe him. He was why Gil was still drawing air. A vigilante crowd was going to hang Gil up in the Oklahoma territories for something he hadn't done, and when

Cap showed up unexpectedly and backed down the ringleader with the muzzle of that Spencer shotgun, the town marshal asked him to take his boyhood friend back to Texas to stand trial.

Gil expected to be turned loose once they were away from town, but his hardheaded old friend had given his word to take him back. Determined to get Gil safely back to Texas, Cap stood up to a murdering family running a boardinghouse, Comanches, and the Gluck family that wanted revenge, not to mention saving a woman named Esther and a tough little fourteen-year-old Choctaw girl, Gracie.

Cap was much of a man.

Gil was both pleased and surprised that the steeldust mare was still standing beside the pool, grazing as if she didn't have a care in the world. In the time they'd been back from Oklahoma and settling into life as deputies, he'd worked with Cap to learn how to train horses and to get the buckskin to act like the mare.

It was obvious it hadn't worked.

The wooden grip of Gil's Colt was sweaty in his hand. Tucking it into his armpit, he wiped his palm on his shirt and gripped it again. A grasshopper buzzed past with a dry rattle and landed on a stem of grass not far away. The sun was lower in the sky, and the shade finally reached his position.

The dry air cooled fast up on the caprock. By

dawn it would be chilly, only to heat up again the next day. A pair of doves fluttered in, wanting to land on the shallow slope on the pool's far side, but flared at the last minute when something scared them. Eyes fixed on where they'd seen movement, Gil readied himself for another attack.

CHAPTER 4

The sun's angle burned into the top of my head, and I missed my hat that was lying back beside the water. The sun would set in the next half hour, and that could be both good or bad for me and Gil.

The prairie was so quiet I began to think the war party had gone—that was, until I heard a horse snort. Closer to the ground than a snake in a wagon rut and hugging the pump shotgun, I inched forward until a slight depression offered me a little more cover. Breathing through my mouth, I settled in and listened.

Voices speaking another language not too far away rose in an argument. I couldn't understand their words, but the intensity of their argument was clear. It sounded to me like two or three of the Comanches were trying to get their point across to the others and it almost made me smile.

"*Kee!*"

"*Haa!*"

They were arguing all right, and it was heated. One of the warriors said yes, followed by a firm no from someone else. Over the years I'd learned a few words in Comanche, though I was far from fluent. The word "*sarri*" came across loud and clear, and I wondered if they were calling us dogs, or each other. It didn't matter, in my mind; some of them wanted to resume the attack and chop us to pieces, and others wanted to cut their losses and go on their way.

The angry voices rose, sounding as if they were coming to blows. I'd always thought the Comanche language was almost peaceful, like soft Spanish spoken by a woman in the dark, but these guys were downright mad, and it no longer sounded like anything I wanted to hear.

I hoped the cooler heads would prevail and they'd ride off, but one distinctive voice took over. The argument grew hotter and heavier until someone cut it off with a firm shout. A minute later the sound of hooves came to me as part of the band mounted up and thundered away.

I couldn't take not seeing what they were doing. I raised my bare head until I could barely see over the waving grass and glimpsed a number of warriors on horseback, growing smaller in the distance, probably going to look for easier targets. My spirits dropped when I saw four others standing together maybe fifty yards away, intent on their disagreement.

They were all younger men, and I realized the argument had been between two camps.

It was the age-old play of young men wanting war and blood, with the older and wiser preferring to use common sense and hunt down easier prey. We'd already hurt them too bad, but these four young men wanted to prove themselves and avenge the deaths of those lying back there on the creekbank.

They didn't see me, because I'd come in a wide sweep around behind where they'd expect us. Even so, I lowered my head and broke off a handful of long grass. Sticking it in my sweaty, matted hair, I raised up again, hoping it would break up the outline of my dome.

One taller man waved a hand toward the pool and Gil's position. It looked to me like he was all wound up like a watch spring and ready to kill. I watched some more; the others nodded, and I figured they'd come up with a plan.

Full of confidence, they advanced on the creekbank and pool in a swagger, proving their bravery to each other. The wind was strong enough in their face that I could smell the grease on their bodies as they angled across. It also carried any sounds I might make away from them.

Letting them get farther away, I rose in a crouch and wiped the sweat from my eyes. The others were gone into the wind, and there were a lot of them, already dots growing smaller and smaller. Five horses grazed a hundred yards away, and one of them was Gil's buckskin. They'd caught him as he fled the original fight. Comanches valued horses more than anything else in the world, and they'd gather as many as they could. I once heard a war party had collected more than a thousand head and the herd slowed them down so much they had to abandon them when the cavalry threatened to catch up.

I bet it killed their souls to leave those horses and scatter.

Giving the main body of warriors time to gain some distance, I followed for fifty yards in order for them to get close to Gil.

When they closed in on where they thought we both were hiding, they knelt and conferred before spreading out, keeping a few feet of separation from each other. A pair of doves peeped into view and headed for water. Seeing the Comanches, they flared off and disappeared. I noted their positions and knelt so that only my shoulders rose above the grass.

It was two to four, and I'd learned long ago there was no such thing as a fair fight. I intended to kill as many as I could before they had the chance to do the same. I shouldered the shotgun, and stood in a high crouch to get a clear view of the four.

They had no idea I was behind them. Putting the twelve-gauge's bead right between the closest man's shoulders, I shot the first one in the back. The impact of a full load of buckshot knocked him forward, and I shucked another load into the chamber and swung on the next man to his right.

"Gil! Now!"

Shocked at the unexpected attack, the warrior in

my sights stiffened and whirled to catch the next load. The distance was enough that the buckshot pellets had a little more time to spread out, dimpling the bare skin of his chest, stomach, and arms, which he threw wide and fell backward, a bow flying from his hands.

It was like shooting field larks off a line of fence posts, and I shucked in a fresh round and fired again, as steady as rain.

Six fast rounds came from Gil's pistol, and the other two turned to run, long hair flying. One only took two steps and fell flat onto his face. The last one figured out that the shots were coming from behind.

He whirled and found me, raising a battered old Winchester with brass brads driven into the stock for decoration. Gil's shot hit him at least once, and the slender warrior staggered as he pulled the trigger and threw a round in my direction. It buzzed past several yards away, sounding like an angry yellowjacket. The warrior fumbled with the lever to load another round, but his arms didn't seem to work well and he fumbled with the rifle.

I shouldered the twelve-gauge and pulled the trigger at the same time a bullet from the Henry now in Gil's hands blew out part of the Comanche's chest. The impact threw him forward and into the pattern of buckshot going the opposite direction. He went down hard, and I swung around to check out the area behind me in case there had been more I'd missed, or some of the mounted warriors had doubled back.

All was quiet.

"We got 'em!" Thumbing more shells into the shotgun, I checked the bodies to make sure none of them had any fight left.

The Henry resting on his shoulder like we were bird hunting, Gil followed a small-game trail up the bank and walked in my direction. "What happened to the rest of 'em?"

"Cleared out. They were smarter than these four." I jerked a thumb over my shoulder. "Their horses are back there and your buckskin's with them. Must have caught him as he was running past."

"I oughta shoot him and ride one of their ponies." He stopped beside one of the bodies and bent down to pick up a sheath knife. Studying the beadwork for a moment, he tucked it under his belt in the small of his back.

Once I was sure they were all dead, I stuffed fresh shells into the Spencer and rested the shotgun in the crook of my arm. I held out one hand for the Henry. "Better reload your Colt."

"Thought you said they were all gone."

"You still need to reload." My dad taught me to always reload the minute I finished shooting, either when hunting, or in a gunfight. That lesson had served me well through the years.

Another pair of doves flew in to the cottonwood

and lit in amongst the limbs. They reminded me of hunting with Dad and shooting enough birds for our supper. "That other pair of doves gave away they were almost on you?"

"Sure did." Loading with one arm was a slow process, and I kept an eye out, just in case. He thumbed the last shell in the Colt's cylinder and slipped it back into his holster. "You know what I need now?"

"Whiskey?"

"Nope."

"What, then?"

"*Several* whiskeys."

CHAPTER 5

Baking under a white-hot sky, the two-story wooden Occidental Saloon was the most impressive building in Angel Fire, Texas. The dusty little burg started as a hide camp for buffalo hunters and grew as traders arrived to buy buffalo skins. From tents to adobe, then plank buildings, the town surrounded by the plains sprawled out.

I'd heard a stage came through three times a week, hauling passengers and mail. Most new arrivals were sure to have been disappointed to find accommodations were still scarce, and the few little boardinghouses were scant on proper bedding and meals. Only an occasional diehard lasted more than one night, and they usually left tired, sleepy, and scratching at livestock they'd acquired during the night.

The single-wide street itself had a ways to go before it looked cosmopolitan, but the painted saloon with the ornate sign above the overhang seemed to promise future prosperity for the town perched north of the Salt Fork of the Brazos River and on the eastern edge of Comancheria.

It was the first time I'd been so far into the Llano, and most other people in their right minds avoided such country that killed in a thousand ways. Only rough men who knew enough to survive Comancheria were tough enough to carve a living from the harsh wilderness of the plains that gave little and took all. But as life there became less perilous, more *civilized* people arrived to separate the hunters from their money and the town expanded.

Beyond the wooden structures warping in the heat, the grasslands stretched to the horizon, bisected by a wagon road running east and west. Vultures floating high in the air oversaw fractures in the ground that were watercourses weaving between low, rolling swells reminiscent of waves on the Texas gulf. The runoff creeks seldom held water, but flowed thick and heavy whenever it rained, providing moisture for sagebrush, cedars, willows, and tall, rustling cottonwood trees.

The country baked during the day in the harsh summers, only cooling in the evening when darkness fell over the land. Winter was treacherous when icy north winds scoured the plains, bringing ice, snow, and, more often than not, death.

For me and Gil, once we left the twin cottonwoods behind, our hats had provided most of the shade for the past two days after the attack. We were glad to see relief in the shade of overhangs covering plank sidewalks on either side of the street.

I finally relaxed once we rode into town, for nothing more than the comfort of others around us to dissuade Indian attacks. That didn't mean a war party wouldn't come riding through, whooping and killing everything they saw like they did in Austin back more than thirty years earlier, but our odds of survival were better by a damn sight with all those guns in town.

Dust hung low in the still air, kicked up under shod hooves and sifted back onto the ground as they passed. An occasional gust picked up a cloud of dust and deposited it in another location. Wagon wheels added to the thickness of the air.

We pulled up in front of the Occidental's hitching post partially shaded by an overhang. Instead of the batwings Gil and I were used to in most bars, the false-fronted Occidental had a single-wide front door that stood open to the dusty street. Large windows on either side were open to admit fresh air, that same dust, and flies.

Gil glanced up at the sign and tilted his hat back. He read it to me, as if I couldn't make out the lettering above the windows and door myself. "It says 'whiskey' on that side, 'The Occidental' in the middle, and 'beer' on the other. I declare, that's the prettiest sight I've seen since we rode out of Fredericksburg."

He'd been talking about a whiskey since the fight. Back home he'd taken to drinking a little more than he had several months earlier, but that was because having only one arm left to manage with took a toll on a man's tolerance.

Even something as simple as getting dressed took longer, though he was getting better at it as time went on.

"You can get that drink and a steak now." I studied the buildings around us. "But I wouldn't expect too much out of the whiskey." The steeldust mare under my saddle adjusted her stance and snorted. She smelled water in a plank trough only a few feet away.

I let her walk over to sniff the water. Satisfied it was sweet, she snorted and then drank in long, loud gulps. Also thirsty after our long trip, Gil's buckskin followed suit and drank from the other end of the wooden trough. As water went in the front end, both horses raised their tails and dropped piles of digested grass, adding to the bushels of muffins left by hundreds of others.

I watched a dusty cowboy walk into the saloon. "I 'spect they pour snake juice in there instead of real whiskey."

He grinned at the thought. "Long as it burns on the way down."

Though you could find real whiskey west of Fort Worth, most of what we'd seen was corn whiskey with prune juice and molasses, a few Mexican peppers for more burn, and colored brown with a plug of tobacco. We'd heard all our lives that peddlers sometimes put a rattlesnake head in to "spice it up," and that wouldn't have surprised me at all.

Personally, I wasn't about to gamble on a beefsteak either. If they had meat, it would likely be buffalo or venison, or something I wouldn't recognize. Once up in the nations when I thought I was about to starve to death, I came across a couple of old boys cooking mule, and I was thankful it wasn't horsemeat.

When our mounts were finished drinking in front of the saloon, we stepped down and slip-tied them to the rail only a few feet from the door. I'd already seen a livery a few doors down and planned to stable them there for the night. I've known some men who didn't mind leaving their horses saddled and at a rail all night, but neither me nor Gil was cut that way.

I pulled the Spencer from its scabbard and handed the Henry to Gil. Resting it against his shoulder, he followed me. Grit crunched under our boots as we stepped onto the gray, weathered boardwalk and into the saloon. The inside was almost empty and surprisingly cool and well lit from the windows. Thick shutters opened inward, allowing sunlight to fill the interior. Heavy wooden bars leaned close to hand to secure them in case of an Indian raid.

The floorboards inside were just as sandy as the plank walk, and the sound underfoot was loud as we stepped up to a polished mahogany bar running the length of the left-hand side. Our reflections in the large mirror on the back showed two dusty cowboys toting enough guns to start our own country.

Spittoons were scattered about, telling me the owner preferred to have someone wash them out than for patrons to spit on the floor. It was something I hadn't expected in such a backwater town.

Gil tilted his hat back, revealing a white forehead. "Hey, barkeep. There's something wrong with your looking glass back there."

The man's face would hold a two-day rain if there'd been a cloud in the sky. His mouth was hidden by a huge gray mustache stained with nicotine that covered his entire mouth. He turned to check the big mirror to see what was wrong. Finding nothing of interest, he faced us.

"What's that? Cain't do nothin' about all them flyspecks. I wipe 'em off and they're back in a day or so. They swarm all them buffalo hides at the far end of town."

Gil grinned. "Well, it ain't that. The mirror don't show both my arms. Just one."

The man didn't have much of a sense of humor. "That ain't funny. You lose that limb in the war, or did somebody chop it off because of your bad sense of humor?"

"Nope, my friend Cap here cut it off one day up in the territories." Gil's voice was cheerful at the thought of whiskey. "Taught me not to reach for his plate when he's eating."

He told only half the truth. His left hand suffered a bullet wound when we tangled with a family of bad brothers, a posse, and two backshooters who killed a Texas Ranger right in front of us . . . all at the same time. That hand went bad up in the Oklahoma territories and blood poisoning set in. I did the only thing I could do to save his life. I amputated it with the help of a woman and girl riding with us, Esther and Gracie.

I reckon I made a pretty fair surgeon, along with Esther who'd been there to help, because Gil survived. Sometimes I wished I could cut out what passed for his sense of humor, though.

At the time I never would have known Esther would come work with us on our ranch outside of Fredericksburg; over the past few months, she'd grown sweet on Gil. They made a pretty good pair, and folks in town thought they'd tie the knot at some point.

Now Gracie was a different story and the toughest little cuss of an Indian girl I'd ever run across. The first time I met her she was a barefoot little gal with hair so black it looked blue. In wore-out overalls held up by one strap over her skinny shoulders, she could have been mistaken for a boy, and was in jail with Gil, for theft.

She now worked for us on the ranch too, and had buffaloed a couple of the hired hands with her sharp remarks and predisposition to fight anyone of any size for any reason.

Inside the Occidental Saloon, sweat still ran down the back of my neck, despite being out of the sun. I rested the pump shotgun against the bar and plopped my hat on the smooth surface to let my scalp cool. Flies rose, buzzed around, and lit again. "Just ignore him. You have any beer?"

"Nope. Water and whiskey. Tequila too, for the Mexicans who come through on their way to Santa Fe."

Gil leaned the Henry against the dark-panel bar, bumping the spittoon with a loud clang. "Well, how about whiskey, then."

"You knock that bucket of spit over, and you'll clean it up. We run a clean business here."

Gil paused, and I wondered if he was thinking of a quick comeback, or a mad. It took a lot of pushing to raise his ire, but there were times he'd flash like gunpowder at something said in jest. "How about that drink?"

Instead of turning and reaching for a bottle, the bartender looked us both up and down. He went back to wiping the bar with a rag so dirty I wondered if he used it to scrub the floor and turned his attention to me. "What's wrong with your eyes?"

His question was nothing new. It's been that way all my life. More than one person, male and female alike, have said my eyes are piercing green, uncomfortable to some, and interesting to others. They're a light shade that's as rare as hen's teeth and they startle people at first before they get used to them.

I had no intention of discussing or arguing something I had no control over. "Nothing wrong with them from this side. I see just fine, and that includes all those bottles you have back there."

"Well, I don't like 'em."

"Sometimes I don't either."

He watched me for a moment, as if expecting I'd explain myself, but I remained silent. He waved at the flies circling above the bar. "Y'all need to know I can only take hard money, silver or gold if you're totin' that. We don't take currency here."

The reflected expression on Gil's face was probably exactly the same as mine. His mouth opened and closed like a beached catfish, so I spoke for us both. "I've never heard of a business not taking cash."

"Didn't say we didn't take cash. Only hard money. That was cash the last time I looked. Don't take paper or outside bank script."

I reached into my pocket and pulled out a few coppers and a single silver dime. They rattled on the bar. "That's all we have. We're carrying paper to save on weight."

He shrugged. "It's not my idea. Mr. McGinty don't like paper. Says it can burn up, or there's people back east printing their own that ain't worth a cent. Says paper ain't real money."

A hot breeze blew through the open door as Gil licked his lips, looking at all the bottles lining the shelves. "I never heard of such a thing." Reaching into his shirt pocket, he withdrew the deputy badge my dad gave him and pinned it on his shirt. "Does this make any difference?"

"Not to me. It's just tin, and we take silver or gold, like I done told you."

Gil didn't get the joke. "We're lawmen here for a wanted outlaw your marshal has in jail."

"That the feller who was picked up in Corrente?"

"I have no idea." I figured it wouldn't hurt to pin on my badge too. "Legally deputized. We're out of Fredericksburg and have the papers to take him back."

"I hear he's a bad man, hide hunter that turned to making money on scalps."

"Well, that's not the charge we're carrying."

The plains were full of former buffalo hunters who decimated the great bison herds. Millions of the big beasts were slaughtered, their hides sent back east to be made into everything from saddles to drive belts for industrial machines. Once the southern herd was gone, many of the hunters moved north to finish off those remaining bison.

Shooting bison from long distances didn't teach many skills other than killing, skinning, and survival, and those rough men who made their living with a Sharps .50 turned to a variety of other violent careers.

I could have said his name was Wilford Haynes, and why we were there for him, but such a discourteous bartender was beginning to wear on me. "Well, he's in jail and the marshal's holding him for us. That's all I know. I'd appreciate it if you can make an exception this time and sell us a drink."

He jerked a thumb at a sign I'd missed when we came in. "Says no bank notes nor paper money."

Some banks issued their own notes that acted the same as currency and could be traded for same. I had a few notes from Texas banks stashed back at my home in Fredericksburg, but none on me since I suspected it would take too long to trade them in by wire if I was to spend them.

Gil's own irritation was showing itself as his fingers drummed on the bar top. "No it don't, it says silver or gold coins only."

"Same thing."

There was a wad of folded bills in the money belt under my shirt. I never went anywhere without enough cash to buy what I needed, whether it was a horse, food, ammunition, or a train ticket. Any other time I'd have a seated liberty or two in my pocket, but we'd spent it back in Concho for Arbuckles, bacon, and flour to outfit our trip.

"This is all aggravatin'." I drew a long sigh.

"So is working for McGinty." The bartender licked his thumb and scratched at something on the glass he was polishing.

"Well, I guess we need to exchange some paper at the bank."

A fly landed on the barkeep's hand, and he slapped it with the thin towel. Wiping the squashed body away with his thumb, he kept on polishing. "It's owned by McGinty too, just to let you know. You're in luck. He don't own the livery, nor the drugstore a ways down. It's run by a sour old man who takes too much of his own patent medicines." He picked up another shot glass and went to polishing it with the filthy rag.

I had to study on that one for a while. "McGinty doesn't like paper money, but he owns a bank."

"He's Irish." The barkeep offered that explanation as if it answered everything. Holding the glass up to the light, he studied the smears he was rearranging.

Understanding dawned. The banker was manipulating the economy for only his gain. Requiring only gold forced customers and travelers alike to change their currency for his own coins. "Can I see what we're trading for?"

"You don't know what gold looks like?"

"I'd bet he's exchanging gold and silver for his own coins."

The bartender shrugged. "What of it? He takes care of the town."

"He owns the town, then."

"Call it what you want. We make a good living here."

"Owning his mercantile?"

Another shrug.

"The town store owns everyone." I was talking to Gil. "It makes life comfortable for folks living here and keeps them from worry, but also from hope."

What the man was doing wasn't illegal; it just smelled skunky.

Gil leaned on the bar and looked out the front door as if he hoped someone would open another saloon across the street right at that moment. "Is there another watering hole in town? Maybe they take bills."

"Nope." Barkeep rested both hands on the top after wiping it down. "This is the only saloon in town. McGinty bought out the Sycamore Bar and shut it down. This one's bigger and he didn't want the competition, and don't think about going to the mercantile for a bottle. They don't take currency neither."

"I bet it don't, because McGinty owns it too."

The bartender repeated my statement. "McGinty owns it too."

I was right, and Gil was disgusted. "Damnedest thing I've ever heard."

"You won't like what I'm gonna tell you next. There's a transaction fee as well, so you won't be trading dollar for dollar. Everything in this town costs."

I picked up the shotgun, and Gil's eyes looked hopeful. "You gonna shoot this weasel?"

"Not worth the price of a shell." I reset my hat. "Come on, Gil. Let's do some banking."

CHAPTER 6

We left the Occidental and walked into what felt like a blacksmith's furnace. Stopping in the shade of the overhang, we took a minute to absorb the activity on the hot street. We were used to the heat, but this one was a hot summer. It would end soon, though. Birds were gathering in swarms back home, and that signaled that cooler weather was on the way. Right then, though, we needed some relief.

The ringing of a hammer on an anvil came to us, and I wondered how anyone could stand over a forge in such heat. I took a deep breath and waved away a fly that was interested in my nose. Looking around, I took in the boomtown that was both shabby and, in some strange way, metropolitan.

Unlike more established towns, Angel Fire was under construction. In Fredericksburg, stores and businesses were built right up against one another, shoulder to shoulder, separated occasionally by blocks and alleys leading to back streets. Angel Fire was an odd mix of adobe buildings alongside plank walls that gave the town an odd, almost temporary feeling, as if the builders weren't sure if the town would even last at all. Two or three of what I took to be older structures were made of sod that seemed to be melting into the ground.

It was now a boomtown instead of a hide town that sprouted around good water. The route was attracting people traveling west along the Overland Trail leading through the New Mexico Territory to southern Arizona.

Here in that sunblasted West Texas town, instead of rubbing shoulders with other businesses, there was space between buildings like missing teeth. Through those gaps between buildings were dozens of white tents. Some were operating as small businesses, while others served as temporary housing.

I could tell it wouldn't be long, though, before those empty lots would fill in because piles of lumber in the streets, hauled from great distances away, were waiting for men with hammers and saws. There were few trees in that part of the country, so someone's optimism proved there was still money coming in from somewhere, but I wondered how long they would last the way this mysterious McGinty operated.

Maybe a rail line was on the way. If they had a stage that came through several times a week, then rail would be next.

Directly across the street churned to fine powder by feet, hooves, and wagon wheels was the W. H. White Mercantile and Hardware store. Signs were everywhere on mostly false-fronted, wooden structures: GROCER, PROVISIONS, DRUG-STORE, DRY GOODS & CLOTHING, SADDLERY, CORRAL, LIVERY, and even a small bakery fea-turing pies and cakes.

More than half contained small script at the bottom that read, J. C. MCGINTY, PROPRIETOR.

Across from us on the opposite side of the street, and three-quarters of the way down, was a square building that didn't have an overhang, just two stone steps leading up from the street. Bank of Angel Fire. I paused, considering the usefulness of a bank in such a place. The man who built it, McGinty, had more vision than most folks, and I had no doubt when the town finally grew into its britches with the arrival of a train sometime in the distant future, they'd rebuild with bricks.

But so much of that was in the future. Right then it was a flyblown town baking in the late summer sun. Gil walked over to the horses and pulled the knot to free his buckskin's reins. I stayed where I was. "The bank's only a few doors down."

He looked disgusted. "You know as well as I do that a cowboy worth the salt in his beans rides everywhere."

"You have two good legs, and we're not cowboying much anymore. Walking won't hurt you none."

"I was made to fork a horse, and most of those

I've seen in my life have four good legs to take me where I need to be."

"Go ahead on and ride if you want to." Shotgun resting in the crook of my arm, I started down the street. "I need to stretch my legs."

"I ain't wearing no socks. If I walk too much, I'll rub a blister. You remember Old Man Williams, he walked a blister on his heel that turned to gangrene and they had to take off his foot. Carved a peg leg and couldn't hardly mount a horse after that."

"He quit walking and got too fat to ride. That's what happened."

"Well, Miz Ruby Green's daughter got that pimple on her chin and popped it. Got blood poisoning and died a week later."

"What's that got to do with us walking to the bank?"

"Nothing, I reckon. Just talking about blisters and gangrene reminded me of her."

I struck out down the street, and with a sigh loud enough to be heard over a wagon rattling past, Gil retied the buckskin and hurried up to step in beside me.

He changed the subject. "You ever hear of some place taking only hard money?"

"Yep, up in those Colorado gold camps. Most of what they trade in is gold dust."

"We're a long way from there." Gil stopped talking when a crow on top of the mercantile's false front cawed.

He worried about signs even when we were kids, because a great-aunt considered herself in touch with what she called the other side. She was forever cutting open fruits and seeds to read the weather, watching caterpillars and insects, and warning us to stay away from places where people died, or were buried.

One winter day when we were sitting in front of the fire in her little cabin after dark, she told a story about seeing a specter walk through the wall over behind us, cross to the other, and disappear through the chinked logs. I thought it a great story that was fun, but Gil believed every word.

Such superstitions were common back where we came from. It was rooted in folklore brought from Ireland, England, Scotland, and mixed with beliefs from Indians and especially Germans in our part of the state.

The sun was low, and the bird's shadow fell on the saddlery across the street, looking like some giant evil omen. I could tell the crow bothered him. I wasn't superstitious, but after one quick look, I went back to studying the busy street.

"I dislike crows. They're almost as annoying as a blue jay, and that one's lucky we're in town, or I'd use it for target practice."

Gil shook his head as if I'd suggested that we eat the bird, feathers and all. "Hope we don't need anything from in that saddle shop, 'cause

I don't intend to darken *his* door. It's marked now." He shivered as a group of horsemen came loping down the street in our direction. "I never saw such a thing."

Big hats, scarves, and loose-fitting shirts with wide sleeves sticking through their vests, they were obviously cowboys from some nearby ranch. They all carried handguns, and more than one displayed a rifle riding under one leg.

He watched the lead riders go by. "I hope those boys are carrying rattling money, or they won't have much fun tonight. Wonder which brand they ride for?"

I always liked cowboys, and worked closely with ranchers and waddies back home when someone needed a horse broke. Before I wore a badge, my stock in trade was raising horses.

Gil stepped off the boardwalk and studied the brands as they passed. Once the first few were past, he continued across the street. "Let's get on the other side and in some shade. Walking makes me hot."

I followed, and we were almost to the other side before a second crew with the same brand closed the distance at a high lope. One of them, a glaring young man with long blond hair down over his collar and a wispy mustache, peeled off and reined up close to be as rude as possible, throwing dirt and dust at us.

Back home in my earlier life, I would have

dragged him off that little mustang he was riding and taught him a lesson. That would have likely involved the riders with him, for outfits like that always stood beside their men, but that would have tangled Gil and his gun in the mess, backing down the rest of them. He could have used my shotgun to hold them still while I whipped some manners into that young man, but right then it was too damned hot to be fighting, and I liked to think I'd mellowed some by then.

Besides, I had to honor the badge and tolerate his rude behavior.

Blondie's high-spirited horse fought the bit when he yanked him back too hard, and it took him a second to get the gelding under control. It was still another reason not to like the arrogant cowpuncher who was going to ruin a good horse if he wasn't careful.

He waved a hand for emphasis, swatting at us like we were irritating mosquitoes. "Why'n't you two get out of the way when working men come riding through."

We turned as one, bringing the badges on our shirts into view.

"Well. A couple of big guns." He hesitated. "At first I thought y'all were box herders."

The boys riding with him snickered at the thought we were men hired to keep prostitutes in line at a brothel or saloon. "I's just funnin' you boys." He soaked in their admiration and what he considered a sharp tongue. "Y'all been hired here in town to take over for Skinner?"

"Nope." Gil's dander was already up. "Here to pick up a prisoner, or more'n one if we need to arrest anyone."

Blondie rested a fist on his thigh, inches from the revolver in a cutaway holster. "Y'all better be careful of what you're tangling with in this town. Most folks here don't bend none."

That told me he fancied himself a gunman, for no cowboy wears a pistol on his good-hand side without it being tied in with a thong over the hammer. It was too easy for a gun to bounce out of the holster when riding in rough country, or working cattle.

Both Gil and I wore ours in a cross draw on the opposite side of our familiar hand, and in his case, his only one, of course.

Blondie raised one corner of his upper lip. "Y'all don't much look like lawmen to me, though."

I was done with talking in the hot sun. "If there's nothing else, we'll be on our way."

"Just don't get in front of Panther Creek riders."

I wondered if I needed to put a chip on my shoulder so he could knock it off like a schoolboy. Maybe we should have spit between our fingers or over a line in the sand to see what would happen next. Not interested in such, I chose not to answer and stepped around behind his horse to cross the street. It was the worst thing we could have done, ignoring him like a pesky fly.

Gil followed and Blondie had to twist around in his saddle to see us, and that annoyed him. "I wasn't finished with *talking* to you."

We kept going, because I had no intention of squaring off with him.

"Hey! I said I'm not finished with you."

Uncertain what to do, his buddies adjusted their mounts with spurs to one side or the other to keep an eye on what was happening. Probably more interested in getting a drink than Blondie's little show, they stayed together as riders for the brand should.

Men going about their business around us slowed to watch. The street continued to be busy, since we were only talking, but those who did notice the look on Blondie's face gave us some room. It was common for men to settle their differences quickly with fists, guns, or knives in that part of the world, and the entertainment was always an extra value when coming to town.

I was carrying the shotgun in the crook of my left arm and turned so the big bore was pointed in his general direction. "You may not be done flapping your tongue, but I'm finished with you."

He saw my right hand resting over the shotgun's grip and quieted. "No man turns his back and walks away from me."

"One just did." I stepped up on the narrow boardwalk and opened the bank's door.

"Are you afraid?"

There was no need for any more posturing. "Good God." I went inside.

CHAPTER 7

The Panther Creek riders tied up at the hitching rails out front of the Occidental and stomped inside. One cowboy named Bill Scott slapped his hat on the bar. "Beer! The boss says put it on the Panther Creek tab."

Barkeep shook his head. "Mr. McGinty canceled all tabs till he gets back tomorrow."

Bill frowned, then recovered. "All right, boys. Dig in them pockets and play some music on this wood."

Change rattled on the bar top and their evening started. By the time Blondie, real name Bright Bolton, arrived, the first round was gone and the boys were working on the second. His entrance was met with a chorus of shouts and warnings.

"You got some catching up to do, Bright!" Bill met him at the counter. "But McGinty put the quietus on the Panther Creek tab."

The news was a shock to Bright. "But it's the end of calving season. Mr. Shank always treats the boys this time of the year."

"I know it, but that's what the barman back there says."

Bright threw a glare at the mustached bartender who caught the look and shrugged, knowing the young cowboy was angry. Bright dug into his pants pocket and produced a single silver dime, knowing the Occidental didn't take folding money.

"I'll take care of this." He pushed away from the bar. "I'll go back to the bank and trade with Callie for some money."

"You're carrying folding money?"

Bright gave him the grin that first caught the young teller's interest when she first came to town. It didn't last long, only until Callie realized Bright was so full of himself that he didn't have any room for anyone else's needs, including hers. He was the kind of man who'd get a girl to fall for him, then once she'd made her intentions known, he'd keep her on the string and move on to the next one.

Only there in Angel Fire, Callie was the only available young lady within a hundred miles, not counting the girls working above the Occidental. Unless Bright wanted to quit his job as a top hand for the Panther Creek ranch and ride farther than that into Fort Worth to see if there was anyone he could interest, it was just her, and she'd already let him know she was done stroking his ego.

Half-lit, Bill leaned on the bar and slapped him on the shoulder. "Bring her back with you, if she'll come."

Anger flashed in Bright's eyes. "She ain't that kind of gal, and you know it."

Bill backed off. "I didn't mean no disrespect toward your girl."

Bright flicked his fingers toward two silent cowboys. "Harvey, you and Shorty can come if you want, or stay here."

The hands shrugged. Harvey nodded. "We'll go with you. It's too stuffy in here till the evening cools."

The trio left and stepped out on the street at the same time a pack of wolves in men's skin rode into town. The cowboys watched them pass. They'd worked as hunters and skinners at one time, much like those who ignored them. The plains were full of men who made a living killing the great beasts, but this bunch was different.

One of them was black as the night. He cast dead eyes on the cowboys who watched them pass. They all fairly bristled with guns, and Bright kept a wary eye on them as they reined up in front of the mercantile.

Men up and down the street paused to watch the newcomers. More than one took note of all the guns and quietly faded away. Harvey and Shorty fell slightly behind their leader as he turned his back on the men who radiated menace. Bright crossed the street, stepping in front of a rider who thought about saying something until he saw the other two, and clenched his jaw.

CHAPTER 8

I was still jittery mad, though I didn't show it. Some things get my goat, and smart-mouth men were high on that list. Blondie was lucky I hadn't lost my temper. There were times when I got so mad the world turned red. When that happened, I didn't recall what I did until my head quit pounding and the echoes of gunshots were all gone.

Gil followed me into the Angel Fire bank and closed the wood-and-glass door behind us. "Well that got interesting real quick. He's just sitting there."

"He'll get hot and go away."

"You know they're heading for the saloon and so are we, eventually."

I swallowed down the anger and looked out through the door's glass. "I think we should just shoot him and get it over with, then."

A young redheaded woman behind the teller cage looked up with shock. "Who are you going to shoot?"

Her frightened voice broke the spell, and I gave her a grin. "Nobody. My buddy here's just rattling the teeth in his head." I stepped up to the window and leaned the shotgun against the wall between us. "We're here to change some cash."

Something flickered in her eyes. She looked uncomfortable. "I understand, but there's a problem."

"What's that?"

"We're running low on hard money, and I'm afraid I can't make any exchanges right now. We have to wait until the bank president returns."

"He out to lunch?"

"No, he left yesterday and said he would be back tomorrow."

I was confused. "So what does that have to do with us?"

"He has to approve of all exchanges from people who don't live here."

Gil chuckled. "That's no way to do business, especially when he owns half the town."

"You know that?"

"Heard it from the bartender."

"Well, I don't know how to help you. Mr. McGinty will allow an exchange of funds if you open an account, but he insists on two hundred and fifty dollars as a deposit to do that." Her fingers flickered over the white collar on her blue dress. "Most people don't have that kind of cash." She shrugged. "And I'm not supposed to do any transactions such as that when he's not here either."

"So you're just supposed to stand back there behind those skinny little bars and look pretty?" Despite my frustration, I almost laughed. "We're not here with enough cash to buy land. We're in town to pick up a prisoner in your jail here and then head back to Fredericksburg tomorrow. We'd just like a drink, some supper, and a bed for the night."

She licked her lips, and I couldn't take my eyes off them. They looked soft and warm, and a little like they'd been glazed with honey. "Sir, I still can't help you. Mr. McGinty has clear rules about bank business, and I'm just an employee."

"How about a little exchange to give us enough for a few drinks and you don't have to tell him."

"I can't do that. Mr. McGinty keeps excellent books and lists every transaction. He knows to a penny how much paper we have on hand, and what coins and their denominations are in the safe each morning. He'll have my job if I don't follow his instructions to the letter." She lowered her voice as if it wasn't just the three of us in there. "And this is a *very* good job for a woman, if you know what I mean."

Gil joined me at the teller window. He took off his hat and scratched at the matted hair underneath. "What are we supposed to do?"

"You said yourselves you're not here but for one night. I bet you can stay at the livery. Jeter don't care what you pay him with. He can feed and water your horses, and y'all can sleep in one of the stalls." She looked embarrassed. "I don't know what else to tell you."

"I have an idea that might work, if you'll consider my suggestion." I reached into my shirt for the thin money belt wrapped around my waist. It was easy to access, so I plucked out a two-dollar bill and slid it under the cage that wouldn't keep a child out. "Do *you* have an account here? You know this is a real bill, so maybe you can exchange it for yourself. I bet he wouldn't argue with that. A young lady such as yourself might need a ribbon for her hair to match that pretty dress while he was gone, or maybe a piece of licorice."

She maintained eye contact and gave me a slight grin when she picked up the bill. She furrowed her brow at me, and the little ripple between her eyebrows made her even more attractive. "It isn't script, is it? We don't take script from other banks."

"Genuine U.S. currency."

She studied it for a minute and looked around as if someone might be watching. Nodding, she opened a drawer I couldn't see and slid it in. Closing that one, she opened another that was filled with rows of stacked coins lying horizontally in a tray. "You want me to mix them up?"

"Sure."

She flicked through the coins and slid them in front of us like poker chips.

I wondered at the bright coins in her drawer. "These are the shiniest things I've ever seen."

"Newly minted silver and gold. Mr. McGinty has a special arrangement with the New Orleans Mint. That's where he's from. He was a banker back there. It's a good thing he's going to Gainesville too, because we're getting low on coins."

"It looks like there's a lot in there."

She hesitated, looking at the drawer and back up at me. She closed it and brushed a strand of stray hair off her forehead. Her gaze flicked around, looking for somewhere to rest. "What I meant was, we do a lot of town business when he's here and these won't last long."

She stopped to take a breath, and I knew she wasn't telling me all she knew. She had more to say, and I could tell she was trying not to talk as much, but since I was just standing there, waiting, she felt she had to fill in the silence.

"I have several people who're waiting for his return so they can do business, folks who live here in town now, or have moved here recently and taken up residence in those tents I'm sure you've seen."

The redhead swallowed and kept talking. "And that'll probably take all I have. I wish he wouldn't leave like that, but one of these days we're gonna be big enough to handle bank drafts and maybe he'll change his way of doing things. We're not quite there yet, though."

I scooped up the coins and dropped them into my pocket with a satisfying jingle. "Thanks for helping us. By the way, I'm Cap Whitlatch. This knothead here with me is Gil Vanderburg."

"Hi. I'm Calpurnia Weathers."

"Mrs. Weathers, we sure appreciate this."

"Miss. I'm not married, and Mr. Whitlatch, if I might say, you have the prettiest eyes I've ever seen."

Gil cleared his throat. "That's the best part of him."

He quit talking when the door behind us opened. I turned to see Blondie stepping inside, followed by two other cowboys who gave us cold looks. He removed his hat and shuffled his feet on the floor to clean off anything sticking to the soles of his boots.

Setting his hat back into place, he gave her a sheepish smile. "Howdy, Callie. Didn't want to track in any mud or horse tur . . . biscuits. Horse biscuits, I mean, on your floor since you're the one who has to sweep."

Her eyes went flat. Despite the long sleeves she wore, and her high collar, she'd looked cool and relaxed up until that moment. Now her face flushed with heat, and I expected to see smoke come from her nostrils.

"You oughta wipe them off outside, not in here. Like you said, I'm the one who has to sweep up your mess. Drag them clean out on the boardwalk where it'll fall into the street with all the other dirt."

He took her scolding as if it wasn't the first time. "Came in to see you." He twisted up his face in thought. "I was just making sure everything was all right."

Her blue eyes went flat. "Why wouldn't they be?"

"Well, these two strangers have been in here a long time, and it concerns me when my girl is all alone with men she doesn't know. They could be bank robbers for all I know."

"They aren't strangers, Bright. And if you haven't noticed, they're both wearing badges, which I doubt robbers would do. This is Cap and Gil." Her voice lifted, and I wondered what was going on. She tilted her head for emphasis. "We're already on a first-name basis, so there's no need for worry."

His expression went blank. "I don't like it when you tease me like that."

She addressed me and Gil. "Mr. Bright Bolton here thinks we're an item, but I'm afraid he's misreading our relationship."

Knowing anything I'd say could put a match to the fuse she'd just stuck in the dynamite that was our situation, I didn't mumble a word.

The two cowboys behind Bolton separated themselves, and it irritated Gil. He shifted his position to face them. They took in his missing arm, and the oiled Colt on his belt. "You boys might need to rethink your thoughts."

Bright tilted his head back and stuck his nose in the air. It was one of those haughty habits of men I'd learned long ago to despise. I'd seen it more than once in saloons, or out back with men shooting dice.

He wrinkled his forehead. "I bet you two are finished, since Callie has orders not to do business with anyone who isn't from around here."

Anything I had to do in the bank was none of his business. I changed the subject to the brand on their mounts. "Who owns the Panther Creek?"

"Mr. H. R. Gage."

"Big outfit?"

"Big enough to take this country from the Comanches and bring in enough cattle and money to get this town to growing."

"Y'all hiring?"

The look on his face told me he didn't like the idea of us considering a job on the Panther Creek ranch. I had no intention of doing so, but it was the first thing I could think of that would get him off balance. It was easy to do, for what would two lawmen want with a ranch job?

I felt better for twisting him up.

Gil saw the trail I was on and followed. "Might need to ride out to their ranch house, Cap, and see if I can get on." He opened and closed his hand. "Not much good at roping all lopsided here and such, but I'd made a fair hand at rustling grub."

He nodded toward Bright and flexed his fingers again to make sure they saw. "Good, hand. That's funny, ain't it? If I can't get hired on with y'all, I might have to join one of them traveling companies and be their funny man."

For a moment Bright looked confused, then realized what we were up to. His smirk returned. "No. Full up right now, and besides, I'm the foreman and do the hiring, not Mr. Gage. I wouldn't hire you two to muck stalls."

"You look perfectly capable of doing that job yourself." I turned back to Calpurnia. "Thanks for the conversation. I'll be back to see you again tomorrow."

Blondie's brow furrowed as he struggled to understand. "What's that?"

"The bank president'll be back then, so I can do some more banking."

Calpurnia's eyebrow rose slightly, and I read in that cute little expression that she understood what I was doing . . . and approved.

Just for spite, I hung around a little longer. I leaned one elbow on the counter and gave her a smile. "You have any idea why they named this town Angel Fire?"

She gave me a big smile and rested her elbows on the counter only a few inches away. Had there not been teller's bars between us, I might have touched her hand. Tilting her head in my direction, she laced her slender fingers and ignored Bright. "I heard it's because of the sunsets out here on the plains. Story goes that some traveler got here late one evening and saw the sky all orange and pink and full of sundown blazes and said it sure looked like the angels built a fire to him. The name stuck after that."

She made a face. "It beats what they were calling it before the stage started coming through. Buffalo Waller."

"It does sound a little better." Having made my point, I moved toward Blondie, intending to walk him down if he didn't get out of my way. "Good day to you, Bright."

We were the same height; our gaze met, and he waited until the last moment. Just before I roostered him out of my path, he moved to the side.

Gil shouldered past the nearest cowboy to him who was shorter than both of us, but he looked tough as nails. We left the bank without the smell of gunsmoke following us outside, though Bright's voice came to me.

"I'm not finished with you yet!"

CHAPTER 9

Bright, Harvey, and Shorty watched the two lawmen take their time in front of the bank after they left. The strangers stood there for several minutes, talking, and Bright was sure it was to annoy him.

Harvey went around behind McGinty's desk and sat in the president's chair as if he owned it. Shorty half sat on the desk, twiddling his thumbs.

Calpurnia frowned at them from behind the teller window. "You lose something, Bright?"

He turned to Shorty. "Why'n't you go outside and keep an eye on that bunch that just rode in."

"They don't interest me."

"No, but I don't like their looks."

"I doubt they like ours neither."

"Just do it. Harvey, you watch the street from in here."

"Don't you think that's a little much?" Tall and lanky with a huge Adam's apple, Harvey rubbed the three-day growth of whiskers on his jaw. "They're just hide hunters."

"I don't think so." Bright leaned on the service area in front of the teller window. "Callie, for some reason McGinty shut off this year's tab at the Occidental. I have a bunch of thirsty buddies that're gonna get real mean when they can't get a drink." He took off his hat and plucked out several folded bills from the inside of the band. "Would you change these for me?"

She sighed and raised both hands to her sides. "I'm sorry, Bright. That's what I was telling Cap and Gil when you came in. McGinty said I can't change any more bills until he gets back tomorrow."

His face darkened at the mention of their names. "I don't like you to use their names like they're old friends."

"You don't get to tell me what names I can speak." The tiny little frown line between her eyes that he loved so much made an appearance. "I don't know what else to call them. Should I say Two Arms and One Arm so you can tell the difference?"

He saw there was no way to win such an argument. He'd never understood women. Cattle were easier. "But you know as well as I do that this bank is full of gold. Just change out what I have here."

A soft growl of frustration came from her chest. "I would, but he'd fire me."

"For doing your job?"

"For going against what he told me." She leaned forward. "He left with a grip and loaded a cashbox on the stage. Said he'd be back tomorrow. He made me repeat that I wouldn't open the safe and would limit what I traded to just a couple of his own businesses in town. I can't even take deposits from the livery, Red's saddle shop, or Mr. Brown's barbershop, though he doesn't do much business in here."

All three were independent businesses in town, along with a handful of others not owned or beholden to McGinty.

There was forty dollars in sweat-damp bills spread out on the polished mahogany under the bars separating the two of them. Half a year's wages for a top hand. "You know these are good."

"I can see that, but what can I do?" She shook her head and used a finger to arrange the bills she couldn't take. "I'm employed by this bank, and Mr. McGinty is the manager and owner." She thought for a minute, the familiar frown again wrinkling the skin between her eyes. "Look, I've done all the business I can cover for the day."

"What does that mean?"

"It means I've already done my good duty for the day. I can't stretch my luck any further."

He saw she had more to say, but hesitated. A wave of dark jealousy washed over him when he realized what she'd said. She'd exchanged money for those two lawmen in a way that wouldn't get her in trouble, and now she was trying to hide it.

Seeing the black cloud gathering over him, she held up a hand. "Look, I have some money at home. When I close the bank at three, I'll go get it and bring it to the Occidental for you. I can take these and bring it back to you."

Bright's face reddened. "No gal of mine is going into a saloon, nor even to the front door. I'd expect you to pass by on the walk across the street."

Her eyes narrowed. "You need to clean out your ears. I'm not your girl, and I can walk wherever I want to in this town, just like you, and furthermore and all that, I've seen you come sneaking down the staircase beside the Occidental. I know what goes on up on that second floor, and even if I had been your girl, that'd be over now that you've laid with one of those gals who only come down at night."

The expression on his face made her nod. "Hit a nerve, didn't I?"

Embarrassed and mad, Bright licked his suddenly dry lips and looked for the words. "Well, you ain't said hail ner farewell to me in a month of Sundays."

"You've been working cows that long and I don't intend to take a buggy all the way out to Panther Creek just to say howdy. Of course we haven't spoken, because I don't go riding around outside of town. We both know it isn't safe."

He nudged the bills an inch closer. "I don't take loans from nobody."

"It's not a loan. It's an exchange between friends."

"No. McGinty had gold right here in this bank. None of this makes any sense."

"Then you're out of luck until tomorrow."

Bright turned to see if Harvey had been listening, and heat rushed into his face when he saw both he and Shorty were watching with their arms crossed, taking it all in.

Anger rose, and he took it out on Harvey. "Instead of sitting there, you oughta go get a shave or something."

"I ain't going to no dance, but I'm about tired of waiting for you to get turned down some more by a little bitty ol' gal that ain't interested in none of us."

Bright slammed his hand down on the bills and wadded them in his fist. "Let's go!"

Stuffing them into his pants pocket, he stomped toward the door to the jangle of jingle bobs rattling against his spurs.

CHAPTER 10

When we got back to the saloon, I didn't like how the steeldust mare was crowded in amongst the Panther Creek horses tied up stirrup to stirrup in front of the Occidental. She stood there as patient as Job, but Gil's buckskin wasn't having it. With the mare on one side, he kept shoving a lathered-up paint out the way to give himself more room.

The two of us understood. There was no reason to jam horses together other than arrogance and aggravation on the part of the Panther Creek outfit. It looked to me they were the cock of the walk, and apparently nobody in town had ever called them on it.

The horses were so tight against one another I had to step up on the boardwalk to untie the steeldust from the rail. Relieved, she backed up on her own until she was in the clear. Keeping one hand on Gil's buckskin to remind him of who I was, I stepped away from the snorting horses and led her into the middle of the street.

The others shifted to get more room when Gil pushed his way in and untied the buckskin. His jaw set, he threw a glance back over his shoulder at the saloon. "I oughta cut the reins on all these soap bones and let 'em head on back to the barn."

"They don't all belong to the Panther Creek boys. I don't want to get into a shootin' fight right now. Let's steer clear of these boys, pick up our prisoner, and get shot of this place."

"I don't like being crowded, in any way."

"Me neither, but I say we let it go right now."

"Let's get over to the livery and get these two rubbed down and fed."

We hadn't gone more than a few feet when I heard a loud voice full of annoyance behind me. "Hey you, Cap!"

Knowing what was coming, we stopped and I led the mare over to an open hitching rail and tied her with a slipknot. Gil did the same, and when we walked back around the horses' rears, I came face-to-face with Bright standing there in the hot sun with his fists bunched.

He looked mad as a hatter, and I was taken somewhat aback by his determination to start a fight. "I said I wasn't through with you. You don't walk away from Panther Creek boys."

Trying to cool him down, I kept my voice as soft and even as possible. "I heard you, but we're heading down to the livery."

The tall cowboy with an Adam's apple as big as my fist answered. "That's where *we're* going."

If looks could kill, the one Bright shot at his friend would have dropped him in his tracks. "Shut up, Harvey." He glared at the cowboy until he looked down. Bright's hand opened and closed into a fist. "The fact of the matter is, I want you to stay away from Calpurnia."

Gil sighed. "You know, Cap, this is just like in fifth grade back in Fredericksburg when Mitch Cavendish squared off with you over that girl, what was her name . . . Iona Staples. You remember what happened?"

Bright took half a step forward, tensed up. "All you two do is yap."

"That ain't *all*," Gil said. "You see, Iona really was interested in me and gave me some sugar right here." He pointed at his cheek.

Bright looked at Gil the same time I cracked his jaw with my right fist. He staggered back and I followed him with a left jab, and came back with another right. His eyes glazed and rolled around in his head, his knees went weak and loose, and he landed flat on his back in a puff of dust.

"Hey, that ain't fair!" The shorter, stocky cowboy headed in like a mad bull; he hit me with his shoulder and we staggered sideways. Instead of fighting, he threw an arm out and caught me in a head hold. Gil was right. It was just like kids in a schoolyard.

I'd done my share back when we were little shavers, because that was how we survived in a world of tough farm boys. Shorty dropped his shoulder and bent me down, intending to bulldog me, I guess. An old hand at that kind of thing, I twisted enough to get my leg behind his. That gave me the leverage to snake my arm between us and throw him backward when he was off balance.

When he landed, I kicked him in the face, breaking his nose, which poured blood. When I straightened, there was Gil with his fist full of Colt, holding Harvey and a handful of Panther Creek riders back. Without that revolver, I'd have been fighting the whole bunch of them.

Gil's voice was even and smooth, as if they were watching us shoot marbles or play mumbly-peg. "This is between Cap and them."

Harvey bunched his fists. "You wouldn't shoot any of us for pitching in on a fistfight."

"You don't know that, do you?" The grin Gil flashed at them wasn't made for girls or fun. It was pure hellcat, and they knew it. "Like you said, though, this is just a fistfight, and it's between them, and not all of you."

I picked up my hat, slapped the dust from it, and set it just right. Bright and Shorty still laid in the dirt. "Y'all were headed for the livery?"

Harvey looked confused at my insistence on talking and not fighting. "We were. The owner's changed paper for gold a time or two. I believe it's the only way we're gonna get any whiskey tonight."

I wondered if Calpurnia sent them down there, as she did us. "Well, here's the deal. I don't have a problem with any of y'all, but we don't need to be standing around too close to one another the way everyone's feeling right now."

I pointed at Shorty, who'd rolled over and was spitting blood, and Bright. He was stirring, trying to find a way to get easy. "Let these boys get their air, and by that time, we'll be finished stabling the horses and y'all can make your trade."

Bright rolled over onto his knees, forehead resting on the dirt. He spoke through the dust. "Let 'em go. He won." The cowboy blew snot and blood from his nose.

Without waiting for permission from the others, I led the steeldust away from the growing group of onlookers that gathered around Bright and Shorty to help them up.

Going down the street, we passed several dark buildings and came to a corral holding half a dozen horses. Across the street was a squatty box made from cement and rocks. It had a single door and thick barred windows less than a foot tall running up along just under the roofline for ventilation. I had an idea it was the structure that served as their lockup.

Not in the mood to check on the prisoner we still hadn't seen, I flicked my fingers to tell Gil we'd come back later. We came to a tall, unpainted barn with both front doors swung wide to admit light and air into the stable. A couple of straight-back chairs and a handful of sawn stumps provided places for loafers to sit and visit out front. There was no one out there, so we led the horses into the darker, cool interior.

A hall wide enough for two wagons stretched nearly a hundred feet to a second set of wide double doors leading out back. A rat scuttled out of sight, and dust motes danced in the beams of light streaming between wide planks that had dried and separated after the barn was built.

A line of stalls filled the right-hand side. A room with a rolltop desk sat immediately on the left when we entered. Beyond that were three doors where I figured the owner stored tack and feed. Further along, two wide pens took up the rest of that side.

A lanky man rose from a chair in front of the desk and came out into the hall. "Help you gentlemen?" He saw the badges on our shirts. "Y'all Rangers?"

"No. Deputies here to pick up a prisoner your marshal has locked up."

"Ah, the *cibolero* named Wilford Haynes is in there. He's *muy malo*. It was the last thing that Joe Skinner ever did, putting him in jail." He stuck out his hand. "Name's Charlie Jeter."

We shook. "Cap Whitlatch, and this here's Gil Vanderburg."

"You lose that arm in the war?"

"Cap here cut it off."

"Oh." Jeter studied on the comment for a moment. "Good to have friends like that."

I liked the little guy. "Skinner the marshal?"

"Was. Haynes stuck him with a knife when they got to fighting. Skinner buffaloed him with the butt of his pistol and managed to tie his hands before he bled to death. Haynes must've nicked one of them big veins inside him and he went pretty quick. You here to hang him for the murder?"

"Nope. Taking him back to stand trial for stealing a pig, mostly."

Jeter frowned. "Just a pig?"

"Looks like more, now."

He agreed with that. "Skinner has a deputy—J. W. Gipson. He's the one who locked him in the hoosegow and sent word to y'all."

"Good. Where's Gipson?"

"Probably laid up with one of them whores over the Occidental, or sleeping one off under a porch or building somewhere. He takes to the bottle pretty regular, especially after Skinner got killed. He ain't much punkin at being a lawman." He scratched his cheek. "Never was, really."

"We'll find him later. We'd like to board the horses for the night."

"Sure enough. Grain's extra."

"That's fine, but we found something out about this town . . ."

"Most places want hard money."

"That's what we hear."

"I don't care. I'll take paper, rattling money, gold and silver nuggets, hell, I'll even barter. Don't matter none to me, 'cause I don't do business with McGinty or his thievin' bank."

"Good. We didn't come prepared for that oddity, so we'll sleep in here, if you'll allow it."

"Sure can, and I won't charge you another penny. That right rear stall's empty and there's some fresh hay in there. Smells sweet as spring. If y'all are fastidious enough, I can set a washtub of water out there in the sun for a bath. Won't even charge you extra. All water should be free, in my opinion."

I had a notion and grinned. "You don't trust banks."

"Nossir."

"And you don't care if we pay with folding money."

"Long as it ain't Confederate." He barked a laugh. "Done said that."

I exchanged looks with Gil. "If you'll take anything, maybe we can talk you into exchanging some of our paper for gold so we can go get a drink."

He grinned back, showing several missing teeth. "If you boys'll go spread your bedrolls back there, I'll kick around here a little bit and maybe find a can with some change in it." He held out a hand, and I reached inside my shirt for a couple of bills.

He took them and waved toward the interior. "I'll have it for you when your beds are made. Turn them horses into that big stable back there on the left if they'll tolerate one another. They'll be in out of the weather and I'll give 'em a bait of oats in a little bit. There's already water in there."

We led the horses to the back, unsaddled them, and hung everything on a couple of saddle stands just outside the enclosure. By the time we'd unrolled our blankets in the stall across from them and returned to the front, Jeter had our cash.

He clinked the coins in my hand. "I won't even charge you boys for the exchange, but I'd appreciate a cigar when you come back, if you think to ask for one. I 'spect you're going to the Occidental, since that's the only saloon we have here."

Gill chewed his bottom lip. "Which is kinda strange. I've never seen a town with only one watering hole."

"That's McGinty for you. Came in and bought everything up and closed down anything there was two of. Tried to buy me out, but I wouldn't deal, so he built a livery on the other end of town. I reckon he intends to try and force me out, but that's fine. I have enough business and don't need any more money that what I've already got."

"He might try to muscle you around someday."

The look in Jeter's eye told me that man was once a lobo wolf. "He knows better than to mess with me. I'll shoot him deader'n a beefsteak and piss on him. I won't tolerate any man who intends to take anything from me, or do any harm to me and mine."

Gil grinned. "I believe you would." He turned to me. "Can we go get that drink now? I'm dry as a powder magazine."

I jingled the change in my hand and picked up the pump shotgun. "You bet."

CHAPTER 11

The Panther Creek boys were out of money, and the looks on their faces matched the mood inside the Occidental. Bright Bolton and Shorty carefully sipped what little whiskey they had left to avoid aggravating their sore faces. Bartender John was still adamant about not taking currency, and the rest had consumed just enough liquor to hang on the sharp edge of fun, or violence.

An equally irritated band of rough riders occupied the first table just inside the door. They'd made it known they were down from Denver and had fought two engagements with Comancheros before arriving at the Occidental to toast fallen comrades they'd buried out on the Llano.

The four of them bought a bottle of Old Overholt to split with the last of the silver from their pockets, and were becoming more and more sulled up over the saloon's insistence on payment. The bank had refused to trade with them, irritating them further. Bright heard them talking about the redheaded gal behind the teller window who stood her ground and looked relieved when they said they were leaving.

One was a hawkish-looking man who reminded Bright of a crane. The man beside him possessed an abnormally long neck, and the other two featured the worn, weathered look of men who'd spent their entire lives moving from one place to another.

Instead of a saloon that was usually full of laughter, cards, and celebration, it was dark and gloomy, despite the hot sun outside that seemed to hang low in the sky without moving. At the back, a pair of Panther Creek riders played cards with a couple of strangers in dusty suits who were ironically using U.S. currency for the pot. The useless tender piled in the middle, and in front of the winners, taunting them with the knowledge the paper couldn't be traded for liquor, or even beer.

Horse hooves hammered the hard ground outside, and a cloud of dust rolled in the saloon's open doors. Saddle leather creaked, and loud voices shouted and laughed. The card game and quiet conversations inside ceased with the arrival of a band of hairy, filthy, and heavily armed men that put a final damper on the evening.

Outside, the hitching posts in front of the Occidental were already thick with horses, but through the open door and flyspecked windows, the Panther Creek boys saw the new arrivals shoving horses that weren't theirs to the side to make room.

The only Black rider in the bunch untied a waiting horse and slapped it on the hindquarters.

It walked off toward the livery, and he knotted his own mount in the space. Others laughed at the sight.

Bright Bolton and Shorty stiffened when the door filled with a large, bearded man under a beaten-down, sweat-stained hat that was mottled with suspicious soils and greasy spots.

He stopped just inside and shouted with a heavy German accent. "Is that bank manager McGinty in here?"

Bartender John's face went white at the flood of disheveled humanity squeezing in and flowing around the oblivious beast of a man who was in the way. "No, he, uh, I hear he's out of town."

"Well, that's what that little split-tail said over dere at the bank, right before she shut and locked ze door behind me. No matter." He chuckled and swaggered up to the bar. "If I vanted back in there, I'd kick zat door into flinders. Me and my boys vant vhiskey, and make it fast."

The foursome at the table just inside the door finished their drinks, rose, and slipped out as the last of the gang pushed inside. Though they all carried pistols and rifles, Bright wondered if they were cowards and blowhards that lied earlier about their dangerous trek to Angel Fire, or maybe they were smart enough to get away from such dangerous men.

As they passed by the big windows looking out onto the street, they paused to talk. Lots of fingers pointed and hands waved before they seemed to come to some agreement. Each man led a horse away from the hitching post and went down the street at a slow walk.

Shoving their way to the bar, the newcomers displaced a couple of Panther Creek riders who gave way probably more for the putrid smell than the menace radiating from them. Confident in their abilities to stand up for themselves against anyone who crossed the outfit, buffalo hunters, or any raiding band of Comanches, the cowboys nevertheless preferred to breathe cleaner air than what surrounded the unwashed men who reeked worse than anything they'd ever smelled.

As soon as he heard the German's voice and got a good look at the men with him, Bright slipped the thong off the hammer of his pistol and saw Shorty do the same. Using his left hand, he fought the fear clenching his stomach and reached out to take a sip from the almost empty shot glass on the table in front of him.

Two Panther Creek men who'd been scattered out across the saloon strolled over and joined them at the table. Bright noticed they'd all shifted their guns to provide quicker access.

Curly, who got his nickname from the uncontrollable hair sticking out from under his hat, pulled out a chair and positioned himself to keep an eye on the bar. "You know, Bright, I'd just as soon head on back to the ranch, instead of drinking with this crowd. We're out of money anyhow."

"I was thinking the same thing." Bright glanced at a windup clock at the far end of the bar and noted the time. "Let me finish this drink and walk Callie home, and we'll get gone."

Curly rose. "You finish up. I'm gone." He walked out the door, followed by two others.

Bartender John licked his lips and addressed the men burned brown from the sun. He spoke to a Black man who came in with them and leaned against the bar with a mustached Mexican, as if talking to them was safer. "Uh, just so's you'll know, McGinty owns this saloon and I have orders to take only gold and silver. Currency won't do."

The big-bearded German with yellow teeth rubbed a hand over his mouth in thought. "How about I pay in lead."

"Works for me." The bartender reached under the bar and produced two bottles of unlabeled whiskey. When the German didn't move, he brought out two more bottles. "That enough?"

"For now."

CHAPTER 12

My irritation out in the late evening heat increased when we returned to the Occidental. I'd raised horses all my life and never liked to see them mistreated. Mixed in with the well-kept Panther Creek stock were mounts that'd been rode hard without much care for their well-being. They were dirty, lathered, and full of tangles in their manes and tails. I couldn't understand how men whose lives depended on the horses they rode wouldn't take care of them.

The odor of death filled the air around us, and I couldn't find where it was coming from. It seemed stronger on the opposite side of the street, and when I passed a knot of horses tied there, I realized what it was.

The rigging on all the mounts was a mix of worn-out saddles and blankets. Each had full saddlebags and, the closer I got, the more they reeked. One of the horses on the end had a long-haired scalp hanging from the horn.

The hairs on the back of my neck prickled when Gil flicked the hair with his fingers. "Look at this."

I felt my face flush. "Indian?"

"Maybe. Could be Mexican hair too."

"Scalphunters. Not buffalo hunters."

In my opinion, they were the lowest version of life I'd ever heard of. It was rare to run across those men who lived on blood, and never in our part of the state. It was still whispered that one outlaw part of our government still paid for scalps, but those tales were old. The Mexican government in Chihuahua paid bounties on hair, though, in response to the ongoing Apache wars. They also paid for Comanche scalps, and heads brought even more if there was identifying beadwork woven in.

The ongoing war between both tribes and the Mexican people had cost thousands of lives and millions of dollars through the years as the Apaches preyed upon those who tried to press them off their land. For the Comanches, it was simply a part of life and they loved to fight. It was bloody and brutal on both sides of the line, but seeing those scalphunters' horses and their gruesome trophies . . . this was the first time I'd ever come across anything like that in person.

"Looks like it to me." His eyes narrowed when he saw my expression. "Cool down."

I looked toward the Occidental to make sure no one was coming out to challenge us for spending too much time looking at their mounts. I figured that was where the barbarians were.

He came around beside me. "Right now this is no business of ours."

"Maybe it is."

"I hate it when you do that."

"I don't like this one little bit, but I think the best thing to do is go on in there and see what's what."

CHAPTER 13

The German apparently decided not to shoot the bartender when he cooperated by providing free whiskey. He uncocked the revolver and returned it to the wide red sash at his waist as his men collected the bottles and started doing their best to empty them.

One pulled a cork and pitched it onto the floor. "Pletz, this will get us started, but I'druther drink the good stuff."

The German grunted. "Whiskey is whiskey. Go back and get what you want, if you take a notion, and let me think for a minute." He squinted across at the terrified bartender. "Where's the marshal? Skinner's his name, right? I've dealt with him before to collect bounty. I have plenty of business tied on them horses out there, so we'll have gold in a few minutes. Get these boys what they want."

Bright saw the skin around Bartender John Hooper's mouth go white. It was the first time the Panther Creek foreman ever saw Hooper give in to anyone.

To avoid eye contact, Hooper absently wiped at the bar top with the stained rag. He stopped, reached to a shelf in front of the mirror, and thumped a bottle of Old Grand-Dad in front of Pletz, who passed it to the man next to him.

Hooper swallowed. "Skinner's dead. Killed by a buffalo hunter named Haynes. He's locked up out there in the hot box, if the deputy ain't forgot to feed and water him. If he did, I reckon Haynes's dead out there."

"Wilford Haynes?" The German's eyes widened.

Hooper paused, thinking, as if it'd just occurred to him that no one had tended the prisoner in the past few days. The barkeep snapped back to the present. "I believe that's the name."

"He used to ride with us, and in fact, the sonofabitch still owes me money."

Hooper shrugged. "Well, I don't know nothin' about that, and I can promise you right now he ain't got nothing in his pockets."

The German picked at something caught in his mustache. He scowled. "Say you don't take gen-u-ine paper money."

Confused that they were discussing payment after he'd been threatened with a pistol, Hooper patted his shoulder, looking for the misplaced towel that usually rode there. "Nossir. Can't, or I'll lose my job."

The German turned to a man beside him. "Schaefer."

"Yup."

"I'm getting to like this man. Go get the possibles bag off my saddle horn."

"Sure thing." The man who carried four visible guns pushed outside and returned in seconds.

"Two lawmen out there looking at the horses."

"They mess with you?"

"Naw." He handed a hide bag to the boss man who stuck a hand inside. "They were lucky."

"They better stay out of our business." The German withdrew a scalp with long black hair and pitched it on the bar. "That's worth a hundred dollars in gold. Trade it for them bottles the boys have and get your money for this hair from whoever took over for Skinner."

Horrified at the sight, John raised both hands and backed away. "I can't take that! And J. W. Gipson took over for Skinner, and he ain't worth the salt they put in beans." He pointed at another sign on the wall that read, NO BARTERING. "And furthermore and all that, I don't know where he is and don't care; besides, I haven't heard of him buying scalps now nor never."

"Pletz."

The gang leader swung around to his man Schaefer. *"What?"*

Schaefer nodded his head at Bright and the Panther Creek riders who'd drawn together and were watching. "It ain't just us in here."

"I don't care about a bunch of waddies." Pletz straightened. He was done with being civil. "I'll get my own."

John started forward to stop him, and the big man put a ham-sized palm against his chest and pushed. John fell backward with a rattle of glasses while Pletz grabbed a labeled bottle and slammed it on the bar.

"You just made money, son, and I'm gonna let you keep living. That hair's payment enough for what we've drunk, and what we're about to drink." Pletz thumped one bottle after another within reach of his men, who pushed forward and grabbed them. "Drink up, boys. This whiskey's done bought and paid for with that Comanche scalp! The rest of y'all, too!"

Two figures stepped inside the saloon, catching Bright's attention. It was Cap Whitlatch and his partner Gil. The cramp in Bright's stomach loosened at the sight of them, and he marveled at the experience. Whitlatch'd whipped the two of them without hardly having to breathe hard, and the confidence the man possessed pushed away some of Bright's fear.

Despite the addition of two more experienced guns that might get them all out alive if somebody started trouble, he'd had enough. "Boys, let's go."

Whitlatch had that pump shotgun riding over his right shoulder when they came in, and he tensed at the sight of a hairy giant passing out whiskey from behind the bar. Bright wanted to wave and get his attention, but that would draw attention to himself and right then he preferred to be one man in a herd of others.

Their eyes met across the room, and Bright gave Whitlatch a nod that could have meant any number of things. Howdy. You're right. Or, there's a door behind you and we intend to take it right now."

One of the scalphunters shouted. "Lawmen!"

The saloon went silent. Looking like a pirate with two pistols stuck in a red sash around his waist, Pletz paused, a whiskey bottle in each hand and a startled look on his face. Tension was thick enough to cut with any of the bloodstained knives at the scalphunters' belts.

Gil's hand hovered close to his pistol. "Well, hell."

With a sick feeling of dread, Bright saw the pump twelve-gauge come off Cap's shoulder as his eyes darted around the room, probably trying to decide who to shoot first, and wondering what in the hell was going on.

No one moved for three heartbeats; then a yelp came from outside.

"Robbery! The bank's been robbed!"

"Calpurnia!" Bright shot up from his chair. Concern for his redhead replaced his fear of an enclosed gunfight inside of the saloon. "Panther Creek riders!"

Pletz dropped his bottles, which exploded at his feet. "My *money's* in that bank!"

The two deputies spun on their heels and rushed back outside, followed by a stampede of drunks who wanted to shoot somebody, and scalphunters who killed for a living and had the opportunity to have some more fun.

CHAPTER 14

The late evening prairie sky was white hot with no clouds in sight. It graduated to a pale blue on the horizon before grass took over and changed the color to mixed tan and green.

The stage rocked on the rough two-track road and dust filled the interior as Joseph McGinty reached down between his feet and touched the heavy cloth grip packed with cash. Satisfied that it was still there and hadn't vanished in the five minutes since he'd checked last time, he settled back and crossed his arms to provide more room for those sitting on either side of the hard seat.

Riding backward, he was squeezed between a quiet dark-haired young woman on his left and a drummer, looking directly at a worn-out old cowboy across from her, a doctor staring straight at him, and a man who looked suspiciously like the law across from the salesman.

Two more passengers rode on top, men of undetermined professions who bought their tickets late and were determined to reach Gainesville as fast as possible.

The stage's big wheels thumped over a hole, and the entire vehicle threatened to come apart around them. Tired and frustrated by all the dust, McGinty leaned over the dozing salesman on his right and rolled down the nearly useless canvas side curtain.

The blinds were attached on the outside of the coach, and to be effective, they were usually required to be tied down to the sides. Dropping them the way McGinty did still allowed dust to roil up inside, and the flapping noise was an irritant as well. It also cut off half the air circulation that kept the inside from being stifling.

The drummer started awake and glared first at McGinty, then at the blinds. "We're gonna roast in here with that down."

McGinty took note of the man wearing a derby. It was coated with dust, and so much had already blown inside that his hair visible under the brim was caked. "You oiled your hair before we left, didn't you?"

"I did." The middle-aged man tilted his hat back, revealing a clean line running across his forehead and hair. "Why do you ask?"

"Because you're working on a pretty good tater patch there."

The lawman across the way snorted at the weak joke. The salesman reached into a pocket on the inside of the coach, producing a dark brown bottle. He twisted off the cap and held it out. "Well, if we're gonna cook in here, I 'spect we should go out happy. Would you like a drink, Mr. Banker?"

They'd exchanged small pleasantries after first getting into the coach, and McGinty made the mistake of telling the strangers just passing through what he did for a living.

"I'll trade you a drink of my tonic for some of them gold bars you're carrying." The man snorted at his own joke and swallowed a good bit of the bottle's contents.

"Merely papers, sir. A satchel full of bank documents that I need to deposit in the Bank of Gainesville. Were I carrying gold, it would be in a locked box under the shotgun's feet."

"So be it." The drummer took another sip. "This is some of the best medicine west of the Mississippi, and I think it would benefit us all. I'll allow a sip or two for everyone in here to get a taste, and there are six more bottles right here." Using the sole of his shoe, he tapped at a hard leather grip between his feet. "Available for pennies."

The gray-haired doctor across the way squinted. "What's in it?" His voice came out rough and gravelly.

The drummer seemed surprised at the question. "Well sir, I can't say for sure, because I only sell these wares and am not a part of the manufacturing process; however, I will tell you that it burns like fine liquor on the way down and is good for what ails you. It's full of herbs and root medicines that come from an old Indian recipe my employer stumbled across over forty years ago."

The cowboy leaned forward with a twinkle in his eye. "I'll give it a try."

The bottle went from hand to hand diagonally across the coach, and the wrangler took a swallow. His eyebrows rose, and he gulped again before passing it back. "That's some fine elixir."

"The finest." The dusty salesman held the bottle out. "I'll share with any one of you."

McGinty glanced at the woman to read her expression. It was one of ambivalence. He kept his arms crossed. "Bread upon the water, huh?"

Easy to laugh, the drummer chuckled. "You may have your suspicions, but I'm simply sharing my good fortune. The small bag at my feet and a larger case riding in the boot are full of this wonderful medicine that treats all ailments including female vapors, sour stomach, and headaches. I'll share what I have here, so you can see the benefits of Dr. Olson's Black Draught."

"May I?" The doctor reached out and took the container. After examining the label, he sniffed the contents. "I detect a hint of sassafras, but I suspect it contains opium and alcohol."

"All good things for the human body."

Despite his misgivings, the doctor took a tiny experimental sip, and then another before passing it back. "Addicts to the dragon might argue that point."

"On both merits, I might suggest." The drummer took the bottle, examined the content's level, and offered it to the lawman. It was hard for him to read the man's expression under a stiff, wide hat brim resting on his eyebrows, and the huge gray handlebar mustache that hid most of his lower face and mouth.

The man's light blue eyes rose from the container to the drummer, and his right eyebrow arched slightly. "No thank you. Don't wish to be impaired on a dangerous road, but I appreciate the offer."

More talkative now that the elixir's ingredients were coursing through his system, the drummer corked the bottle for the moment and slipped it into the inside pocket of his coat. "I pride myself on being a good judge of character and an individual's profession." He pointed at the wrangler. "You're a cowboy, of course, for I see the rope burns on rough hands and a face carved by the weather."

The wrangler picked at a broken thumbnail as the coach jumped and jolted again. "That'd be pretty good, except I said when we were talking earlier that I was headed up to a ranch out of Fort Worth for a job breaking horses. Not much magic in that."

"Ah, but I detect a slight accent that makes me think of Appalachia."

The man shrugged. "Tennessee. Came out here when I was a kid."

The drummer pointed across the coach. "I

know you're a doctor, of course, and this young lady to my far left I'll allow is a schoolteacher. Am I right?"

For the first time, the woman made eye contact and appeared startled. Pulling her dress's collar higher on her neck, she frowned. "How do you know that?"

"I've not encountered a lot of women on stages. The ones I can recall are military wives going out to join their husbands at some fort or military post, fresh widows looking for a new start, teachers traveling on pennies, or some female of ill repute being run out of town."

She gasped, and the lawman growled in warning and tilted his hat upward. "You're overstepping your bounds, sir."

"I'm so sorry. I didn't mean you were a woman of rough means; I merely used that example to demonstrate my deductive abilities of elimination. My decision rests on you being an educator."

"Well, I'm not."

The interest of all five men in the coach was piqued, for she didn't offer any other suggestion as to what she was doing riding a stage headed east.

Apparently feeling dry, the drummer's hand slipped back under his coat like a tree squirrel going into a hole. It emerged with the bottle again, and he went through the process of uncorking and drinking again.

"This bottle is getting low." He sipped again. "Anyone else want another taste?"

The cowboy accepted his offer. The doctor tilted it next. "Sweet, too. Molasses, I suspect, and some other flavor I can't detect, though it's familiar." He passed it back to the drummer who held it out again.

"Feel free."

The lawman and McGinty refused. It was not offered to the lady a second time.

The sun-scorched landscape outside refused to change. It was still wide prairie drooping in the heat, occasionally broken up by strips of wooded creeks and draws. The driver kept the horses at a steady pace that ate up the ground.

McGinty noticed the cowboy's head nodding, but that was nothing unusual. The rocking motion either sedated some of the passengers, or gave the others a feeling sailors called seasickness. Sleeping was better, because puking out the side of the coach was uncomfortable for everyone and there was no hope that the driver would stop only because someone was sick to their stomach.

It was dangerous to stop anyway. Indians and robbers were a constant concern, and though they weren't on a Butterfield stage that regularly carried cash or gold, it was still subject to the predations of road agents who preyed upon travelers.

McGinty buried his smile with the confidence

that the other passengers had no way of knowing that the man riding shotgun was employed by him to protect what was in the bag at his feet, as well as the strongbox riding up front. The guard only knew someone had hired him through a third party to protect the passengers in Indian country, and through the more settled areas of north-central Texas until they reached Gainesville.

Stops weren't frequent, but necessary. It was the previous stage stop called Scorpion Springs that the lawman came aboard, though he still hadn't identified himself as such, and that worried McGinty. As they continued east, he wondered if it wasn't planned circumstances that brought the man onto the coach.

The doctor's eyes were growing heavy when McGinty's concerns got the best of him. Ignoring the drummer who was also nodding, he shifted his knees and bumped that of the mustached man. "We haven't met. Name's McGinty. A banker in Angel Fire."

Those pale blue eyes held his. "What's a banker doing out here?"

That wasn't the response he was looking for. His well-practiced lie came easy. "Well, I'm heading to Fort Worth to meet with others about future finance. I have to ask. Are you a sheriff?"

"No. Texas Ranger."

"Ah, I wouldn't have expected to see you on

a stage. Most of the Rangers I've ever met have their own mounts and travel at will."

It was several moments before he answered, as if judging the merits or intention of the question. "Horse went lame. Sold it, and I need to get back to the station in Duck Creek."

"Never heard of it."

"Not far from Embree, a day's ride northeast of Dallas."

"Ah. *That* town I've heard of. Urgent business?"

"All law business is urgent."

"Well, I for one am glad you're here." The young lady with blue-black hair smiled, bringing deep dimples into view. "There's so much Indian activity around here."

The drummer perked up for a moment. "Ma'am, I don't mean to be contentious, but it's common knowledge passengers don't discuss religion, Indians, or point out where heinous murders have occurred along a line."

The woman's dimples disappeared at the mild scolding. "I didn't mean any harm, sir."

For the first time since they'd left the station, the Ranger leaned forward. "Miss, my name is Malachai Holman, and yours?"

"Amanda Dorsey."

"Miss Dorsey, feel free to bring up any appropriate topic of discussion you wish, and we won't let mister, what's your name, drummer?"

"Augustine Dewey."

"We won't let Augustine here impede our enjoyment any further. You won't, will you, sir?"

The drummer stuttered twice before he could gather his wits. "Of course not."

A shout came from up above as the driver leaned over to make himself heard over the thunder of his horses' hooves and the rattle of the stage. "Guns up, gentlemen! The station's burned out. Looks like Indians, but they're gone. No matter, we have to stop and rest the horses."

Amanda gasped as the cowboy and doctor settled into a deep sleep instead of reacting to the danger. McGinty was shocked when the drummer reached back under his coat and, instead of the bottle, drew a small revolver that he swung toward the Ranger, who slammed a boot in the man's chest, produced a .44 from under his own coat as fast as lightning, and shot the man square in the chest.

CHAPTER 15

Close to sundown, the opposite side of Angel Fire's main street was in shadow. The saloon side of the thoroughfare was a little brighter, and I noticed the false fronts of the buildings were the only places still catching light. In less than an hour, all would be dark.

It was dusk, and all Gil and I wanted was that drink, but inside the Occidental, it looked like we'd walked into a dark rattlesnake den. There were men all around, and every one of them had a mad look on their face in the oil lamplight. I couldn't tell if they were cross with each other, or like us, they'd found out that the saloon didn't take any form of payment other than rattling money.

It sure looked like they were about to start shooting something—or each other—and Gil spoke under his breath. "Oh, hell."

Mouth suddenly dry from the situation we'd walked into, I took in the bar that looked much different from the last time we were in there less than an hour earlier. It was filled with the hairiest, dirtiest, most dangerous men I'd ever seen, and I figured out real fast I didn't want any part of them.

Beside me, Gil spoke aloud again, though I doubt he realized it. This time it was louder when the pirate back behind the bar glared at us as if his miserable life was our fault. "Uh-oh."

The pump twelve-gauge came off my shoulder at the sight of those men who all looked as if they wanted to cut out my liver. I knew most of them were seeing the badges on our chests and those little pieces of cheap tin were about to get us killed, or shot up at the very least.

It's funny what goes through your mind at a time like that. Was there a doctor in town to treat us? Would Jeter take care of the steeldust mare if I was hurt for weeks? Would Calpurnia come rushing to check on me?

Then my mind split once again, and Calpurnia, the woman I'd only just met, was suddenly in my head. The man behind the bar sure wasn't supposed to be there, and I wondered about the bartender pulling himself upright from the floor.

My blood went cold, and no one moved for three heartbeats; then a yelp came from outside.

"Robbery! The bank's been robbed!"

To my right, Bright shot up from his chair. He and his partners Harvey and Shorty were surrounded by cowboys who looked like they were fighting stomach pains. Bright hoofed it around the table. "Panther Creek riders!"

The prairie pirate behind the bar, who looked like he ate raw meat for every meal, forgot me and dropped his bottles with a wet crash. "My *money's* in that bank!"

A man like that has money in a bank?

No matter, somebody was robbing the local depository, there wasn't a marshal in town, and I wore that damned star. Calpurnia was there too, in that bank, and she was in danger. I didn't have to say anything to Gil, who'd already read my mind. We whirled and headed down the boardwalk at a dead run.

A one-armed man runs differently, but Gil matched me pace for pace. "The horses woulda been faster!"

I didn't need to answer him, because both were in the livery. Once past the thick clot of horses tied up in front of the Occidental, we angled off across the street. Other folks in town were headed in the same direction.

Gil wouldn't stop talking, though. The many times us kids ran through the darkness with stolen melons, he chattered like a magpie the whole time. "I don't see that knothead deputy anywheres about."

"Said he was likely laid up somewhere sleeping one off. It's just us."

"I didn't sign up to marshal this place."

A gunshot came from somewhere ahead, but I couldn't tell if it came from inside the bank, or another location. It became clear when a man wearing a suit staggered out of the bank, holding his stomach.

He shouted and dropped to his knees, bracing

himself with one hand on the boardwalk. "Robbery! Murder!"

A shifty saddle tramp with a long turkey neck waited beside four horses tied to the rail. He produced a pistol and shot the wounded man. We heard a loud grunt as he took another bullet in the gut. Shying away from the robber, he stumbled against the wall and saw us running. Holding out a hand for help, he took two more steps in our direction before his knees gave out again. He fell and lay still.

The lookout who shot him shouted through the open door. "Here they come! Hurry up!"

The muzzle of his pistol flashed as he threw a shot in our direction and the hot slug buzzed off to my left. Most of the people still on the street at that hour ducked and ran. A few others drew weapons and hunkered down behind any cover they could find.

The outlaw ducked back behind the horses, preventing us from firing back. Gil and I split up. He continued straight and I cut back to the left, trying to get an angle on the man trying to kill us.

I hadn't taken two more steps when a bullet sizzled past my head and slammed into the shop to my left. It came from the wrong direction, and not the lookout. I dropped to a knee against the wall only inches from the freshly splintered bullet hole and tried to find where it came from.

The world turned into noise and sounded like a

battlefield skirmish. The gunfire came from the Panther Creek boys, but they were firing not at the bank or the lookout, but at the roof of a false-fronted building across the street, yellow in the long rays of the disappearing sun.

The outlaws had staked a man up there with a rifle to cover for them. Dozens of bullets splintered the plank front hiding the rifleman, exploding with little puffs of powdered wood. Through the little holes, I saw a shape move past as he scrambled for some distance between him and the boys in the street.

It wasn't but a second when his hat flew off and we heard a thump, followed by the sounds of a body rolling down the roof's slope. It landed with a crash on a pile of lumber beside the building.

There was no more return fire, so I concentrated on the outlaw in front of the bank. Horse hooves thundered on the packed street, and I thew a look over my shoulder to see the mob of barbarians charging in my direction, firing into the air and at anything taking their fancy. Their guns flared in the dim light like a photographer's powder flash.

An onlooker wearing a flop hat grunted and clutched his stomach. One of the gang's bullets missed its intended target, which could have been the bank window, the lookout, or even the bank itself, and struck the innocent man.

Across the street, someone yelped and I caught the image of arms and legs falling through the paned window of a small shop. He could have been another victim of a wild shot, or diving through the glass to escape the irrational gunfire. Either way, he'd be looking for someone with a needle and thread soon.

It reminded me of a book I'd read on a trail drive several years earlier titled *The Secret History of the Mongols*. It described the way they arrived in hordes and sacked Chinese towns. Looking at those savages coming down the street, I wasn't sure they had any different idea. Once they finished with the bank robbers, they might not stop until the whole town was ashes.

For a second time the saddle tramp stepped into the open and this time threw a rifle to his shoulder. He shot at me and missed again. That guy should have given up the rifle for a shotgun, for he was no good with it. I dropped to one knee, and he jacked the lever just as Gil appeared behind him. Gil fired, and the outlaw flinched, hit in the back. He twisted around to face his attacker.

The Spencer in my hands came up and I pointed more than aimed, but couldn't fire because Gil would have caught part of the charge. Any other time the expression on his face would have been funny as he looked down the big bore of the twelve-gauge. The man darted away from Gil to my side of the horses, giving me a clear shot, and I took it.

Most of the load took the man in the chest and

stomach, the buckshot puckering his shirt in half a dozen places. He fell half on and off the boardwalk and was still.

I raced to the bank and took a quick peek inside through the big window. The front glass shattered from a gunshot, and I whipped back out of sight. At first I thought it was one of those hairy men shooting in that direction and barely missing me before realizing the bullet came from inside. Another shot came, and I flattened myself against the wall.

The men I assumed were hide hunters passed the bank like a Comanche war party, throwing lead into the front of the building, then kept going. I was sure they'd circle the bank like that over and over again, if they could.

I waved them back. "There's a woman inside, you idiots!"

Gil made his way around the other side of the front door and matched my position. He pointed at the dead man almost at our feet. "I saw these guys leave the saloon as we were coming up. There were four of 'em."

One on the roof, and he might've still been kicking, but not for long with several holes in him, and this one cooling on the boardwalk. That left two more inside.

"Go around back. There might be a door back there. No matter what you do, don't let 'em take Calpurnia as a shield!"

Bright's voice came from behind me in all the chaos. "Shorty! You and a couple of the boys go with them, and be careful of my girl!"

That arrogant fool irritated me, but right then was no time to argue about whether she felt the same about him or not. More guns in the rear meant they couldn't get out the back. We had 'em trapped.

I sensed men scrambling around me, taking up positions across the street and anywhere else they could get a clear shot. It was mostly the Panther Creek riders, and at least they weren't throwing lead at anything they saw. A few townspeople arrived, taking up positions where they could see the front of the bank.

I couldn't say that for the scalphunters. They'd wheeled around and were coming back, and I did something that shocked even me. As they rode past for another crack at the bank, I ran out in the street with the shotgun pointed at the first person I saw, and that was the pirate.

It was the worst place I could have braced those men, for they reined up right in front of the building and between the cowboys who'd just found a place for cover. If the bank robbers had taken a notion to start shooting, they could have mowed down a good number of those men sitting atop their horses.

"Hold up!" I didn't have the pump twelve against my shoulder, but it was pointed in the general direction of half a dozen men sitting above me.

The man wearing a red sash started to point his pistol at me, and I stopped him. "Uh-uh! We're in a pickle here. If you start shooting at me, those fellers in the bank might want a crack at you and you'd be in a crossfire. I don't believe those boys around us would like that, either."

"You fool!" He threw a look at the bank, then back at me. His German accent was heavy, reminding me of back home where Gil and I came from. "You have us sitting here right in the open."

Now wasn't the time for discussion. I just wanted them to stop shooting at the bank and in the direction of Callie. Good Lord, now I was calling her by a familiar name she hadn't given her permission to use.

"There's an innocent woman in there. Y'all just ride on past and help us instead of acting like this."

"Lower that thing in your hands."

It hadn't occurred to me that they'd never seen a pump shotgun before. It was fairly new, and I'd only gotten my hands on it a year or so before. I liked it, because it held seven shells, giving me much more firepower than a traditional double barrel. After firing, one pumped the sliding fore end to eject the spent shell and then forward to load another. It was a deadly weapon in close quarters and had been by my side since the day I bought it.

"This thing's a shotgun and it'll spray you and a couple of those boys behind you." I stepped to the side closest to the bank so they could pass without getting behind me. "Now, y'all either join us, or get the hell out of my way."

I swear he thought about pointing that revolver at me, but changed his mind. "The hell with you, then!" Spurring his horse, he rode past and down the street, leaving the smell of death behind them. Mad as a yellowjacket, I walked over behind the robbers' horses where they couldn't get a shot at me.

"Y'all in the bank! Turn that woman loose and come out and throw up your hands. You ain't getting away, and if you hurt her, you won't hang—I'll shoot every damned one of you right where you stand!"

The street was quiet for a moment, and the next thing I knew, a rattle of gunfire came from behind the building. I flinched at the sound, but no shots came our way.

Gil's dim voice came to us. "Cap! They went back inside!"

CHAPTER 16

It was chaos in the coach as the driver reined up beside the blacked adobe walls of what had been a way station. At the sound of the Ranger's gunshot, the groggy cowboy and doctor jerked up right from their sleep with shouts of fear.

The drummer's little pistol went off, the bullet punching a hole near the front of us in the stage's roof.

"Sonofabitch!" The Ranger's right boot came up and pinned the drummer against the back wall. He fired a second round into the drummer's chest only a half inch from the first. The dying man groaned and collapsed in on himself.

A shout of pain arose from up above, and the driver's voice, full of shock, came to those inside. "Thompson's been shot!"

McGinty threw himself away from the gunfire, squeezing Amanda into the corner in an effort to avoid being shot himself. Panicked, she screamed, slamming a fist against his head to get him off. Shouts of alarm came from the two cowboys riding on top.

The driver reined the team up, throwing everyone forward. Still unaware of what was going on around them, the cowboy and the doctor, whose knees were interwoven with Amanda and McGinty, reached out to brace themselves, tangling even more with the banker and schoolteacher.

"Aggghhh." The shout of pain filled the air as the guard thrashed around on the seat beside the driver. He jumped to the ground, followed by the two men who'd spent the entire ride hanging onto whatever would anchor them on the rocking coach.

"One of y'all shot Aloysius!" His face full of fury, the driver yanked the door open. "What'n hell's going on in here!"

The Ranger swung the big .44 on the startled man. "Back off there, hoss. I ain't sure you're not in on all this yet." He flicked the barrel at the two dusty cowboys behind him who climbed down from the roof. "You boys back off until I sort all this out."

Holding up both hands, they took two steps back, and the driver looked confused. "In on what?"

"This robbery."

"I don't know what you're talking about, but y'all just shot a man up there who'll be handy if them Comanches show back up."

"Round must've gone through." The Ranger took the little pistol from the dead drummer's hand. "One thing in its time. Banker, you and Miss Amanda get out on her side and stay with the driver." He studied the two cowboys outside, who kept their hands away from the pistols on their belts. "You boys can keep them revolvers, but if I see a hand even touch the butts, or if y'all get somewhere I can't see you, I'll shoot you down. Y'all hear me?"

Silent, they nodded in unison, and the Ranger saw for the first time they appeared to be brothers. He grabbed the doctor's elbow. "Sir, are you yourself?"

Rubbing a hand over his forehead, the doctor frowned. "I'll not be manhandled."

"Forgive me, but I need your attention. Is your mind *clear?*"

He nodded. "I believe so. What happened?"

"This drummer knocked you out with that damned snake oil of his. Can you get enough wits about you to see how bad the guard's hurt?"

Trying to rid himself of the cobwebs, the doctor shook his head. He pointed at the drummer. "How'd *he* get hurt?"

"I shot him a couple of times."

"What? How come you do that?"

"That's what you do to a snake, and I didn't want him breathing no more, but there's time for explaining and this ain't it." Not knowing the groggy cowboy's name, he addressed him in a familiar way. "Buck, shake yourself awake there and give him a hand. You might keep that hogleg on your hip limbered up in case there's trouble. Driver, get that shotgun up there and keep it handy."

"Soon's I puke." The cowboy now known as Buck stepped out and leaned over, throwing up everything he'd eaten since he was a kid. He wasn't quiet about it, and arched his back like a cat with each explosion.

Amanda and McGinty moved away from the sick man to join the other two topside cowboys who were studying the burned-out station. McGinty had his cloth grip in hand and threw a glance up at the guard, who lay groaning on the coach's bench seat.

She looked at the banker with wide eyes, pulling a strand of black hair from her face. "What just happened?"

"I have no idea, but I think the Ranger knows." McGinty started to set the grip down and changed his mind. He switched it to his left hand and turned to study the way station along with the brothers.

Bullet holes pocked the adobe near the doors and windows on either side. The fire burned everything that served as fuel. The roof had collapsed, and blackened timbers stuck up above the walls at the far end. He walked to the shattered door and peered inside.

Charcoal and ashes covered every inch of the dirt floor. A body lay curled up under a long, scorched table, as if the man had crawled under there in an effort to protect himself. McGinty turned to survey the nearby empty corral that contained another body. Animals, coyotes likely, had been at that corpse.

The fire hadn't been out long, though the ashes were cool. The interior still smelled of fresh smoke, though. McGinty considered the timeline. The stage went through three times a week, and it had been three days since the last stop. Three days for the coals to die.

A heavy thud caused McGinty to turn and see the Ranger dragging the drummer's body out of the stage by the collar. One worn shoe came off as the dead man's feet thumped over the high doorsill and landed on the hard ground. The Ranger unceremoniously dragged the limp body to the edge of the corral and let it drop.

Seeing that the doctor needed help with the wounded guard, one of the brothers climbed up on the driver's seat and helped the moaning man down. He kicked the cash box and McGinty winced as if it held fine china. The other brother reached up, and they lowered Aloysius Thompson to the ground.

The doctor knelt and looked at the guard's leg. He grunted and rose. "I'm too old to be doing this on the ground. I need to get him higher so's I don't have to curl up like a grub to work on him."

Only slightly taller than his brother, the cowboy who appeared to be the older of the two brothers pointed at the building. "Can we get him on a table in there?"

McGinty shook his head. "Nope. Burned out and there's a body under a table. Wouldn't be right to work on someone right above a corpse. Besides, it stinks in there."

Annoyed and pale, the doctor shook his head. "Is it all plumb burned up in there?"

McGinty paused, confused. "The body, or the table?"

"The table," the doctor snapped. "The body in there's no use to me right now."

"We might be able to brush the soot and ashes off enough for you to use it."

"Y'all do that, then. Bring it out here so's I don't have to work in amongst all them ashes."

Once they had the groaning guard propped against the stage's front wheel, the brothers followed McGinty to the station's gaping door. He still held the grip, bringing curious looks from the others. Regaining control of his stomach, Buck joined them, pale and shaky.

The older brother stuck out his hand and they shook. "Say your name's Buck?"

"That'll do for now."

"I'm Garry and this is Larry, my brother."

"Figured y'all for kinfolk."

"Give us a hand?"

"I'll try." Buck wiped his mouth with the purple scarf from around his neck.

Together, they carried the table outside and used a burlap sack Larry found on the ground beside the corral to wipe it down. Seeing the table, Amanda hurried around to the stage's boot and came back with a rolled piece of canvas.

"Use this to cover it."

"Good idea." The doctor circled around back to the boot and plucked his black bag from the pile of dust-covered luggage. By the time he'd returned, the brothers and Buck had Aloysius on the table.

The wounded guard rallied enough to point at his knee-high boot. "Y'all, see if you can get it off without cutting the top. I'm mighty proud of these boots." He raised his leg and blood poured from the top. "Dang it. I 'magine they're rurnt inside, though."

Doc paused for a moment, suddenly pale. He leaned away from his patient and gagged, then waited to see if he was going to really throw up. "That damned snake oil's rough on a man."

Seeing the moment had passed, he straightened, opened his bag, and came out with a pint bottle. Unscrewing the cap of Beech Tree whiskey, he took a long, deep swallow and then handed it to the wounded man. "This is good for you, Aloysius. High-grade whiskey."

"How do you know that?"

"Says so right here on the label. Take a couple of swallers. You'll need it to take some of the edge off." He waved at the three cowboys. "Y'all heard him. Get that boot off and be gentle. Don't go to yanking on it. Two of you hold this broke leg in place and the other work it off."

"I thank you for not cutting my boot. It's fairly new and not cheap. I don't have many fine things."

"Son, you've already said that. I believe you're getting delirious." Doc took the bottle from Aloysius and swallowed a considerable amount. Whiskey bubbled as he drained half the bottle and passed it back.

Doc plucked out an assortment of tools, including a dark brown bottle, while the cowboy and brothers held the leg and pulled the boot off as easy as they could. Aloysius yelped, bit his shirt collar, and groaned.

Buck worked the tall boot free and marveled at the hole behind the calf. "Must've punched through that drummer and hit a strut, from the angle I see. Then on through the calf."

Once it was off, Doc produced a pair of scissors and cut the trousers to the knee. Folding the edges back, he poured some of the contents of a brown bottle onto the bullet wound.

Aloysius hollered right out loud again. "Goddlemighty! It hurts bad enough already."

Instead of answering, Doc put a fingertip in the bullet hole. "Finish that bottle. Your shin's broke. I can see the bullet in there and it'll be easy to reach, but I'll have to set your leg and put a splint on it, so you boys get on each side and be ready to hold him while I set this stem."

He went to work, and McGinty walked over to the Ranger standing with his back to the way station's exterior wall. "What was that all about in there?"

The Ranger took a moment to scan the prairie around them. There was only one tree in sight, and it was a tall cottonwood well beyond the station. He pointed to the valise the banker still held. "That drummer wanted whatever you have in your case."

"He was gonna *rob* me? No one knows what I have in there."

"He was, when he got the chance, and he must've known there's money in it. Even I figured it out after you said earlier you were a banker, and you haven't stopped touching the damn thing since we left. But this was all planned from the start. I figure he had a friend here at the station, waiting, but they hadn't planned on the Comanches who showed up and tore that playhouse down."

McGinty shook his head. "I still don't understand."

"Whatever's in that bottle the drummer passed around was supposed to knock everyone out. You know as well as I do stage lines suggest that if somebody brings a bottle on board, they're supposed to share in order to be neighborly. Whiskey don't work fast, but opium does. Only problem, he hadn't counted on being turned down by so many of us, and having a decent woman in the coach. The idea was to wait until everyone was asleep and when we stopped, him and his partner was probably gonna kill us all while we slept.

"But I reckon things went bad from the start, to see those two brothers riding on top, and an armed guard, which I still don't understand, because this isn't a Butterfield stage hauling money or mail."

McGinty kept his expression even. "So when the rest of us, and especially you, didn't drink, he had to change his plan, but what I don't get is why *he* didn't pass out."

"He wasn't really drinking, and that's what I got onto first. Oh, he looked like it, but he just let it run in his mouth and then back into the bottle. The level barely went down."

The Ranger paused, thinking and keeping an eye on the waving grass around them. "I 'magine he must drink enough of that stuff, so that what little he took in didn't affect him. The only time the level went down was when these guys drank."

McGinty shivered, glad he hadn't taken the man up on his offer. "You knew he was pulling a gun, and that's why you shot him?"

"Saw the bulge under his coat when he'd take the bottle out." The Ranger paused and looked startled. He suddenly snatched the Colt from its holster and thumb-cocked it. Extending his arm, he aimed it at the men working on the guard. "Driver! Hands up and step back from those others."

Instead of complying, the stage driver reacted faster than an innocent, startled man should. He reached for the pistol on his belt. The Ranger's gun belched smoke and flame, and the driver threw up his hands and fell backward. Amanda screamed and crouched while the others froze, lest they also became targets.

Doc threw a look at the driver, then at the Ranger. "Dammit. You gonna shoot people as fast as I can patch 'em up?"

"Boys, draw your weapons and check around this house. This wasn't Comanche doings, or maybe not at first. This was a robbery plain and simple."

Seeing the driver wasn't dead, the Ranger took his gun and left the moaning driver where he lay as a thick river of blood poured from his stomach.

Used to following orders on a ranch, the brothers and Buck unholstered their guns and spread out to look for anyone hiding nearby. As Buck passed the guard's sawed-off twelve-gauge leaning against the stage's front wheel, he slipped his Colt back into its holster. Picking it up, he broke it open to check the loads. Seeing twin circles of brass, he snapped it shut and disappeared around behind the adobe.

Doc glared at the Ranger. "You gonna just leave him there to bleed to death?"

"That's my intention." The Ranger stuck the man's unfired revolver in his belt. "We'll move him to your table when you finish up that leg, if he's still sucking air."

"You're a hard man, sir."

"That I am."

Hands to both sides of her head, Amanda backed away from the table. "I don't understand any of this."

"The driver and the drummer were in cahoots." The Ranger continually surveyed the area as he talked, not making eye contact with anyone. "The drummer had to act when the driver hollered that the stop was burned out. That's when he threw down on me. Now, I'm not sure about Aloysius, but I can talk to him when the Doc's finished with his leg. He's no danger now if he's with them. He doesn't have a weapon."

The guard had passed out from the pain before the shooting started and was still unconscious.

McGinty shook his head. "The guard wasn't in on it. He's in my employ."

"Why do you need a guard?"

"You were wrong about not carrying cash. I have a strongbox up there. Money heading to the bank in Gainesville. We don't tell people when we're moving it, and I didn't even want him to know what was going on. I have a third man who hired him for me without knowing who he worked for."

The Ranger sighed. "It's always about money."

Buck and the brothers came back around. Buck held the shotgun in the crook of his arm. "Nobody, here nor there."

Frowning, the Ranger thought for a moment. "No more bodies?"

"Nope. No blood. No nothing."

"Maybe I was partly wrong. There should be another man involved in this."

"Maybe the one inside." Buck pointed at the adobe and the body within. "Or that one by the corral."

"Could be, but they usually have two people. One to switch teams, and the other manages the stage stop itself, food and such. That accounts for those two. I'd suspect the third who did all the killing and burning. That's the one working with the drummer and that driver laying there, and I'd expect him to be somewhere around here."

Doc straightened from splinting the guard's leg. "That'll hold him. He'll live. A couple of you boys move him over against that wall and heave the driver up here so I can work on him, and Ranger . . . what is your name?"

"Malachai Holman."

"Don't shoot anyone else for me to fix up, Malachai. I'm already tired."

They all jumped when one of the coach's horses on the left side screamed in pain. It rose in its traces, pawed the air, and then collapsed with a gurgle. Unable to comprehend what was going on, they simply stared until another soft thump came to them and the horse in front went sideways, throwing the right lead animal off balance. The remaining two on the right side fought the harness until the second horse fell and went still.

It finally came to the Ranger. "Comanches! They're killing the horses! Everyone inside!"

He grabbed McGinty's coat and thrust him toward the burned building. The banker hesitated, looking back at the driver's seat where the strongbox sat, hidden.

Malachai threw a shot just to get the attackers' heads down and grabbed Amanda by the waist. She yelped as he almost threw her toward the station. "You boys get Aloysius!"

The brothers grabbed the moaning guard off the table. Barely missing them, an arrow shattered when it hit the adobe wall, showering them with pieces of grit and wooden shards. The metal arrowhead hammered from a piece of tin can ricocheted and cut the Ranger across the cheek.

Shifting the shotgun to his left hand, Buck used his revolver to throw two shots at movement not far from the cottonwood, a distance greater than the effective range of the short two-shoot gun. He grabbed the bleeding driver by the collar and dragged him inside as gunfire rattled and bullets struck the adobe in showers of powdered dirt that glistened in the dying light.

CHAPTER 17

Inside the dim Angel Fire bank, Calpurnia crouched in the shadows behind the half wall containing two teller windows. Terrified, she kept her head low, fully expecting to be shot at any moment. The day's last light came through the window, illuminating the two outlaws sitting on the floor not far away.

One was cursing and using his good hand to tie his scarf around a wound in his upper left arm. Taking one corner of the silk in his teeth, he made a loop with the other hand and pulled the knot tight, shutting off the blood seeping through his shirt. "Dan'l. You hurt too?"

"Naw, they missed me." Daniel stayed back away from the windows. "Frank's dead out front, though."

"See Harlan?"

"He was on the roof across the street, but they run him off of there. He hasn't made a sound since. I'm afraid he's done for."

"This was supposed to be easy."

"Well, it ain't." Daniel Morgan thumbed fresh shells into his Colt's hot cylinder. "I didn't expect everyone in town to show up shooting!"

"You said we'd get in and out quick."

"Well, that didn't happen."

"Are the horses still there?"

"Hell, I don't know, Nate." Daniel risked a peek through the shattered glass. Frank's body lay still, leaking a great river of blood in front of their ponies. "Still there."

Nate finished tying the scarf and rested his eyes on Calpurnia. "I have an idea."

Daniel's hands fluttered over his pockets, searching for the spare rounds he knew he'd need. "I'll listen to anything right about now."

"We're going out with this gal between us. They won't risk hitting her. She'll ride behind me and we hightail it out when it gets dark."

The sun was almost down. Leaving under the cover of darkness was their best bet, in Nate's opinion.

"I have a better idea." From behind the counter and the teller window, Calpurnia's soft voice was still full of fear, but confident.

"You?" Daniel frowned.

She nodded in the growing gloom as if they could see her. "As long as you do what I say."

"Why would you help us?"

"Because I need to get out of this town and you can help me."

"I don't understand."

Staying low, she crawled around the counter and flicked a finger at the croker sack lying beside Daniel. "That little bit of money you got

148

in there ain't a dust mote compared to what I have in the safe."

"You said you didn't have the combination."

"I lied."

Always a quick thinker, Calpurnia stared past the muzzles of two guns when the pair came in with the intent of robbing the bank. She saw the perfect opportunity to get away with a valise full of cash waiting in the safe.

McGinty's insistence on taking in only gold and silver had a purpose no one understood. He really had nothing against cash money, because it was so easy to carry. More than once he'd left Angel Fire on business in Gainesville and Fort Worth, carrying valises full of cash to squirrel away in one of the biggest banks in Texas. The Liberty Bank in Gainesville was considered unrobbable, and his friend owned the establishment.

He always returned to Angel Fire with a heavier valise, filled with coins, but they weren't what they seemed. Exact copies of double eagles and silver dollars in both appearance and weight, the money was nothing more than stamped copper alloy and coated with gold and silver veneer worth only a fraction of the money's denomination.

He bought the planchets from the Davis brothers in Fort Worth for twenty-eight cents a pound, and that included delivery charges to a metallurgist in Gainesville. Copper prices were falling, and the cost of stamping their own counterfeit coins gave them a profit of more than 40 percent per pound.

The cheap counterfeit coins were traded for real paper and circulated throughout the town when travelers arrived to do business. They also bought real hard money, which funneled into McGinty's safe along with everything else.

It was a perfect scam. Insist on hard cash. Travelers had to exchange their paper for counterfeit coins. The real cash went into the safe, then on to Fort Worth, and the cycle continued.

McGinty didn't know Calpurnia was a watchful girl. When it was time to travel to Gainesville, he'd fill a valise with the paper money and put it into the safe until the next morning. A small strongbox holding real coins also went with him on each trip.

Confident that only he knew what was going on, he never checked the grip's contents when he left, simply opening the door and taking it with him.

That morning she'd substituted one valise for another with the exact weight and appearance. He was gone with a cloth grip full of stacked paper, and she had enough money to start a new life, along with the gold and silver they'd taken in the day before.

But these guys had messed up the works and

were there to steal the money she'd already stolen. It was a bet that she needed to get out of town before McGinty found out what she'd done, and she wanted that cash for a new start.

They wanted to live, and the only way for the three of them to be successful was to work together.

"You boys get me out of here, and you can have all the gold you can carry." She pictured the stacks of counterfeit coins in the safe. "I'll take a grip with that little cash you have in there, and the few bills that are left. We'll all be tickled."

Daniel shook his head in amazement. "A woman bank robber. Nate, you ever hear of such a thing?"

"I haven't, but you haven't got all this worked out, missy. We're still in here and they're all out there."

She presented him with the smile that melted Bright every time he saw it, and had almost hooked Cap Whitlatch, who she found interesting. She hoped it would work on those two holding guns on her. "McGinty don't trust anyone. He has another way out of here."

"A trap door in the floor?"

"No. You can't get away with digging something like that in a small town. But if you're a carpenter by trade and own more than half a town, you can cut a door into the building beside you. That's McGinty's drugstore through the wall right there. It's not open yet, so no one's paying it any attention. Move that coatrack out of the way and there's a little door we can use."

"They'll still see us leave."

She chuckled, a harsh, sour sound that few men had ever heard. "Another door on the opposite side of that building leads outside. They'll be watching this way, and we'll go the other."

"Our horses are out front. We can't *walk* away from here."

"Webb Jefferson's blacksmith shop is right past there. He always has a few head in the corral out back that needs shoeing, or he's finished with. He keeps a couple of worn-out old saddles in a little tack shed out back."

"You came up with all this right now?"

"No." She gave Daniel that dimpled smile. "I like to think ahead."

CHAPTER 18

The cottonwood's shadow not far from the way station was long across the grass. Already the dry air had cooled, and insects came to life with a chorus of sounds. A pair of doves appeared out of nowhere and took a bead on the tree. They flared at the last minute and lit on a bare, dead limb jutting out the side to coo at the world. Somewhere out of sight, a mother prairie chicken clucked and made a *brirrrb* sound to gather her chicks.

Other than an occasional war whoop, the Comanches surrounding the burned-out station settled in for a siege. From time to time, one of the warriors took a shot at the roofless building, more to keep the defenders on edge than in the hopes of hitting anyone.

McGinty thought they were in the worst place imaginable, and would have preferred to be holed up almost anywhere other than the burned-out station. Their clothes were black from soot and the charcoal they'd handled to clear out enough space to fight, throwing unburned timbers into the end farthest from the door.

Only a foot or so away from his valise full of cash, McGinty knelt against the wall and studied the little pistol the Ranger had taken from the drummer's body. Only four rounds remained in the five-shot. That left three available, if things went bad either with the Ranger or the Indians. He could use those to defend himself, and maybe four if it came to killing the white men around him, but if it was Indians who got in amongst them, that last round would be for himself.

Aloysius was out of his head, and it wasn't the whiskey the wounded stage guard had consumed. The shock of the bullet wound and such a shattered shinbone worked against him. He was delirious and had been talking loud out of his head for more than an hour, getting on the nerves of everyone who was wound as tight as a watch's mainspring.

Doc sat cross-legged on the floor near the dying driver named Leonard. "We're gonna need water soon." For an elderly, gray-haired grandpa of a man, he was surprisingly limber. His big, soft hand flicked a finger at the man lying beside him with a bullet in his gut. "A man hurt this bad dries up inside pretty fast. I don't know where Malachai's bullet went, but it tore him up pretty bad. They both need to drink as much water as they can hold and the rest of us are gonna need some before long, too. This dry air's sucking moisture out of us awful fast."

Leonard lay against the inside wall. He was conscious and surprisingly free of pain. "I could drink a gallon." He'd quit bleeding from the bullet hole in his stomach, and though the wound was worse than the guard's leg, he looked to be in pretty fair shape for a dying man.

"It's your own fault," the Ranger told him. "I wouldn't have shot you if you weren't a thief."

"I don't feel like arguing with you right now, Malachai." Both hands lay limp in Leonard's lap. "There's a couple of canteens out there on the stage. I'm dry as a gourd."

"I don't intend to go out there and get 'em right now while it's still light." Buck finished counting the extra rounds in his pocket for the Colt he wore. "How'd they water the horses around here? I didn't see anything but a trough."

"Hauled it in from a spring over by the cottonwood." Leonard hadn't been overly friendly when they loaded up the stage back in town, and was now downright surly with a hole in his stomach. "I saw a bucket sitting outside when we got here. Feel free to stroll down there and fill it up if you have a mind to. I'm sure them Comanches won't mind."

Buck ignored the sarcasm. "They hauled water for the horses?"

"When they didn't lead them down to the spring there by the cottonwood. Planned to dig a well over by the corral, and might have started it for all I know. This stage line ain't a big operation, so these stations fend for themselves on whatever they make on feeding and putting up travelers."

His voice was weak, but still fairly strong. "Hey, Doc. I've quit bleeding. That's a good sign, right?"

"Not at all." The doctor shook his head and looked up from Aloysius, who'd thankfully gone silent. "I suspect you're bleeding inside. I see your belly's a little bigger than it was."

"I'll be damned. It sure is." Leonard looked at his stomach and kept talking as if he was just fine. "Aw, I 'magine the company gives them a little money each month, but they won't pay to have someone to dig a well." He stopped talking and rubbed at his dry lips. "We still have two horses out there in the sun too. I sure hate to see 'em suffer in this heat."

"I'd dearly love some coffee." Amanda spoke up for the first time. "And something to eat. We haven't eaten in hours and we're gonna need food pretty soon."

"We can eat one of the horses out there." Malachai couldn't stay still. The Ranger moved from place to place, looking out at the waving prairie and watching for Comanches. With his lips pressed together, his mustache hid most of his lower face. "That is, if we can whittle a hunk or two off without getting killed."

"*Horse*meat?" Amanda twisted her mouth in disgust.

"Tastes all right when you're hungry," Garry said and nodded at his brother, who nodded back. "Course, that's hearsay. Larry there ate dog once."

"Didn't know it at the time." His brother tilted his hat back in thought. "Those old boys had a good stew going and said it was rabbit. Hard to tell in a boiling pot, but they might've been funning me too, for all I know." He paused. "Tasted all right, though."

He rose and went to the fireplace to poke around after checking to make sure the mud-and-stick structure wasn't about to fall. Though scorched with a big crack on one side, it still looked serviceable. "There's a useful kettle here. Maybe some kinda food in one of these boxes survived the fire. Might be something we can cook, if I can find it."

"I don't like having that stage right there neither." Malachai moved again, annoying McGinty, who wasn't fond of having a lawman around.

McGinty was afraid the Ranger would start asking questions that he didn't want to answer. He needed to get that money safely deposited in the Liberty Bank, and then wire it back east where he intended to move so he could get away from Indians, cowboys, and buffalo hunters and an endless swarm of flies.

Malachai paused and looked down at the wounded man for a moment before continuing to pace like a cat in a cage. "For all we know, there's a dozen Comanches wadded up there behind the stage where we can't see them. That's too close for me."

As if to punctuate his statement, an arrow sizzled through the open door and buried itself in a fallen timber at the back of the station. Amanda cried out with a startled yelp, and the men ducked for cover in case they were rushed.

A whoop came to their ears as a distinctive Comanche voice taunted them again. McGinty's blood ran cold, and he realized the little pistol in his hand was going to be of little use if they attacked. He looked at it, wondering if he could hit anything with it.

He stared out the window as the evening quieted again. More doves swooped in to drink from the spring under the cottonwood tree, and the air came alive with birds that needed to water before dark. It was a common, peaceful sight that belied the death and danger around them.

After a moment they relaxed. McGinty's eyes flicked from the people inside to the stage. "I hear they start fires with arrows. What if they set the stage on fire."

"It ain't much use to us right now." Leonard grunted and winced. He kept one hand over the hole in his stomach. "Two horses dead in their traces, it ain't going nowhere." He paused and twisted his mouth in thought. "I don't much care anymore, nohow."

"How about we cut them two out and team up the others." McGinty absently pointed with the pistol. "Two can pull it, right?"

"At a walk." They could see Leonard working on the problem in his head. The driver was the only one who knew anything about handling a team, and his pale face told that he might not be conscious much longer. "It's hard for me to think straight. Let's see. The stage is heavy, and you add all our weight together, it'll be a chore. At the very least, you'll have to dump all the luggage and cargo, and anything else you can throw out to lighten the load, and that's if the Comanches leave on out of here. Two horses sure won't be able to pull fast and long enough to outrun a war party."

Startled at the statement, McGinty's voice came out high and shrill. "I have a box on there we can't abandon. The one that was under your feet."

Leonard mustered up enough energy to snap at him. "You will, and that grip of yours right there'll stay, too."

McGinty's face flushed, and he gripped the butt of the little revolver harder than necessary. "You ain't the boss of me, and that stage is no ship. There's no captain here in charge. You're a damned stage robber, Leonard."

"But I'm a captain." The Ranger's voice was hard as flint. "You'll all do what I say so we can stay alive."

McGinty had a sudden thought. "Hey, Malachai. Where's your badge? I suspect you need a badge to prove who you are and to take charge."

"We don't all wear 'em. Folks think we do, but I bet half the Rangers in this state don't own one. A badge costs money, and the state don't issue them, so if I wanted one, I'd have to get it made, and besides, sometimes I don't want anyone to see who I am right off. It helps when arresting miscreants from time to time."

The Ranger waved a hand in the dying light. "Besides, y'all are getting ahead of yourselves, anyhow. We're not going anywhere for a good long while. At least until we kill enough of them savages to lose their taste for fighting and leave. That's a task that's gonna take some doing."

CHAPTER 19

It was near dark in Angel Fire when Gil left Shorty and a couple of Panther Creek men to keep an eye on the rear of the bank. He circled back around to the main street to meet up with me and Bright, who'd packed away some of his arrogance, probably figuring that it would take us all to get Calpurnia out of trouble.

We were standing in the shadows against the front of the building west of the bank. To the east was a drugstore and beyond it, a blacksmith shop. Smoke still rose from the forge, but the smithy was gone, like the majority of the people who were going about their business when all that mess started. To anyone passing on the street, we looked like loafers standing around passing the time of day.

Someone in the Occidental a little farther down laughed and a bottle broke. I shook my head. "Those men beat anything I ever saw. Riding around and shooting everything that moves, then they go in there and take over. I'd wager they're not paying for a thing. McGinty's gonna have a fit when he comes back and finds out what they've stole, and damaged."

The look of disgust on Bright's face told me he felt the same about them as I did.

"That big guy named Pletz tried to buy drinks with a scalp. Saw him pitch it on the bar." Bright almost chuckled, but it came out as a mixture of fear, awe, and disgust. "The bartender almost died right there when that thing landed in front of him."

Gil's eyes narrowed when he saw my reaction. "Don't."

I feigned innocence. "What?"

"Don't get it in your head to go and arrest them boys. These badges are rooted in Fredericksburg, not out here. We're not Texas Rangers, and they're no business of ours."

"Neither is this bank robbery, but we represent the law."

"That's what I was afraid you'd say. I swear, Cap, you beat all I've ever seen. I reckon I need to remind you that we're here to pick up Wilford Haynes and take him back. That's our *only* job."

"Well, when a crime's committed right in front of me, I can't look the other way. If I did, you'd be looking at the grass up there in the territories from the wrong side. I can't abide meanness or criminal behavior."

His face fell, and he knew I'd won. "So we take care of this little . . . situation here, and then you plan to march down the street and do what?"

"I don't know yet."

"Scalphunting's not against the law. Cap, the state's apparently paying the bounty."

"Yeah, but I don't like it, and they're breaking the law taking over in that saloon, as far as I'm concerned, and somebody has to do something about it."

"I don't like a lot of things, but I try to stay out of other people's business."

He was right, and at that moment I glanced down the empty street at the rectangles of yellow light spilling from the doors and windows. I realized with a start that it was almost full dark.

"We're done with this." The voice that came from behind us was unfamiliar. I turned to see a group of men I didn't recognize. It finally occurred to me that townspeople had gathered and wondered why I hadn't paid them any attention. I saw little Jeter standing there with a double-barrel ten-gauge in his hands, along with soft-looking folks I took to be shopkeepers.

The speaker with a florid face looked both angry and afraid. I liked that about him. Anger leads to bad decisions, and fear acts like a set of reins, making a man think before he acts.

He held a Winchester in his hands. "I own the saddle shop over there, and my money's in that bank, the same as everyone else here. We need to root that bunch of outlaws out of there."

"What's your name?"

"William Cork."

"Well, Mr. Cork, if you have a way to do it, then root away." I tried not to let the memory of that crow's dark shadow on his sign influence the way I felt about the man. It was none of his doing, though I knew Gil was probably about to have a rigor thinking about what we'd seen, and that this man owned the business. "I don't intend to just go charging in there, and I doubt many of these other men here are interested in it neither. Just let me think."

Of course the townspeople would be there, and concerned about the robbery. It was their town and their money. The weight of what I'd taken on pressed on my shoulders. Here my sense of right and wrong had blinded me to what was going on around us.

Cork's face was so red I thought he looked like a tomato. "That little gal's in danger too! She's just as important as our money. We need to get her out."

I wondered at that odd statement, weighing Callie equal to the town's money. "That's what I plan to do, mister. Jeter, you said there's a deputy somewhere around here who took over for Marshal Skinner."

He pointed to a doughy-looking feller standing nearby under a slouch hat. He had the hangdog expression of a man wishing he were somewhere else. "That's J. W. Gipson over there nursing a headache."

It was still quiet over at the bank, so I walked on down to where Gipson stood. "You J. W.?"

The man possessed the largest bags under his eyes I'd ever seen. He struggled to bring me into focus and nodded. "I am, but I'll tell you right up front. I ain't much of a deputy." His gray tongue poked out and wet his lips as he scratched at a week's growth of whiskers. "You're the ones here from Fredericksburg to pick up Wilford Haynes."

"That's why we were here, but this takes precedence."

"What's that? Presidents?"

"It means we have to deal with this first." I squinted at his stained, dirty shirt. He wore a rusty pistol stuck in his belt. "Where's your badge?"

"Laying back there in front of the jail box. I done quit."

"You were duly sworn in by the sheriff and the people of this town to uphold the law. They paid you a fair sum; I'd expect you to do that."

"Keeping the peace is one thing, but Skinner's murder kinda soured me on dealing with other people's troubles. And before you ask me about returning the money, it weren't much and I done drank up the last paycheck, what there was of it."

Shaking my head at the useless man, I turned back to Bright and Jeter. "Forget this fool. We have to get Calpurnia out of that bank without killing her or anyone else, other than them outlaws in there. Y'all have any suggestions?"

To a person, they all looked lost and ready to wander away.

I was about fed up with the whole town. "How about you, Saddlemaker?"

"I say we shoot our way in and kill 'em all."

"You've never been in a gunfight, have you?"

He gave a sheepish shake of his head. "Never even been in a *fist*fight, but I know what needs to be done."

"Your enthusiasm is well founded, Mr. Cork, but that's where you stop." I pointed at Gil. "Take Saddlemaker here and a couple of others and go around back. Get a few pieces of stove wood once you're there. In five minutes, stand away to the side of the back door and start chunking wood at it. They'll think you're trying to kick it in and either face that way, or shoot. No matter, when you do that, we'll go in through the front."

Saddlemaker frowned, and I jerked a thumb at Gil, then a couple of others. "I need men out here in front who're experienced. Go with Gil and help him."

"He only has one arm."

"That's right, and he's fought Indians and outlaws. That one-armed man'll stand with you. Gil, go on now."

He nodded and left to make his way around to the rear. I picked up a straight-back chair that was sitting in front of the closest store and handed it to one of Bright's men with a *wait a minute* flick of my hand.

"Jeter, work your way around to the other side

of the front door and one of y'all get another chair. I see a couple over there at the blacksmith's shop. When you hear a commotion out back, throw them through the windows and we'll go in. I hope Calpurnia ducks when it all starts and we can catch those two that're left in a crossfire."

"Why don't we just wait 'em out?" A bearded man crossed his arms as if challenging my authority.

"You want to sit out here for the next couple of days while they have a woman in there against her will?"

"McGinty'll be back and he'll know what to do."

"He's a banker. Not a lawman."

Beard seemed determined not to quit arguing. "What if they shoot the woman?"

"I intend to move fast enough to stop that."

Bright and his men moved in during our exchange, covered by the more cautious townspeople. A mountain of a man reached out for the chair in my hands. He addressed Beard in a firm voice.

"Shut up, Bentley. Let this man do his job. Mister, I can throw harder, but I'm not much good with a gun. I'll go in behind you, and if I get my hands on one of them fellers, I'll twist the life out of them."

The biceps on that man told me all I needed to know. "I bet you will. You're the blacksmith?"

"I am."

"Stay close to me."

Shouts came from the rear, followed by the bangs of stove wood against the door. The big guy heaved the cane-bottom chair through the shot-up window at the same time Jeter broke out the one on his side with a crash of breaking glass.

I went through the empty window frame, shotgun ready. Men poured in the other one, and a hard thump out back told me Gil and the others had kicked the door in.

It was dark inside, and I almost shot a figure that came out of the gloom. What we hadn't counted on were the shadows. I was about to pull the trigger when I saw Gil's one-armed silhouette backlit by the open door behind him.

It was silence in the bank, except for a lone cricket chirping somewhere in the dark.

Crouching with the shotgun ready, I searched the area I could see. "Calpurnia?"

"It's us! No one shoot!" Gil called from the back. "We're building a light."

I waited, sensing men pushing inside behind me. Someone scratched a match, and a lamp came to life. One of the townspeople to my right rustled around, and soon Jeter was holding a lamp himself. The bank was empty, and before long there were two more oil lamps providing light.

Around behind the banker's desk, Jeter pointed at a tall, wide, mirrored hall tree pulled partway out from the wall. "There's a little door back here cut into the next building. That's the drugstore." Holding the shotgun with the muzzles pointed at the ceiling, he pushed his way through the gathering crowd and unlocked the door and went out.

Beard went around back to the teller area and yanked open the drawers. "There ain't a penny in here, and the safe's standing open."

The blacksmith gave the hall tree a good yank and it fell out of the way. He and a couple of others pushed through, and we heard sounds of footsteps as Jeter returned. He came back around to where I stood. "They went out the side door of the drugstore. No telling how long ago, while we were all standing out here arguing. They're gone."

The fear in Bright's voice was deep with anguish. "My God, they stole Callie!"

CHAPTER 20

It was full dark, and the Comanches around the stage stop kept up their periodic whoops and yelping above the crickets and night birds. A wash of stars twinkled overhead, and the glow of the rising moon spilled silver light across the land. The night would have been peaceful elsewhere, but within the walls of the burned-out way station, it was full of fear, thirst, hunger, and death.

As the temperature dropped, the air cooled and smelled of charred bodies, burned wood, dust, and blood.

"Is it dark in here?" The stage guard's voice was high and weak. Aloysius sounded like an old, old man, though he was barely forty, the Ranger guessed.

He knelt beside the man lying on the ground. Doc was tending to the driver, Leonard, who was finally unconscious and moaning in his sleep. Buck and the brothers Garry and Larry were positioned at the windows and door, watching for Indians.

"Yep." Malachai put a hand on the guard's forehead, which was hot and clammy. "Full dark outside, Aloysius. Don't worry."

"I can't see anything."

"No one can." On one knee, Malachai talked

to Aloysius without looking at him. He couldn't help but keep watch through the open door and windows. "We dasn't have a light because of the Indians."

"Who's talking?"

"Me, Malachai Holman."

"I don't know no Malachai."

"I'm the Ranger."

"Oh, now I remember. Getting fuzzy. I wish I was back home in Harlan. I don't belong out here where there ain't no hills nor trees. Kentucky's where I'm from and I was a fool to leave. I shoulda stayed there and dug coal like my old man." He was silent for a long moment. "I wish I was back up in a cool, green holler."

"Don't we all." Their only saving grace, in a sense, was the full moon, though it gave the Comanches enough light to attack, and Malachai figured they'd wait until the early morning hours when everyone was tired and sleepy.

"Malachai." Aloysius reached out for an arm, a leg, or some physical humanity. "Is that little gal okay? The one riding with us?"

"She's fine."

"Can she come hold my hand?" The dying stage guard's voice cracked. "I don't want to die alone."

"You ain't dying."

"You don't know nothing. My leg don't feel right and it's going to sleep."

The Ranger paused for a moment, listening to the wounded guard's labored breathing. Malachai had seen many men pass through the years, some harder than others, and though he'd told the man he wasn't dying, it was probably a lie. "I'll get her."

He rose and crept around the half-burned roof supports scattered across the floor. They'd moved some of the tangle to one side, blackening their hands and clothes in the process, but it made movement easier. He'd pushed Amanda into a corner to protect her as much as possible.

"Miss, would you care to go sit beside that guard?" Malachai spoke low so as not to be heard. "He's in pain and asking for a woman's hand to hold. I believe he's getting close to meeting his maker. Mind, his name's Aloysius."

"Of course." Gathering her skirts, the black-haired young woman rose and felt her way to the back wall where the man lay on the dusty canvas she'd brought from the boot. She dropped to her knees and felt in the darkness until she found the guard's hand. She took it in both of hers. "I'm here. It's Amanda."

"No. I don't recognize your voice."

"Yes it *is*. Feel my hand." She ran her fingers lightly across his sweaty forehead and down his cheek. "See, it's smoother than some old smelly cowboy's paw."

His calloused thumb rubbed her skin. "It *is* you."

"Sure is." She was silent for a while. "You hurting?"

"Some, but I'm going fast."

"It's just a bullet wound and a broke shin."

"I saw my cousin die like this." Aloysius swallowed, a dry, painful sound. "A friend of our'n accidentally shot him while they was hunting rabbits and it was the same wound. He lingered for a day, and then his heart just stopped and we put him in the ground the next morning. I wish my leg had been a different place. Then that bullet woulda missed me. I don't want to go into no grave."

"Well, that won't be happening here."

"I'm afraid you're wrong." His lips and tongue crackled with dryness. "You see that little light?"

Close by and listening, Malachai saw her look upward. "That's the moon coming up."

"No, the bright one with all the colors." Aloysius pointed to a burned timber. "Right yonder."

She hesitated. "Sure do. I see it now."

"It's coming from the angels. They're gathering close around us. I can feel the breeze off their wings."

The Ranger stifled a shiver. He was glad for the darkness, for he wouldn't want anyone to see his fear, or awe. Malachai swore that once he saw a man's soul depart his body. It was a young farmer left for dead by bandits not far outside of Austin. When he and others accidentally came up on him early one morning, they all agreed a mist rose and lingered above the body for a long moment as his last breath escaped his lungs.

Aloysius continued to hold Amanda's hand. "That pretty angel right beside you has yeller hair. She looks familiar."

She touched her blue-black hair with her free hand. Her soft voice broke. "Is it a woman angel?"

"It is, and she looks a lot like . . . oh."

"What?"

"I don't know who the fat little boy is with her, but he's round as a punkin and looks like my baby brother who went to heaven when he was only a year old. Hey, Chester, is that you standing there beside Leonard?"

Everyone inside the walls listened to the eerie conversation, not making a sound. They were still in danger of attack, so the Ranger scanned the area around the way station. The stage outside glowed silver in the light of a half-moon, and the two remaining horses stood with their noses almost touching the ground.

"Leonard?" Amanda's voice came soft and low. She turned to look where the quiet driver lay in the shadows. "Malachai. You might want to check on Leonard. He's awful still and quiet over there."

The Ranger moved close and knelt. Doc looked up from where he knelt beside the body. "That's because he's dead. Went just a few seconds ago."

Malachai rose and turned to the dying guard, wondering if Leonard's ghost really was there and not gone on to wherever spirits were supposed to go.

Amanda visibly shivered. She leaned close to the dying man. "You really *do* see the angels." It was a statement, not a question.

"I do, and they're beautiful. Leonard's gone now." He pulled at her hand. "They say I have to tell you something. Come close. This is only for Luciana."

"Shhh." Feeling for his forehead, she leaned in and turned her head so he would whisper in her ear.

From where he stood, Malachai couldn't hear what Aloysius said, but she drew in a long, slow breath. The next sound was a death rattle as his last inhalation escaped.

It was all quiet within the walls until Amanda rose with a rustle of skirts. "He's gone."

From his position at one window, Garry spoke. "How come? A man don't die from a fresh hole in his leg."

Doc stood with a grunt. "I've seen it before. I've lost more'n one good cowhand to a broke leg. Sometimes it's not the wound, but a man's own body that kills him."

The Ranger studied Amanda's shape as she returned to where she'd been sitting. Malachai wondered if she'd heard the man's last confession, some unreal sight from his dying brain, or something else. He didn't like it when he didn't have everything gathered in one neat pile.

Malachai was a planner, and that's what made him good at his job. He shrugged. "Buck, help me tidy these two up back there."

They bent to drag the two men Malachai had killed to a spot back in the darkest part of the burned-out station.

CHAPTER 21

Her mind reeling, Amanda, also known as Luciana, sat back against the dried mud-and-hay wall and studied on what the guard had told her. She knew his name as Aloysius Grant, a distant relation to the famous general and president. He was a frequent visitor to the rooms above the Occidental when he had a little jingle in his pockets working for various employers in Angel Fire, Santa Fe, and Gainesville, and very popular with the other two girls working there when he passed through.

Aloysius was free with his money, when he had it, and the girls who weren't otherwise occupied when he came in always vied for his attention. Luciana always caught his eye, and through the months, they'd become almost exclusive.

It was in one of those rooms, sitting on the squeaky bed as he caught his breath, that Aloysius told Luciana about being hired by Bright Bolton, who was following McGinty's orders to find a guard for the gold shipment on their way to Fort Worth.

Propped on the pillow and hands behind his head, Aloysius spoke of Bright's offer to ride the stage. "Yep, he rode in from the ranch one day and said he was looking for me. Said they're gonna pay me a month's wages as a top hand to just sit up there with a shotgun across my lap while McGinty rides inside."

Her instincts piqued, she rolled onto her side and let one breast fall out to keep him interested. "Why's that? What does Bright have to do with any of that?"

"Why, I reckon because McGinty's a banker and probably afraid of his shadow." He flicked a strand of long black hair over her shoulder. "Bright says he wants someone close by while he travels, but don't want anyone to know he's hiring."

"Why don't Bright ride with him, then?"

"I figure it's because he's sweet on that little teller that works there and don't want to leave her. You know how these cowboys are when there ain't many decent women in this town. If he's gone, some of them others might think she's available and come a-buzzing around her like bees to honey."

"Decent?" She raised an eyebrow.

"You know, the marrying kind."

"I could be like that." It annoyed Luciana that he thought she intended to be a whore for the rest of her life. If she was out wearing one of those high-necked dresses in the chifforobe only three feet away, strangers thought she was a storekeeper's wife, or a baker, and more than once with her hair up, she was asked by strangers new to town if she might be a schoolteacher.

She always impressed them with her fluent Italian and French, having fun being something she was not. Men out west always fawned over educated women, and if they could cook and hold a conversation about more than cows, buffalo, or hunting, all the better.

"You could be like the marrying kind, but I don't think many of the boys around here'd be interested in hitching up with a Mex." He paused and studied her eyes. "Or a half-breed."

Luciana's dark brown eyes flashed. "My parents were Italian. From Italy."

"You speak good English."

"I was born here, but they always spoke Italian at home. It was my first language, and I'm good at other tongues too. *Sei un villano.*"

"I like the way your mouth moves when you say that. What does it mean?"

"'You're very sweet' in Italian." In truth, it really meant, you're a boor. "*Et tu es tout petit labas.*"

"What language was that?" He turned onto one elbow and pulled the sheet down to her hips.

"French."

"That sounds even better. What'd you say then?"

"I like being with you." Her eyes twinkled, because she'd really told him he was very small down there.

"Ha, I'd bet money you were Mexican."

"Do you speak Spanish?"

"Enough to get by."

"*Creo que te amo.*"

He looked at her without understanding.

"I think I love you."

They both laughed at the ridiculous statement. She didn't comment further. "Does the blood in my veins matter?"

"Not a bit. I don't intend to have kids with you."

Tired of the game, she returned to his new job. "Let's get back to what we were talking about. Where's McGinty going?"

He lay back. "Says Fort Worth."

"When?"

"Day after tomorrow."

"And you're guarding what he's carrying. Money from the bank."

"I'm guarding whatever he puts in that strongbox."

Luciana tapped a finger on his chest. "I have an idea."

"What's that? Wait, I bet it's the same one I have." Crow's-feet formed at the corners of his eyes.

She slapped his arm. "Listen. I've heard that he does this a couple of times a year and he always takes a strongbox that is so heavy two men have to lift it up under the seat."

"How do you know that?"
"He talks to me a lot."
"Ah, he's a customer."
"I'm his favorite."
"There's a reason for that."
"Thank you. He didn't tell me about *this* shipment, but I know there's a lot of money coming through here, and with those railroad men being here . . . what . . . three times to talk about the new line?"
"Don't start me to lying. I don't pay attention to who's in town when I'm here."
"Well, one of 'em came to visit all three times and it's been me he's seen. He always pays twice what the others do." She gave him another soft whack. "And don't you think this one's free either, mister."
"Never crossed my mind."
"That railroad man told me they've surveyed through here and out toward a place they're calling Gallup out in the New Mexico Territory. It's a stage stop right now with good water, but that's why the railroad wants to go through there.
"I'm not supposed to know it, but they're paying McGinty for some of the land he owns here, and are putting more in his bank. It doesn't look like much, but I had a . . . friend . . . tell me he was in there one day and the safe was open. He said it's full of gold double eagles and stacks of money."

"So?"

"You're not as bright as I thought you were. Those railroad men have money in there too, and McGinty goes to Gainesville and Fort Worth with a strongbox each time. They're all moving money around, and it's right there for the taking."

"Taking." Aloysius rubbed a hand through his curly hair. "Are you asking me to stop that stage and *rob* it?"

"No, dummy. Think. You're already guarding it. If you have a partner, say it was me, and we worked together with one or two others, we could come up with a plan to get that money. I grew up in Fort Worth, back in Texas. My daddy owned a store there and I know a place where we can stop the stage and rob it before it gets into town."

"We?"

"Me and you." Luciana sat up, excited. "Think about this. You make the driver stop. No wait, I'll be inside and need to stop. I'll call up and tell y'all I'm feeling faint, wait, better yet." She giggled. "I'll have a ladies' problem and need to go behind a bush. While I'm there, everyone'll be distracted and you take the driver's gun, then get down and point that shotgun at them. I'll come out from behind with a pistol and we'll take their guns and make them walk away. You can drive a team, right?"

"I've never handled four horses, but I 'magine I can do it."

"Good. They walk away, and we drive the stage right close to Gainesville and drop off the strongbox." She started talking faster in her excitement. "Then we go in and tell them we were robbed. They'll round up a posse, and when they're gone, we go out there, get the money, and we catch the train to Fort Worth. Then we'll switch there and they'll never know which way we went. Dallas, Austin, east to Arkansas . . . anywhere."

"That sounds awfully complicated."

"Do you have a better idea?"

"I can come up with one by the time we leave. It'll be a helluva lot more simple, you can bet."

She bounced up and down like a little kid. "So we have a deal?"

"We do."

She thought for a moment. "How do you like the name Amanda?"

"I like it just fine, why?"

"Your new partner's name is Amanda."

CHAPTER 22

The hard slap of a gunshot jolted Malachai Holman from a light doze. For hours the Ranger had moved from one spot to another, peering over first Garry's, then Larry's shoulders out the front before moving on to another viewpoint. Like an animal in a pen, he joined Buck at one of the windows before looking through a shooting port on the back side of the station where Doc kept an eye out.

Well after midnight, they took turns catching a little shut-eye for an hour while the others kept a lookout, using Doc's pocket watch to keep time. By three, Malachai needed some rest, though he knew Comanches were partial to attack in the wee hours before dawn, when everyone was in a deep sleep.

"Wake me at four," he told Doc, who looked as if he was out on his feet.

He settled in close to Amanda so he could keep an eye on her in the event something happened and they needed to move fast, and promptly went to sleep. The gunshot jerked everyone awake and Malachai came up quick, pistol in hand.

It was Buck shooting from one of the two front windows, and he fired again, then holstered his pistol and shouldered the short coach gun. "They're out there. Saw their shadows."

Only a couple of feet away, Larry shifted to see better around the doorframe. "It's so damned dark I don't see much of nothing." He grunted and staggered back, the feathered shaft of an arrow protruding only inches from the red shirt covering his chest. He gasped. "Garry, I'm hit."

The short twelve-gauge in Buck's hands belched smoke and flame out the window, and a yelp of pain told them the buckshot had taken a toll.

Ducked down below the window, McGinty rose enough to see outside. On the far side of the coach, a flicker of light broke the darkness. "They've fired the stagecoach!"

The two remaining horses still in their harness jerked and pulled in terror, but the dead animals on the left side and the brake prevented them from running away. Frantic, they fought the straps, squealing in fear.

"Someone cut the poor things loose!" Amanda's voice rose over the noise.

"That's what they want." Malachai fired at a shape running from the stage. In the growing firelight, he saw they'd crept up despite the defenders' watchfulness and stacked dried brush and wood on the far side.

The blaze was small at first as twigs crackled. The summer-dried fuel caught, almost exploding in the heat, and in seconds the blaze lit the darkness. The light grew as the wooden coach smoked, then the canvas shade opposite the defenders burst into flames. The whole side quickly became engulfed, and fire consumed the exterior before licking inside and finding even more fuel.

Like a blacksmith's bellows, dry air pulled through the coach's open window. In minutes, the entire vehicle was a giant torch throwing off enormous amounts of fire, smoke, and heat they could feel inside. It lit the surrounding area, and the defenders saw painted warriors rushing around the edge of the night.

It also threw light into the station where they huddled. A bullet flew through the open window out front and slapped the wall behind Malachai. The Ranger realized what was happening and pushed Amanda onto the floor. "The fire's lighting us up. Get back under cover!"

Buck used his pistol again. "We can't let 'em get in close!"

At the gunport on the back wall, Doc also fired. "They're behind us." He looked up at the open sky overhead. "Liable to come over the wall any second."

Garry dragged his injured brother away from the front and the glow. Malachai took his position, though the blistering heat kept him behind the wall, instead of looking through the opening where figures moved and flashed in the flickering light. Gunfire flashed in the darkness beyond the ring of light. Bullets slapped around them as the two remaining horses screamed and threw themselves against their collars.

The coach lurched a few feet before two shots ended the animals' pain. Malachai looked to his right to see Buck in a classic shooter's stance, both hands holding the pistol. The Ranger felt his face redden. "We might need those two shots you just wasted."

"Couldn't let 'em burn to death." Buck fired at a warrior's shape and dropped the empty revolver back into his holster. "Here they come!" He shouldered the coach gun and waited.

Hooves thundered outside as mounted Comanches charged the station, coming in from two sides and angling around the burning coach. The defenders fell back, shooting from inside their makeshift fort. A mounted brave threw up his hands and fell, his horse running past.

Three men neared the station and jumped off their mounts, whooping and brandishing axes and war clubs. They rushed the open door and pushed inside, only to absorb both barrels of Buck's shotgun. They dropped in a tangled heap as Malachai thumb-cocked his Colt and saw a warrior at the window, aiming a Winchester at Buck.

The Ranger fired and the bullet hit beneath the

man's eye. Blood sprayed in a mist behind him, and he disappeared from sight. The attack fell off, and then the only sound was the crackling of yellow flames as the coach turned into a bonfire.

CHAPTER 23

You can't much chase outlaws across the dark plains. Once Gil and I realized what those two bank robbers had done, it was too late to take after 'em and there was no way to trail three horses across the Llano until the sun was up.

The undertaker had only been gone with the outlaws' bodies for a short time. He was already making plans to box them up and have a photographer take a likeness at first light. That way folks could see the corpses out front before they stuck them in the ground later in the day, and he could get some advertisement for his business in the local paper, the *Epigraph Gazette*.

A large number of townspeople had scattered to get their gear and some sleep before we gathered at daylight to go after the pair who'd stolen Calpurnia. I'd quickly discovered she was the town's sweetheart, and to a man, they all felt some responsibility toward her safety.

Standing near the empty corral beside the blacksmith shop, Gil kicked at a dried horse turd and shook his head. His hat was tilted back and kinda crooked, the way Esther liked for him to wear it. They'd since taken up with one another back in Fredericksburg, and she tended to tell him ways that she thought he looked better.

Rubbing his mouth, he finally spoke. "You know the last time we had anything to do with a posse, they wanted to hang us."

"That's because they thought we'd murdered someone." I looked into the darkness toward where we suspected the bank robbers went, and wondered if either of those guys was smart enough to circle around and take out in another direction.

A sick ball of worry rested in my stomach. I wondered if they'd tied Callie onto one of those horses, or just threatened her to go along. Riding with your hands tied was rough on a person, and most townspeople weren't used to a saddle, especially women.

"And besides"—I brought myself back to the posse—"this time *we're* leading it, not running away."

"We weren't running away *then*. Them guys back in the territories just showed up and started pointing guns at us."

"Well, if you saw a man hanging from a tree limb, you might think the folks loafing around close by would've had something to do with it."

"Why do you take other people's sides when we talk about things like this?"

"Because I like to look at a problem from both sides."

He rubbed his mouth again. It was becoming a habit, showing he was thinking. "I don't know,

Cap. Why don't we just go by ourselves? We can travel faster."

"That'd work if all these people weren't involved, but they're gonna go anyway. If they aren't riding behind us, they'll likely get in the way or mess up the tracks we need to follow. Besides, Bright and some of the Panther Creek boys will be with us, and that should make it safer, what with those Comanches on the prod."

"Which way do you think they went after they got out of town?"

"I'd say east. It's a little safer than heading out to Santa Fe or Denver. If I's them, I'd ignore that wagon road and head out away from trails."

He nodded, thinking. "We still have those scalphunters to deal with too."

"They worry me more'n the Indians." I didn't like having those men around, not one little bit. They were dangerous as a wad of rattlers, and I wished they'd just load up and ride off. They wouldn't, though, because like everyone else in town, Pletz once had money in that bank that was now in the saddlebags of those two bandits.

On the other hand, some of those hairy ol' boys were carrying Sharps, and if we ran into trouble, they were experienced enough to use them for long-distance shooting. Three and four hundred yards weren't much of a shot with one of those big .50 calibers, and I wasn't opposed to having such marksmen along, even though they were murderers and brigands.

Trouble can change a man's mind about the company he keeps.

"We know what we're getting into with a war party," Gil said, "but these guys might ride along just fine, then turn on us like a pack of wolves."

"There's that possibility."

"On top of all that, we still have to come back here and pick up old Haynes."

"I'd almost forgot him." A bad feeling washed over me. "Let's go down to that little jail of theirs and talk to him."

"*Talk* to him?"

"Yeah. I'm not even sure he's still in there, and if he is, he might've died with Gipson watching him. For all we know, he ain't been fed or watered for a few days, or he might've dried up in this heat. He's our responsibility now."

"You and your responsibilities."

"Yep, besides, we have to go that way to the stable anyhow."

I was looking forward to lying down on that pile of hay across from the steeldust mare and getting a little shut-eye. I was plumb wore out and we had to be up well before daylight. We struck off down the street that was still pretty active for that time of night, and after all the troubles we'd fought through.

The Occidental was lit up like daylight and

working alive with Pletz and his men. They weren't loud, and that was even more worrisome. The scalphunters were doing some serious drinking. We paused in the shadows to see them hunched over the bar and tables full of bottles and glasses. A couple of cowboys were in there too, along with a local or two, probably commiserating about the money they'd lost in the bank robbery.

I stopped in the street to look through the open doors. "If we had enough men, we'd go in and arrest them all for the murderers they are."

"It'll take the cavalry to do that, and the nearest fort's three days from here. Then what would we do with those guys if you did? Chain 'em to a hitching post?"

"I'm thinking we should send a couple of riders to get some help."

"You said yourself we're going after the bank robbers in the morning. You're getting distracted by too much thinking."

"The way they're drinking, half of 'em won't be able to fork a saddle."

Gil laughed. "I'm not sure about that."

A woman's shriek like a panther's scream split the night, coming from one of the rooms above the saloon. Sounding as if it tore something in her throat, it came again before trailing off into what I could only describe as a wail.

"What'n hell was that?"

"A woman, and there's no law here anymore." Drawing my pistol, I ran to the shackelty outside staircase leading up to the rooms occupied by Angel Fire's ladies of the evening.

"Oh, hell." It was Gil's usual response to trouble.

CHAPTER 24

Nate and Daniel, the two cowhands turned bank robbers, used the silvery moonlight to head east on strange horses, followed by Calpurnia, who was already voicing her regret about leaving with them. Part of her problem was the broken-down saddle they'd stolen for her. For one thing, it was a work saddle, and not a traditional side saddle that decent women used.

Dresses weren't designed to ride like a man, and the bloomers she wore underneath were bunching up against the insides of her thighs, rubbing them raw. She felt it was indecent to ride in such a way, and each time one of them glanced her way, she blushed in the darkness.

Calpurnia wasn't much of a rider anyway, and the way she sat in the saddle was going to tire the horse that was already limping. They hadn't counted on them not being properly shod, and she was afraid the gelding had either already thrown a shoe, or had been waiting for the blacksmith to tend to him.

Stealing horses was risky business in several ways, it seemed.

Not trusting the two men with her, she had two bank bags full of her stolen cash slung across behind the saddle horn, and riding across her upper thighs and the seat rise. They'd left the heavy money behind after she convinced the two bandits the coins weren't real.

While the mad townspeople gathered in the street outside to come up with a plan, she showed Nate and Daniel the money she'd switched when McGinty was getting ready to leave. Awestruck by the sight of so many bills all bundled up and stacked in the flowery carpet grip, they realized she'd been planning to rob the bank for months, and her way was likely better than theirs.

Trying to hold back the tears of pain that made her eyes sting, she blinked them clear and focused on the half-moon that lit the flat land stretching in all directions. Where horses and cattle had grazed outside of town, rough scrub had sprouted in an evil tangle.

Acacia, yucca, prickly pear, and scraggly mesquite were taking over the bare ground, pushing the grass away and sucking all the moisture from the earth. The vegetation changed as they moved away from the settlement, turning back into the grassy plains that had baffled, then killed, many of the early Spanish explorers.

The grass had evolved with millions of buffalo eating it down short every season, preventing anything else from growing. Their droppings and urine provided nutrients, and the prairie grasses responded by growing thick and tall. With the demise of the great herds, there were places where the grass was giving way to invasive vegetation, which was changing the landscape forever.

Avoiding any road or path, they cut across the moonlit prairie and covered ground quickly to put as much distance as possible between themselves and their pursuers. Using the silvery orb and eventually the stars to guide them, the robbers pushed generally eastward. As the night passed, the pair drew further ahead, though she could still see them well enough in the moonlight not to worry about being left behind.

They wouldn't leave the money she was carrying, and that was a fact. It was only after the moon faltered did Calpurnia worry that she might lose *them* under the vast expanse of stars that filled the sky from the horizon in all directions.

From time to time she kicked her failing horse into a faster walk, but that was all he could do. After what seemed like hours, they reined their mounts back and waited for her to catch up. When she did with great relief, they split up enough that she could ride between them.

On her left, Nate edged close, his wounded arm hanging loose at his side. "We're far enough away that we can slow down for a while. They won't come after us until dawn."

Daniel chuckled. "If they come at all. They don't have any idea which way we went, and unless they have a good tracker, they'll never find us out here in all this grass."

They'd surprised her when the pair ignored her demands to ride on the road, and instead followed one particular bright star toward the east. She'd never learned to use the heavens to find her way and was completely lost.

She stiffened her legs a little to take the pressure off her thighs, almost standing in the stirrups. "Nate, when are we going to stop?"

"I figure we'll keep going all day. Find us an arroyo or somewhere out of sight and make camp at dark." He gently touched his arm. "Besides, if I can keep going with this, you can get tough and ignore blistered thighs."

"I can't ride that far. I'm miserable *now*."

"You'll be more miserable if them Comanches find us." Despite the wound in his arm, he laughed, soft and mean. "I'm not surprised you're hurtin', though. If you're wearing bloomers under there, peel 'em off and you won't rub as much. We won't look."

Her face flushed with heat as Daniel edged close enough that their stirrups touched for a moment. "I have some liniment I can rub on them blisters when we stop. That'll help."

They were too close and talking over each other, making her head spin. Nate spoke right on his heels. "Let me carry that money. It'll take some of the pressure off your legs."

She didn't know what to do, but it sure wasn't that. "You'll run off and leave me."

"Lady, if I wanted it bad enough, I'd shoot you now and leave your body for the coyotes and buzzards."

Her blood ran cold. "Would you back away, please." She hadn't thought everything out that far. "You're too close and this poor horse is hard enough for me to control as it is."

They separated, giving her room, and kept riding toward dawn that was still hours away. Though the day behind them had been almost unbearably hot, the night air was cool, almost chilly. From time to time they'd kick up a night bird, and once, a sleeping covey of quail startled awake and exploded from cover and whirred away, spooking them all.

Still they rode on under a sweep of stars and the setting moon, keeping the horses at a steady walking pace that put miles between them and Angel Fire.

CHAPTER 25

It was a bright night, and the few yellow windows illuminating the street that anchored Angel Fire did little to take away the thick spray of stars overhead. They twinkled more than usual, maybe because of the high plains heat that was rapidly melting away. It would be cool throughout the night, allowing the world to take a deep breath before the heat returned with the morning sun.

Between the buildings lining both sides of the street full of horse muffins, the shadows were dark. Some of those alleys were blocked with plank fences closing off the spaces from the street. Beyond them were white tents that glowed in the moonlight.

As Gil and I rushed toward the woman's screams, I couldn't help but wonder if anyone was watching us from cover with a gun in hand. There was nothing we could do about that, and we'd cross that bridge when we came to it.

We hit the stairs hard, taking the steps two by two without getting shot in the back. I charged upward, the Spencer in both hands and ready for whatever I might find. Gil was right behind me, hitting every step on the way so that together we sounded like a couple of ponies loping on a boardwalk.

The warped stairs that rocked and bounced underfoot ended at a small landing serving a single door. I grabbed the brass knob and twisted, expecting it to be locked, but the heavy door that looked to be nailed together with cast-off planks swung inward on smooth hinges to reveal a small, foyer-like room with a door on each wall.

Three choices to get killed.

The raw wood they'd used for those walls was warped and twisted, making the area look to be moving. I knew we were in a house of ill repute, but I'd never seen one so drab and disheartening. Any other time I'd have dwelled on how it would take the starch out of a man intent on such business, even a youngster there for his first time.

Decorating wouldn't have mattered none. Wallpaper wouldn't have held on to the buckling enclosure, and no amount of paint would brighten the dark interior lit by the tiny flame of a kerosene lamp on a homemade table in the middle of the "room." It was turned so low the flickering wick barely put out a glow at all. I'd seen hog pens that looked more cheerful.

Gil almost ran over me when I paused, also uncertain which door to enter. "You better pick quick, Cap."

The sounds of a woman crying came from the right, but the one on our left cracked and I saw part of a woman's terrified face. In the dim, flickering light, her eye was black and a split in her upper lip still seeped blood.

That was the first threat. Since it was a woman, I kept the Spencer aimed away from her and hit her door with my shoulder, expecting to find someone waiting behind it with a gun or a knife. It slammed back, and a half-nude woman in thigh-high stockings staggered off balance with a yelp of surprise. The upper half of her body was covered with a thin material I didn't have the vocabulary or experience to describe.

The door struck the wall and bounced back, but I was inside and found her alone in the room. I was pretty het up, looking for a threat that wasn't there and searching for someone to shoot.

"No!" She held out a pale, chubby hand to stop me. "Over there! He beat me when he was through and went across when I wouldn't do anything else for him. He's killing Agatha!" She pointed across the unpainted foyer to the opposite side.

"What about that third room?" Gil had remained in the alcove, pointing his pistol at the other door directly across from the entrance.

"It's empty now that Luciana's gone."

At least somebody was out of harm's way.

Gil stayed where he was, beside the landing's door. The scream came again, weaker this time, and to me, it sounded like a dying gasp. Taking two steps out of the prostitute's room, I raised a foot and kicked the door in. The hasp shattered and the lock bounced onto the floor as the door tilted off one hinge and slammed back against the outside wall with a crash that sounded like someone had knocked down the whole building.

The small room was a carbon copy of the one we'd just left, containing a washstand, iron bedstead with a small table beside it, and small chifforobe. Like the other rooms, not even rugs covered the gritty floor.

Lit by the small flame of a single oil lamp, a skinny, consumptive-looking woman nekked as the day she was born lay on her stomach across the bed, bleeding from more than a dozen slashes across her back and buttocks.

Standing beside her was one of the animals who called himself a scalphunter. Hair to his shoulders and barely covered by a rotting pair of stained long johns, he whirled and threw a leather quirt at my head. When I flinched as it bounced off my forehead and cheek, he grabbed a pistol from a holster hanging on the metal headboard.

Time slowed.

He'd thrown the quirt to startle me, giving him enough time to reach that hogleg. It was in his hand before I could take a step. He twisted in my direction, bringing the pistol to bear.

Blood splattered on the sheets and wall, also covering his hands and long, dirty fingernails that reminded me of claws. Bearded lips revealed

203

rotting teeth that had never been cleaned by a finger or a chewed twig and a mouth twisted into a snarl. The rank odor of unwashed humanity that could have come from him or the woman hit me in a wave, but in that instant, I figured it had to be him, because there was a washstand holding a bowl of dirty water under the room's lone window.

He fired too fast, and the .44 slug went through the thin wall on my left. Unlike a pistol that required aiming, the twelve-gauge in my hands leveled off in his direction and I squeezed the trigger. The detonation felt like someone slapped my head in the small room and damped my ears as his body jerked from the impact of all those pieces of soft lead that tore through flesh and shattered bone.

The scalphunter hit the floor with a groan and landed against the woman's bare feet before folding sideways and hitting the wash table with his head, which bounced once on the floorboards. It tipped over, and the plain white pitcher and bowl shattered, spilling dirty water across his still body.

Even though I knew the man was dead as a scalded chicken, I shucked a fresh shell into the magazine. My ears felt like they were full of cotton from the blast, but I heard the empty hull bounce on the planks with a small, hollow *ticktock* sound.

Gunsmoke floated in lazy swirls as a slight breeze came through the thin, faded curtains over the window that had been propped open in the heat.

The danger was over for the moment. "Gil, watch the stairs."

"I'm a-doin' it."

I stepped to the bed and touched the woman's nearest calf, one of the few places that wasn't whelped, slashed, or bloody. "Ma'am?"

She didn't make a sound, but her leg jerked a little under my fingers.

Barely covered by an untied corset and bloomers, the woman from across the hall rushed past me. "Agatha! Oh my God! He's killed her."

I stepped back. Far from making a doctor when I was young, there was nothing I could do. "I don't believe so, but she's hurt pretty bad."

Putting one knee on the bed, the woman turned her friend over. "Honey! It's Faye. You're all right now."

The side of Agatha's face that had been pressed into the bloody mattress was slashed the length of her jawline. The pressure of her head on the dingy sheets had prevented the wound from bleeding too badly, but it gaped open in the light.

She drew a deep, shuddering breath, and Faye's hands fluttered like moths over Agatha's already bruising body, unable to find a place to touch her. "He slashed her to pieces!"

"Cap!" Gil's voice was sharp with concern.

A gunshot made us jump, and I turned to see him standing halfway out the exterior door. Holding himself steady against the frame with the arm that was missing to the elbow, Gil's right shoulder jerked as he returned fire twice at some unseen assailant outside.

"Things are getting a little busy out here." He shifted his body inside and out of the line of fire as a heavy body tumbled down the stairs. Two more shots came from below, one slug splintering the door facing where his head had been only moments before. Footsteps and shouts told me people were heading upstairs.

I rushed out of the little room with the shotgun held high. Gil saw my intention and stepped out of the way. Reaching the outside door, I stuck the street sweeper around the frame and, without showing myself, pumped two loads of buckshot down into the night.

The first shot sounded deep and hard, like a shotgun should. The second was almost a misfire—the paper shell must have absorbed a lot of moisture, a hazard we were all familiar with. Instead of the *crump* sound I expected, it was a muffled pop, weak and inferior. Still, the powder had enough punch that someone absorbed the pellets and screamed in pain.

The man's shouts were followed by even more heavy thumps and cursing voices. The rattle of pistols answered my shots and I stepped back, in case one of their bullets came through the wall. Thumbing fresh shells into the receiver, I tried to make them stop. "You men! Stay down there!"

A second flurry of gunshots popped down below, flashing like those firecrackers folks back east liked to set off for the Fourth of July. Hot chunks of lead blew holes in the wall and doorframe. Infuriated that they couldn't see us, the friends of the dead scalphunter lying only feet away spread out into the street and opened up on the upper part of the Occidental with everything that could shoot.

Bullets plowed through the planks, pitching splinters into the air. Others ricocheted around the rooms, throwing up dust and powdered wood.

We dropped to the floor. Faye landed hard and gasped. I looked to see a dark, puckered hole through the flesh under her arm. Still concerned with her friend, she grabbed Agatha and dragged her limp friend onto the floor. More slugs punched through the wall before someone down below shouted at them to stop firing.

Recognizing the German accent, I crawfished my way to the stairway door and called into the darkness. "Is that you, Pletz?"

"Whitlatch?"

"It's me."

"Why are you killing my men?"

"Because one of them tried to murder a woman

up here and I did for him." I thumbed fresh shells into the shotgun's magazine as we talked. "Y'all shot another woman up here too."

"Too bad you were not hit yourself."

"Your boys aren't too good with pistols, it seems."

In answer, a buffalo rifle roared down below. The big slug punched through the wall and exited through the roof, leaving a hole the size of my fist. Pletz laughed. "Was that any better?"

"You keep it up and I'll kill a bunch more of y'all before we're through."

Gil's questioning eyebrow almost reached his hairline. "I wish you wouldn't keep makin' them old boys mad."

It was silent for a moment while the big German studied on what I'd said. "I have three dead men on the stairs, you say there's one up there, and two more are shot up. This is a waste of good men."

"There was nothing good about this animal up here. He got what he deserved and I would have taken great pleasure in hanging him, if I'd had the chance."

"You killed these others at my feet!"

"That's because they shot at Gil first." I looked over to see that he was going through the one-armed process of reloading his pistol stuck under his armpit. He didn't ask for any help, and I didn't offer it. The best way to stay good at something is to do it for yourself. "We're only defending ourselves up here, Pletz. There's no fault or dishonor in that."

It was quiet for a long moment before a phlegmy laugh came through the darkness. "You're doing a pretty damned good job of it too."

"That's cause we have the high ground."

"I can burn you out!"

"Then you wouldn't have a saloon. Think about that! This only happened because I couldn't let your man murder a woman."

"She's just a whore, though there's only two left in this town and he shouldn't have done whatever he did to damage her. Who is it you shot up there?"

Gil spoke up. "Took you long enough to ask."

"It just occurred to me. Who did you kill?"

"How'n hell are we supposed to know his name?"

"Of course."

"Big shoulders." Gil looked over at the corpse. "Rotten teeth. Carried a quirt."

"That's Tyson. He's always been partial to quirts."

"Not anymore."

"He dead for sure?"

"As far as I can tell from all the holes in his chest."

"I never liked him nohow. Are you going to shoot any more of my men?"

The gunsmoke had almost cleared from the room, and I didn't want to add any more. "I don't intend to. If they don't shoot at us, then me and Gil are gonna get a doctor for this woman."

"She's only a whore."

I wondered why he had to reemphasize that. "No matter, but she's still alive and needs tending to."

It was quiet enough to hear a horse snort down below. Shouts came from the street as the townspeople came out to see what was going on. I could tell they were staying well away from the saloon, though.

The scalphunter laughed again. "All right. I don't care."

I didn't like his comment. "Pletz!"

"What?"

"I don't give a damn whether you care or not."

He chuckled. "You should join us. I can use men like you, and you'd make up for them you killed."

"Not hardly. Are you going to try and even things up?" I didn't want to be out looking for Callie with that pack of wolves behind us. For some reason, I felt I could get an honest answer from the German, though. "If you are, tell me and let's get this over with."

"Nothing to even up. That was between you and Tyson."

That offered some relief. "There's the others on the stairs."

"They have their own minds. I didn't tell them to come up and kill you. If I'd wanted it done, I'd have done it myself."

"Good."

"If I had, it would be a different story, though."

It felt as if I was talking to the devil himself out there in the darkness. "I don't doubt that."

CHAPTER 26

Hours later, when Calpurnia was about to scream from the pain, the glow of the rising sun gave her hope.

Nate turned to look over his shoulder, back the way they'd come. A distinct line in the grass showed where their horses had walked, but the bent blades were already standing back up. "They'll be on the way."

Calpurnia tried to think through the pain. "I bet they'll start by following the road. It will take a while before they realize we didn't take that route; then they'll have to retrace their steps to the corral and work out the tracks from there. You guys were smart about that. It should give us maybe a day, at least."

"Damn, girl." Nate was impressed. "You're turning out to be one to ride the owl hoot trail with."

Daniel reined up. "I smell smoke."

His partner stuck his nose in the air like a dog. After several moments, he pointed a finger to their right. "Coming from that way."

"I wonder what's over there." Daniel studied the horizon. "Can't be a cook fire, unless it's some stupid settler. War parties make small ones with dry wood so it won't smoke."

"I smell it. Something big burned, I suspect." Calpurnia nodded and pushed a red curl out of her eyes. "Are we still going east?"

"Kinda."

"Then that's southeast." She spoke the obvious but ignored the look they shared between them. "How far off the road are we?"

"Hell, I don't know. Miles, I reckon." Nate pointed with his good hand toward where the smell originated. "It's that way."

"How far do you think?"

"We're headed in the same general direction, so maybe, what, three miles. Could be five for all I know."

She closed her eyes, imagining a paper map that McGinty kept on his desk. "I bet it's the Moynahan way station."

They exchanged looks again. "I remember a way station by that name," Nate said.

"We can go there and get fresh horses, or maybe even wait for the stage to come back through." She bit her bottom lip. "It'll only be a day or so for the next mail run. I can stand a few more miles to get there, but I can't ride much longer than that."

Daniel shook his head. "They'll have a posse after us. If they follow the road, they'll eventually get to the station."

"I'd imagine that's one of the first places they'd check." Nate fiddled with the reins in his fingers.

Calpurnia thought hard. "They'll figure the road." She nodded in affirmation. "If they get hard after us, they'll use the road, figuring we'd do the same to head back east. But we won't stay on it. We'll just ride up, intersect with it at the station, and get fresh horses."

"We want more, though." She saw Nate concentrating on her like studying something new.

She stiffened. "What's that?"

"The rest of that money, and you're gonna be with us when we find McGinty and what was in that vault."

"Isn't this enough?" She was through riding with the men who turned hot and cold as fast as she could turn her head.

Nate looked at her from under his eyebrows. "I done told you what kind of men we are."

She thought back to her trip from Fort Worth to Angel Fire many months earlier. "Look, it's not a through station. The stage from Angel Fire stops there to wait for the westbound stage. They meet there to exchange the mail and passengers going either direction and get fresh horses. After that, they turn around and go back. That posse behind us is going to be looking for two men and a woman. That's what they'll have on their minds. We can't ride up together and get on."

Daniel stuck out his bottom lip, thinking. "Fine, then, Nate can be your partner and I'll split off or hold back and come in a little later. Nobody'll think anything of that."

She gave the bank bags a pat. "This is all we need. A little gold seeded in the right place, and people will tend to forget what they've seen."

"You know, Nate. We're pushing our luck out here with them Indians all around. I wouldn't mind taking a stage. What's the first big town we'd come to? Even if there's already a passenger or two, she could pretend to be a schoolmarm or something, and nobody'll know you and I ride together. I see it all the time," Daniel said.

"Strangers riding on a stage pretending to be something different, and act like we don't know one another." Nate rubbed at the weeklong growth of whiskers on his chin. "Nobody'll ever think of something like that. We pay at the station to ride and get rid of these soap-bone nags. The first stage'll turn around and go back to Angel Fire and all's well; then we show up in style . . . to where?"

"Gainesville."

"Ain't that where they hung all those men during the war?"

The older of the two, Daniel, nodded. He loved reading newspapers, and retained most everything he ever read or heard. "Confederate troops arrested damned near two hundred Unionists and tried them in a citizen's court. Hung over forty before they were done."

"Rough town."

"Not as rough as it is out here on the Llano. That was in the past. We get there, we can get fresh horses and disappear up into the territories. There ain't but a few marshals sent up there after anyone, so we can get gone free and clear."

Nate jerked a thumb at Calpurnia. "She'll draw attention."

"We can make use of her."

"What do you mean by that?" Calpurnia didn't like them talking as if she wasn't right there between them. "You're not using me for anything."

"What I meant was that we can come up with a good story before we get on the stage and you'll sell it. Men lie. Women don't. If you say we're family, traveling somewhere, most anyone will believe it. Besides, that arm of yours is gonna draw attention, Nate. She can say she's nursing you. That'll work."

Licking her lips, Calpurnia squinted her eyes at the sliver of sun coming up over the horizon. She knew a lot more than she let on, like McGinty's true destination. He always bought a through ticket to Fort Worth, but he stopped short in Gainesville each time. He had a friend in the banking business who also had a friend who'd worked in the San Francisco and Denver Mints. The man was a genius when it came to the metallurgical arts, and they'd cooked up a scheme Calpurnia had only stumbled upon when she came to the bank after hours.

McGinty was there, with stacks of coins on the desk in front of him and drinking whiskey like it was water. When he saw who it was at the door that evening a couple of weeks earlier, he let her in without hesitation. "What are you doing out this late in the day? You know it's dangerous for a woman alone when the saloon fires up."

She patted the outside of her full skirt. "Not as dangerous when I have this with me." She was carrying a little derringer he'd given her to keep close in the bank.

"Come in. I'm drinking whiskey. Would you like some?"

"Do you have any water to cut it?"

He looked at her with new appreciation. That wasn't a comment that would come from someone who hadn't ever had whiskey. "Sure do."

She sat in a chair beside his desk as he took another glass from the bottom drawer. He uncorked a bottle of Old Reserve, poured in a couple of fingers, and finished filling the glass with a dipper full of water from a bucket sitting nearby.

He slid it across, bumping a stack of coins that fell with a rattle. "Tell me, Calpurnia. What is it you want out of this town now that your daddy's passed on to his reward?"

She felt a flush of anger. McGinty knew full well that he was the cause of her dad's death. He'd worked and scraped for years to put back enough money to open his own store, but every time he felt he had enough, something came up and drained the well. When McGinty told him about investing, her dad jumped at the chance, investing all he had into Texas Rail and Telegraph, which failed, costing him all that he owned. "Well, he wanted to open a mercantile someday."

"But I ruined that plan. But what do *you* want?"

She shrugged, wondering at his callousness. "A house, when the town's bigger."

"You don't like the boardinghouse?"

The Western Boardinghouse wasn't much more than a dozen rooms opening into a long hall that served as a dining room and parlor. It reminded her of the stable down the street, and oftentimes smelled that way when certain transient guests came and went. Her room to the right of the front door was one of the two largest, and cleanest.

On the opposite side of the entrance was where some of the more fastidious guests stayed. Those at the rear were places she would never enter.

"I'd surely like a little house." She blushed. "And my own privy. That's living in style."

McGinty took a deep swallow of his whiskey. He'd been at it for some time, and his face was red in the light of a single oil lamp. "Single women don't own houses."

"I'll be the first." She saw an opportunity. "Maybe you'll build one and I can rent it from you. Then we would both benefit."

He laughed. "I'd be paying you to pay me. That doesn't make sense."

"Surely others will come in and build. As smart as you are, I suspect you can't own an entire town."

"You're right. I'll need some competition to keep things interesting." While she took a tiny sip of her drink, he tossed off what was left in his glass and poured another. "My house is large enough. You could stay there."

"How would that look?"

"Who cares?" He glanced at the door as if someone might come in. Dusk had arrived, doing little to slow the traffic out in the street. "Besides, if you play your cards right, you might inherit the house, in a way."

"How so?"

"I'm about tired of what we have out here. I require more sophistication, and that's why I'm putting money in a Gainesville bank. By the time I'm finished, I'll have enough cash to buy my own railroad, if I want."

"Aren't you smart?" She grinned at him and sipped her drink. He took another swallow and she grinned wider. She'd noticed that each time she lifted her glass, he did the same, and she decided right then to see how much whiskey

219

he'd drink. "I knew you had an idea no one understood. I've been working here long enough and am a loyal employee. Why do you only take hard currency?"

An insolent grin crossed his face, and he took another swallow. "Here's how it works."

That was when he let slip his plan to get even richer than he was and move back east, and why his businesses only took gold and silver coins. That night, he picked up two of the stacks and let the coins drop onto the table one at a time, listening to them chink together as they landed, like a card player fiddling with his chips.

"This is how I can own one of the biggest banks back east."

"How?"

He gave her a wolfish grin and winked. "Have you ever seen a shell game?"

She shook her head.

"It's a con game in which someone hides a pea under one of three walnut shells. If the man's good, he can switch them around in front of a mark until he's confused. Then the mark pays to pick the shell hiding the pea. But he always loses."

"How, if he's watching?"

"Because the man's a cheat." He bit the word off hard. "He's learned to roll the pea out from under the shell you think is hiding it and slip it under another. Sleight of hand, and that's what I'm doing."

"How?"

He was about to tell her when they saw Bright peeking through the bank window with both hands on either side of his face. When Bright saw Calpurnia, he smiled and waved. Ready to pull the lovesick cowboy's head off, she ignored the remainder of her drink.

"Bright will walk me home. Good night." She rose.

McGinty's mouth formed a hard line as she left, showing his disappointment with the outcome of the evening. "You'll need money, and a husband to make your dream come true."

She gave him a crooked smile. "I've already figured out a way to make money, and without a husband."

She didn't have a clue how to go about it until she saw him leave town with a case full of cash and a strongbox under the feet of the guard, Aloysius.

Then she knew, and it would be McGinty who would fund it.

Her lame horse snorted, bringing her back to the present. A tiny grin curled the corner of her mouth, and she dazzled Nate and Daniel with a big smile that had captured McGinty's imagination. "You're right. Men lie, and women always tell the truth." She turned her horse into the wind and sniffed the air.

Nate frowned. "What are you doing?"

"Following the smoke to that way station. I need to get off this horse, wash up, and get something to eat. We'll work this out once we're there."

Ignoring them, she focused her attention on following the scent, like a bird dog on quail, and struck off to the west.

Shrugging at each other, her new partners followed her across the vast prairie.

With them behind her, Calpurnia's smile grew even wider as she repeated those words to herself again. "Men lie. And women always tell the truth."

CHAPTER 27

There was just enough glow from the rising sun for the defenders in the Moynahan station to see the surrounding area. What was left of the stage smoked in the dawn, and the Comanches had pulled back. Malachai studied the scene with a keen eye on what might come in the next few hours.

Cool air pulled through the open windows and door and over the adobe walls. On the distant northern horizon, a thin blue line told of a coming storm that promised relief from the hot, dry weather they'd endured for months. It wasn't much of a surprise. Malachai expected the weather to change. Starlings and other birds had been gathering for weeks, filling the morning and evening skies with live, feathered clouds that whipped in a dizzying array of directions.

"Larry's gone." Doc wiped his hands on a bloody rag and pitched it on top of his open Gladstone bag, the kind doctors had been using for over fifty years. The only thing left inside were dirty tools, empty bottles, and the few bandages he'd brought. "I'm sorry, Garry."

Kneeling beside the body and sheltered against the wall, Garry's soft voice cracked. "It should have been me. The youngest should never die first. I always promised our mama I'd take care of him."

"There ain't no should or should nots in this." The Ranger stared out at what remained of the smoking stage. "When people get to fighting, you never know who'll get hurt or killed. I've seen men standing side by side when a bullet or arrow came in, and it was only a matter of inches that determined who would live or die."

He turned to the young cowboy kneeling beside his brother. "Sometimes it's only a matter of a slight breeze turning an arrow. Once I saw a bullet nick a man's wrist and ricochet into another's head, killing him dead as a steak while the first man's wrist was only cut and bruised. We ain't promised nothing after we're born, other than we'll die someday."

He finished talking not to Garry, but in the direction of the burned stage. Most of it was consumed, but the heavy, thick wheel hubs continued to smoke. The wood inside the metal rims occasionally flickered to life before going out again. The odor of burned hair and charred horseflesh filled the still air with a nauseating stench.

Malachai wasn't surprised. He figured they'd fire it at some point. That's what he would have done to keep them hemmed up and in one place. He'd seen it done before too, but no white man knew how a Comanche thought, and sometimes they'd leave wagons alone after pilfering them, maybe because the smoke would draw curious Rangers, or the cavalry.

They weren't necessarily afraid of the mounted soldiers, because the army's slower horses carrying heavier men and equipment were easy to outdistance. The Rangers, however, were different. They learned from the Comanches and used their own tactics against them, riding lean and fast. They'd keep coming and not quit until their horses played out, or the weather or lack of supplies drove them back, or the war party simply scattered to the winds to gather somewhere else in a few days.

Still keeping his carpetbag nearby, McGinty shook his head. "Everything on that coach is burned up."

"You worried about your money, aren't you?" Doc's expression was one of disgust. "All these men dead, and we're probably next, and this poor woman here's looking at God knows what if we're overrun, and you're worried about the gold out there in that strongbox."

Trying to recover, McGinty raised his hands. It was obvious to Malachai that the banker wanted to get his hands on what was in the strongbox, but as a man, he needed to show that he was trying to think ahead. "I meant the water in those canteens. We need it."

Aggravated, Malachai turned and studied the

area around them. Three Comanche bodies lay inside the door, and one between the stage and the station. It was probably killing the surviving warriors to leave them there. They traditionally took their dead with them.

They were still making it known, though, that they hadn't left. A coyote-like yelp might come from one direction, and then a different voice on the opposite side brought taunts in a language the defenders didn't understand. Malachai figured they wanted the bodies of their people to give them a proper send-off to wherever such heathens went.

The truth was, he'd like to drag them out a ways from the house before they started swelling and stinking. The same went for the driver, guard, and Larry. It was a distasteful task, but one that would require action before long.

The Ranger glanced around at the burned-out station, hoping to see at least the head of a shovel leftover from the fire. At least they could bury their dead with that. He sighed. If there were any tools, they'd be in the shed out back that Buck told him about, but it was burned to ashes, also. They'd have to use their knives to loosen the packed dirt underfoot to get those corpses underground, and that was a lot of work for men with no food or water.

With a start, he noticed in the gathering light how filthy they all were from the soot and charcoal that surrounded them. It had been necessary to pull some of the rubble out of the way to make room to defend themselves, and to a person, their hands and clothes were black. Their pants, and the sides of Amanda's dress, were extra dirty where they'd absently wiped their hands.

She had several smudges on her forehead and cheeks, and he thought it was somehow appealing. It wouldn't be long until those smudges ran with the sweat they were all about to endure as the day warmed.

Heat returned with the sunrise, and though it was still early, they were already starting to feel uncomfortable. The adobe station's walls provided protection from bullets and arrows, but it also blocked any breeze from reaching them. They got a little relief when the light wind pushed through the openings to briefly take away the nauseating stench of death and replace it with the early morning dampness that brought the pleasant odor of moist dust and crushed grass.

It was an odd, comforting smell in the midst of their dire situation.

Malachai looked northward again, seeing the thin blue line of clouds was still there, and not just an early morning mirage. Could that be a norther?

Northers were fast-moving cold fronts with strong winds and dark, blue-black skies racing in from the north and sending temperatures plummeting. If that was what it was gathering on the horizon, they could experience a wide variety of weather, either refreshing, or deadly.

"Wish I had a rifle." Buck watched out the window opening. "Every now and then I see grass move out there, and I'm sure there's an Indian doing it. It's too far for this scattergun."

Malachai tapped the pistol riding butt forward on his left hip. Most Rangers wore them in a cross draw, making it easier to reach on horseback. For a moment, his mood lightened when he remembered a newly arrived dandy who showed up one day wearing a pistol riding backward, butt forward in a right-hand draw.

He and a couple of friends had asked for a demonstration on how the dandy could draw the pistol riding backward and fire before some old-fashioned gunslinger put two or three holes in his shirt. They'd laughed when the man snatched at the Colt with practiced motions, then dropped it muzzle first into the dirt.

"I've been seeing the grass move too." Malachai rested his hand on the butt of his pistol. "I wish these things'd reach a little further."

"I'm going for water."

Coming out of nowhere, McGinty's statement interrupted their conversation. Doc chuckled. "I'd love a drink too, but I don't have anything to doctor you with when you get shot, banker. You should just stay right where you are and let these fightin' men figure out what to do next."

McGinty's face reddened. "I wasn't always a townie. I've done my share of traveling dangerous territory."

Garry untied the scarf from around his brother's neck and used it to cover the corpse's slack face. No matter what he did, Larry's eyes wouldn't completely close, and Garry felt it was disrespectful to leave him that way. He rose and handed Amanda the pistol from Larry's holster. "You need this. Know how to use it?"

"Yes."

"Good."

McGinty spoke up. "Hey, I could use that."

"So can she, and I'd rather see her live through this than you." Garry rejoined the others.

"The damned truth of it is that McGinty's right—about water, that is." Doc nodded. "It's been twenty-four hours since we drank. We can't go on like this. We'll start suffering before long, and that'll impact our ability to deal with this fight.

"I'm getting a headache as it is and feel lightheaded already. Those are signs we need water. And pardon me, ma'am, for such language, but none of us has made water since we came in here, and that concerns me too."

Amanda flicked a dismissive hand and hefted the Colt. "What are you going to carry it in?

The stage fire was so hot I bet it melted the tin canteens under the driver's seat."

McGinty's eyes widened. "You think it got that hot?"

"I'd say so," Malachai answered for her. "Why?"

"Nothing." McGinty's eyes flicked to the valise.

Buck flicked a finger toward a collapsed pile of charcoal near the fireplace. "There was a shelf back there that had lard tins on it, I reckon. The lids are still on them, and even though they took some heat, I think they'll hold water."

Garry walked back to the blackened, buckled shelves. Two large tins lay in the rubble. He picked one up by the wire bail and shook it. "This one's empty." He toed the other. "This one still has lard in it, but not much."

"How're we gonna use those for water?" McGinty's voice was full of doubt. "We can't get them clean enough in here. Nobody can drink grease water and keep it down."

Amanda snorted. "Men! I swear." She stalked back and took the one-gallon bucket from Garry. "You have everything we need right here under your feet to clean 'em out. It's called sand."

Using her short fingernails, she managed to worry the lid off to reveal recongealed lard in both containers. She scraped the whitish fat from the interior with her fingers, then held out her hand to Malachai.

"Loan me your knife."

He slid a long, thick blade from the scabbard on his belt and handed it to her. They watched as she stabbed it into the ground and worked packed sand free. It came up in clods that she broke up and used to scrub the buckets out. She shook them out, repeated the procedure, and emptied the clotted sand again.

Ripping the bottom out of her petticoat, she wadded the rags and wiped as much sand out as possible. Shaking them to get the last of the grains out, she cleaned the lids the same way and studied her work.

Satisfied, she hooked her fingers through the wire bails and held them out to Garry. "This part was easy and safe. Filling them up's the dangerous work. You sure you want to do this?"

He looked at the others around them. "No, but Doc's right. I think we have to."

Malachai came up with a plan. The Ranger noted the distance from the station to the cottonwood tree. "Buck, you've been wanting to shoot at that moving grass."

"I have."

"That's because you can't see them. We're gonna do the same thing. Garry, if you still want to go, you and McGinty can slide out there the way those Comanches are sneaking around. Once we get away, we'll stay low and crawl while we keep 'em looking at the station here."

Buck considered the suggestion. "How?"

"When I tell you, Buck, throw a couple of rounds that way." He pointed in the opposite direction of the cottonwood. "While they're concentrating on not getting shot over there, McGinty and Garry'll try for the spring."

It was obvious when fear took over and McGinty changed his mind. "That's a long way to crawl, toting a lard can. Maybe there's another way. I'm not sure I want to go out there after a swallow of water and get myself killed."

Disgusted, Malachai spat on the ground. "You stay here, then. I'll go with Garry, but you'll drink only after everyone else, if there's any left."

McGinty's eyes flicked from one to another. "I'm just saying there might be a better way."

"Shut up, McGinty." Amanda shook her head. "Don't, Malachai. It's not worth it. Wait till dark."

Doc stuck out his hand to Buck. "Give me that scattergun. Amanda, I'll need to borrow your pistol there for a while. I'll try and cover for them."

"This is ridiculous." She shook her head no. Malachai knew she'd been mad when she cleaned out the lard tins, probably to show her worth, but now watching those two readying themselves to go out in the open to maybe catch an arrow or bullet, she'd changed her mind. "Maybe they'll leave when they see we're not going to give up."

"They have the advantage and know it'll get

worse as it gets hotter. Why do you think they're teasing us right now?"

Defeated, she held out the revolver. "You'll all get killed."

"We're gonna die anyway, if we don't have water." Malachai peered outside. "Nobody shoot until they see us. That'll be my signal to Buck. Garry, we can't follow that path. They'll be laying for us, so we're gonna swing out and make a wide circle to come in from the other way. You ready?"

Holding one bucket in each hand, he nodded. "Maybe if we can't see them, they can't see us."

"I doubt that'll last long." Malachai crouched and ducked around the door, taking a bead on the cottonwood. Mimicking his posture, Garry followed and they reached the edge of the waist-high grass surrounding the station without drawing fire.

Both men dropped and made their way in a wide arc through the tall grass. Soft rattles from the lard buckets forced them to stop. Malachai's heart beat hard and fast as Garry realized carrying the buckets by the bails wasn't the way. He tucked one under each arm, silencing the rattles but making travel awkward.

The sun felt like a physical hand pushing on their backs and shoulders. Both men broke into a sweat that ran in rivulets from under their hats. The first hundred yards were uneventful, and

Malachai had the idea they'd moved in such a wide arc they were coming in behind where the Comanches might be lying in wait.

Halfway there, and all was quiet except for the sounds of birds, insects, and the rustling grass underfoot. Feeling more confident, they moved faster and were almost to the tree when a covey of blue quail gave them away. Spread out and feeding, the little birds erupted into the air, wings whirring, and flew directly toward the cottonwood tree where they scattered out at the base.

On their knees, the two men froze until a large Comanche stuck his head above the grass to see what had flushed the birds. Malachai's pistol spat fire, and the bullet took the man in the neck. Slapping the wound with his hand, he sank back out of sight.

Running like a deer, Malachai rushed to where the man fell and surprised a second warrior who wasn't expecting to find a Texas Ranger charging into a small nest they'd stomped in the grass.

The Comanche was wearing a breechclout, leggings, and moccasins, and his bare chest, arms, and face were painted for war. A small war club raised to swing, he yelped a challenge and charged. The lard cans rattled as Garry dropped them and grabbed his pistol. Malachai fired a second and third time so fast they sounded as one gunshot.

Both rounds caught the warrior in the torso. He grunted and fell beside the body of his friend and twisted like a snake for a moment before growing still. Behind them, Garry's pistol and the defenders' guns opened up. Malachai hoped the others surrounding the station weren't able to tell their shots came from the spring.

The clear water bubbled up through a mat of green grass only yards away, draining away from the stage stop down a thin stream cut in the last thousand years. A distinct path appeared to their right, packed by hundreds of feet and hooves to the lifegiving liquid. It was that same path they'd avoided in order to surprise the two warriors lying still in the hot sun.

No longer needing to be quiet, Malachai and Garry charged forward. Pistol in hand and cocked for action, Malachai whirled and checked their surroundings as Garry dropped to his knees beside the spring and worked at the tight lids with his fingernails.

Gunfire crackled from the station as Buck and the others triggered their weapons slow and steady. War whoops reached their ears, and return fire scattered from three distinct weapons. The attackers' guns sounded different than those within the station's walls, the pops losing their power in the wide-open spaces, while the defenders' fire bounced off the adobe.

At that moment, the barrage was all directed

at Buck and Doc, but Malachai knew that wasn't going to last. Already, the sound of hooves on the hard prairie came to them.

For one desperate moment, Malachai thought Garry wasn't going to get the lids off the buckets. Panic in his eyes, he glanced around and, seeing they were still alone, got his fingertips under the edge and yanked. The lid on the first one came off, along with a nail, and Garry dipped the bucket deep into the cool spring. He swished it around to remove the leftover sand from Amanda's scrubbing, threw it out, and filled the now clean container with a gush and gurgle of cold water.

He yanked it out, pressed the lid on, and repeated the process to fill the second.

"Hurry up, son." His eyes flint hard and darting around, the Ranger was ready to go. "We're about out of time."

A mounted warrior charged their position, yipping in glee at seeing the two white men crouched beneath the tree. Raising a lance, he leaned over the horse's neck and drew back to throw. Malachai rose, standing as if facing an opponent on a town's street, and stood sideways. The Ranger extended his arm, aimed, and fired.

The bullet took the Comanche in the chest. He collapsed over the horse's withers and landed on his neck and shoulders with a crack of snapping bones. Another mounted warrior appeared several yards away and circled around, shouting to alert those nearby.

Malachai turned to see Garry with his entire face in the water and thought he'd taken an arrow. Relief washed over him when the young cowboy looked up, gulped air, and leaned down to drink again, then rose.

Seeing wisdom in his actions, Malachai took a knee beside the cold water while Garry covered for him. He drank deeply of the best-tasting water he'd ever had in his mouth, leaving both buckets of water for the others. More hooves joined the first, circling them.

"Look!" Garry pointed at the first warrior they'd shot. A Winchester repeater lay nearby.

He grabbed both buckets by the bails, for silence was no longer important. Malachai jumped forward, picked up the rifle, worked the lever, and saw brass in the breech. Closing it, he brought the weapon to his shoulder and looked around.

"Here they come!"

The sound of charging horses said there was no time to run. They had to deal with whatever was coming at them. Gunfire cracked and bullets snapped past. Malachai's heart sank when a second set of guns fired from their left.

They were caught in a crossfire.

CHAPTER 28

The morning sun made its way above the edge of town, pushing the long shadows of the buildings across Angel Fire's main wagon-rutted street and shading the men who showed up to join the posse. It was already warm, and I knew the day would be miserable before sundown. I was hoping for a push of cool air to come in from the mountains and give us some relief, but so far we hadn't felt a thing.

Sitting on the steeldust mare after a good night's sleep in the stable, I watched the collection of men gathering around us. Spirits were high. They'd slept off their mads about the bank being robbed and they were now looking at this posse as one would a hunting trip.

Gil watched Jeter, the stableman, coming down the street, leading a good-looking paint. "You know what I'd like right now?"

"That shot of whiskey we came into town for?"

"Well that'd be nice, but don't you think it's a little early for drinking?"

Tilting my hat to the side to block the sun, I gave him that look I usually reserved for discussions in saloons. "So what would you like?"

"These hot days make me want watermelon soaked cold in a spring somewhere. You remember those big ones with the red meat we used to steal from Old Man Burns when we were kids? I never tasted anything sweeter in my life than a stole melon from a cranky old cuss like him."

"I'll allow you had the best nighttime thumping ear in the county back then, but you weren't that happy the night he put a couple of pellets of birdshot in your rear when we was running."

"Hard to run in the dark when you're carrying the biggest watermelon from a feller's patch." Gil chuckled, and I saw that old look that used to drive the girls crazy back home. He'd lost it for a while, after I had to take his arm off, but him and Esther had gotten together and she brought his old self back.

"Well, we're gonna get a good dose of sun and dust before you eat another watermelon, stolen or not."

Jeter joined us with a double-barrel shotgun in his arms. "Mornin', gents." He looked around. "If I was you, I'd tell most of these fellers to go back to bed and we'll pick two or three of those Panther Creek boys to join us. The way they're waving them guns around, one of us'll get shot before the robbers."

I was afraid Jeter spoke the truth. "Did Marshal Skinner ever have a deputy worth a damn?" I'd already considered Gipson and threw that idea out, but I hoped that someone with more grit, sense, and experience was close by to rely on.

We could see him thinking about who'd served with the late marshal. "None that are still around." He pointed. "Here comes Bright."

I expected him to be the first one there, but from the looks of his eyes, he'd been up all night. They weren't bloodshot, though, and so I figured it was all worry about Calpurnia, which I could understand.

He gave us a nod when he rode up. One lip was puffy from the beating I'd given him and his hat brim curled upward on one side as if he'd slept in it. The two men who'd joined him in the fight were swelled as well. The short man's nose across the bridge was angry red.

Despite their appearance, Bright was more concerned with the others around us. "This is a sorry-looking bunch."

"They'll do." I always figured a man can surprise you, if you give him a chance. Though some of those collected around us wore suits, more than a few had likely fought engagements either in the war, or against Indians.

The looks on the faces of Jeter, Bright, and Gil started me to worrying. I decided I needed to know. "Gentlemen!" The laughter and conversation drifted off. Some came closer to better hear, while others simply waited where they were, as if challenging my authority. "We're riding after outlaws in Comanche country. I'd prefer experienced men. Let me suggest that if you're a family man, you stay back. If you've fought in the war, or against Indians, I'd like you to ride with us, though."

"If we engage with either bands, some are likely to get shot, or killed. If that's a concern to you, we won't turn to look as we ride out of town, and you can stay here without shame."

At least two soft-looking men exchanged glances and came to an agreement. I knew they wouldn't be with us when we left town, and they'd still be breathing when we came back.

It wasn't my place to pick men. I didn't know any of them, but a man with a face full of creases nudged his horse forward. "I didn't have much money in that bank, but I despise a thief and I was once a lawman. I know a lot of these old boys, and I might suggest one or two who're hard enough to ride the range with."

"Pick your men." We shook, and I told him, "My name's Cap Whitlatch."

"Stup Ferguson."

He pronounced it "Stoop."

We looked down the street at a fresh commotion and saw the scalphunters pouring from the Occidental. Gil didn't like it one bit. "Well, hell."

The Spencer across my lap, I nudged the steeldust forward and stopped her in the middle of the street. Saddle leather creaked, men groaned, and iron rattled as the white savages mounted up. Pletz saw me and reined in my direction.

"You look to be in our vay." His German was even thicker that morning than usual. "You vant something?"

"To tell you that these men, and you, aren't riding with us."

"Ve vaited all night. Ve are part of your posse."

"No, you aren't. Pletz, I don't like you, and I don't trust a one of these yahoos as far as I can throw 'em."

The bearded man who was once a buffalo soldier narrowed his eyes and tried to stare me down. I didn't give him the satisfaction of meeting his gaze. This wasn't a bunch of boys in a schoolyard, but I knew good and well if things went sideways, they'd do their best to kill me right there in the street, or out somewhere on the plains.

One thing that made me feel better was there were less men than they'd arrived in town with. One had an arm with a stained bandage. Bloody mucus ran from one nostril, and he looked miserable enough to lie down and die. They survived a rough night at our hands, and I didn't feel one bit bad about it.

The other limped to his horse. The others were likely laid out over at the undertaker's office. I kinda wished that the buffalo soldier was cooling somewhere, because I felt he was one of the most dangerous men there, next to Pletz.

"We ride alone." I waved toward the end of town. "If you want, y'all can leave first and see if you can pick up the trail yourselves. That's your right. You lost money too, you say."

He had other things to say. "You had no money in the bank. Why are you and that cripple in our way?"

"Because I can't turn my back on robbery, or murder. And besides all that, we're lawmen and have a duty to perform." We both knew I was talking about last night. "And there's an innocent woman who was stole."

"That's what I intend to bring back." The buffalo soldier laughed, and the others joined in.

God help me, I thought about blowing Pletz and the buffalo soldier right out of their saddles at that moment. They were a waste of good air, and it would rid the world of two brigands, but I knew if I did, the rest would join in and there'd be a lot of bodies on the ground when it was over, mine included.

Buffalo Soldier's hand was close to the Walker Colt riding on his off side. Others were watching to draw if someone opened the dance, and I wasn't sure Pletz wouldn't be the first one. The Spencer shotgun rested with the butt on my thigh, the muzzle pointed upward. I could get it down and leveled in a hurry, but some of them rode with rifles across their laps and there was no way I could beat them.

Horses and men shifted behind me, and I thought of all those townies and cowboys that would get cut down if shooting started. Some of the anger went out of me, and I settled down in the saddle, realizing only then that I'd been almost standing in the stirrups.

"We're wasting time." I turned the mare around and walked her toward the posse. The back of my neck prickled at the thought of getting shot in the back. Gil, Stup, and Bright were still facing the mob, and I watched their eyes for any sign of danger.

Gil gave me a half smile, and I knew things were all right, for the moment. "Gil, you and Stup lead 'em on out of town. I'm gonna sit right here with this shotgun till y'all are gone, so we don't have anyone riding up our backsides."

"Let's go, men." Gil led the way as I turned the steeldust mare around to face Pletz. The posse flowed down the street past the closed bank, heading east. That was the obvious direction the robbers went, and it was the best place to start.

I was pleased to see Stup still waiting with me. That old man had a Henry repeater with the butt resting on his thigh, and I had no doubt he knew how to use it.

Watching and waiting, Pletz and his men sat there like toads. Dangerous toads.

When the posse was out of town, Stup still hadn't moved. His eyes flicked to the shotgun, then to the mare. "How many shells you have in that pump shotgun?"

"Seven."

"Can't get 'em all."

"They're too mean and tough to kill like this. I just intend to sit here in their way for a few more minutes before we leave, just to make a point."

We were playing a time game. The longer I sat there, the angrier they'd get, and at some point Pletz would have to challenge me. If that happened, we'd lose, so I needed to break it off pretty soon, but I had to drive my intentions home.

"I know a few old boys who'd sure like to help us." Stup pursed his lips in thought, pushing out his mustache. "But they're scattered far and wide."

"We'll just have to make do."

Pletz was one of those riders who rode all rounded forward and slumped over, like that old Comanche they scared us kids with, Buffalo Hump. Instead of challenging us, Pletz nudged his pony to the left and disappeared across a lot between two unfinished buildings. Silently, the rest of them followed and they vanished.

Stup never took his eyes off them until the last one disappeared. "Making do's what I've done all my life."

CHAPTER 29

The air was quickly becoming thick with moisture as Pletz and his men struck out north of town then swung east. His right-hand man, Henry Schaefer, rode up beside him. "We should have killed that damned lawman back there and been shut of him. I've never seen you back down from anyone before."

Pletz didn't tolerate his men questioning his decisions. Once a leader showed weakness in any manner, it was only a matter of time before someone with a little bark on them would challenge his place of authority. That usually resulted in the death of one or the other.

They were like wolves. When the pack's leader was strong and violent, the others submitted. But as he aged, or showed any signs of weakness, the next in line who was biding his time would eventually offer a challenge.

Pletz had no illusions that he'd lead them forever, and he always expected someone to try to take over at some point. Though Pletz didn't touch his weapons, the look in his eyes was one of murder.

Schaefer's face paled at the expression on his leader's face. "I didn't mean you was scared or nothing."

To emphasize his hold over Schaefer, Pletz ignored him for a good five minutes before taking a slow, deep breath. His men had seen and heard that sigh, and it could mean he was about to kill the man who irritated him, or just the opposite. He might be preparing to offer an explanation.

He'd heard that some of the men thought that when he paused like that, he was translating his thoughts from German to English, to make sure he said the right words.

The truth was that the man was playing chess in his mind, trying to decide on the best response. "We could have drawn down on him, but that shotgun is part of him as much as his hands and arms." Pletz never looked at a man as they rode, always watching ahead and to the sides. His men in the rear were required to check their back trail, and he'd let them know at the outset that if they were attacked from behind, he'd kill the surviving drag riders as soon as the fight was over.

"You saw the way he was holding that scattergun. All Whitlatch had to do was drop it level and spray us with double-ought buck like geese on a pond, and I wasn't interested in getting shot this morning."

"Well, that might have been true, but him and One-Arm killed Tyson last night and he wasn't doing nothing different than we've done in towns before. We've never tolerated anything like that as long as I've rode with you."

"Why put that on me?" Pletz grunted. "*You* could have shot them last night when you went out looking for those two and solved your own concern. Looks like we both had to think about what would happen if we drew down on them two."

Schaefer's head snapped toward his old partner. "How'd you know?"

"Because I'm in charge of this bunch and I don't trust a damned one of you. I watched you leave and followed. You shouldn't be so drunk when you're going to ambush someone."

"I don't like you following me." Schaefer scowled and risked a glance at Pletz.

"I don't care." Pletz adjusted the pistol and knife in his sash, causing Schaefer to tense. Instead of producing a weapon, he took out a plug of tobacco that was tucked inside his shirt. Biting off a chew, he tucked it away again and spat to the side after chewing for only a moment. "Why didn't you go on in and shoot those two when you had the chance?"

Schaefer sighed. "Because I's drunk, but not enough to be completely stupid. That little stableman was in there somewhere making it three to one. Saw him moving around, and then when I managed to find a knothole to look inside, Whitlatch and his one-armed friend were still awake and bedding down in a stall with that steeldust mare. She smelled me and blew. They came up wide awake and didn't go to sleep for a good bit after that. There was no way to do it without getting into a gunfight, so I changed my mind."

"Lucky she caught your scent. He'd'a killed you, I reckon. That man's a one-person army and Whitlatch works with One-Arm like they was the same person. When you come up against a pair like that, you'd best have the bulge on 'em right from the start."

They rode in silence, as they often did when on the trail. Pletz was a thinker, and preferred not to engage too deeply in conversation when they were riding. He'd spoken enough for a week, so he remained silent for a while.

Occasionally, he adjusted his route without explanation, heading somewhere only he knew about and moving only by degrees when changing direction.

When he saw Pletz wasn't inclined to talk any further, Schaefer drifted back beside the buffalo soldier named Leroy Booth. They came together, as they usually did on the trail. Though the scalphunters operated as a loosely tied unit, the men usually partnered up with someone for a variety of reasons, safety and companionship being the most common.

Schaefer allowed his mount to ease away from the main body of riders so they could talk. Booth followed. Once he felt they were out of earshot, he kept his voice low. "Pletz is acting strange."

"What do you mean?" Booth chuckled. "He's always strange."

"No, he let that feller Whitlatch live, and then backed down."

"Pletz didn't back down. I've never known him to bend a knee to any man."

"What I meant was that we've always gone where we wanted, and took whatever caught our fancy. He turned away from Whitlatch and don't seem inclined to make him pay for killing Tyson. It ain't like him."

Booth rubbed his mouth, digging a dry crust from one corner. His thick beard was sprinkled with gray hairs and coated with dust. He pulled the wooden plug from a water bag hanging from a strap across his chest and took a swallow. "Deitrich makes his own way. Maybe he didn't want to lose too many more of us." He plugged the bag back up and looked around. "A year ago there were twenty-five riders. Now we're down to less than fifteen, and Sandoval with them holes in his arm don't look too good."

The wounded man rode in the middle of the pack with his bandaged left arm hanging straight down, blood oozing from the rags binding the seeping holes. Half a dozen shotgun pellets found him going up the stairs, and Booth had plucked them out of his arm and shoulder with the aid of a bottle of whiskey and a pair of tweezers he always carried with him.

Sandoval's face was gray with pain, and his nose constantly ran, dripping onto his shirt. Schaefer wondered if he'd broken his nose falling down the stairs after being shot. He kept wiping at bloody mucus that seemed to come from nowhere. His head bobbed from time to time as if he was about to pass out.

He turned his attention back to Booth. "Well, I'm about done with all this." Schaefer adjusted his battered and torn hat to block more of the rising sun. "The scalping business is about finished, and I'm not sure when we're gonna get to sell the ones we have, let alone what we're gonna collect between here and there.

"I never thought I'd see the day when Pletz took any guff from a lawman, but he disappointed me back there in town. We shoulda rode through that tin star and his men, and instead Pletz led us down a side street with our tails between our legs."

"I believe you're drifting into dangerous territory, my friend. All this talk sounds like you're laying for Pletz. You'd better think twice about squaring off with that old Dutchman. He'll gut you in a heartbeat and sleep like a baby afterward."

Schaefer glanced over to make sure they weren't overheard. "Well, I might be considering a new way of life. This business is about done. I'm thinking about heading out to the mines in Arizona and doing a little prospecting."

"You'll never turn a spade full of dirt." Booth showed his white teeth in what passed for a smile. "You ain't that kind of man."

"I believe I'd rather die than have a shovel and pick in my hands all day. I had in mind to prospect in a different way, looking for what's already dug."

Booth's eyes brightened. "I wouldn't mind lifting some of the weight off those miners."

"See? It's a good idea. I say we start early, with that bank gold Pletz is after."

"You know we're going to find them bank robbers before long." Booth poked at a cloth bag full of cured scalps hanging from his saddle. "Once we do, we'll have money again to get us through until we get paid for this hair. Hell, we don't need much. We have enough food for a couple of weeks, and I know for a fact we took so much whiskey from that saloon back there that we have enough to stay drunk for half that time."

"Looks like we're thinking the same. Let's get through this and see what happens."

As was his habit, Schaefer studied the country around him. To the north was a heavy blue line he didn't like. He pointed. "Norther coming in."

A man who hated cold weather, Booth frowned into the distance. "Colored folks don't cotton to the cold. We ain't made for it. That's partly what I like about your idea of heading for Arizona. I hope we find a hole somewhere soon so I can build a good hot fire. If I don't get chilled early, I can stay warm, but I never can seem to catch up if I don't."

Schaefer barked a laugh and bit it off when Pletz looked around. "Well, you're gonna be miserable in a few hours, then. That way station I heard about is up ahead. We can get inside out of the weather if we get there fast enough."

Booth watched the distant line and adjusted his collar, as if the cold wind was already blowing.

Schaefer kicked his horse into a lope. He pulled up beside Pletz. "You see that cloud in the north?"

"I do."

"We're gonna have to find cover soon or we're liable to freeze to death when it gets here."

Anyone who'd lived on the plains for any length of time knew about such storms that plunged the temperature by sixty or more degrees in an hour and brought sleet and snow so fast that men died from the elements or froze to death before they could find shelter.

Schaefer jerked a thumb the way they'd come. "Back in town they was talking about a stage stop somewhere. Said that might be where McGinty came through on his way back east. I heard a feller in the bar say them robbers might be heading there with that little gal too. You think we can find it and get out of that weather?"

"A norther is rough in this country if you can't find a good shelter," Pletz allowed. They rode together in silence for several minutes before he spat a brown stream off to the side. "But I'm more worried about them Comanches over yonder."

Shocked that he hadn't noticed, Schaefer rose up in his stirrups and saw a wide band of Comanches spread out and riding hard in their direction. He looked around for cover and saw nothing but flat country. Not even a buffalo waller broke up the landscape.

The hairs on the back of his neck prickled at the sight of still another band coming in from a different angle. "They see us."

"They do, which means there's gonna be a fight." Pletz adjusted his seat and rested one hand on the butt of his revolver. "Unless I can get 'em to talk with us instead of shootin'."

"Talk? About what?"

"Joining up, of course."

Schaefer was stunned. They'd never considered being friendly with any Indian tribe in the years they'd ridden together. It went against everything they stood for, and if those savages found out what they were carrying, it would be a slaughter and he wasn't sure *anyone* would ride away. "We're not Comancheros."

"Not at the moment, but if we trade them a few guns for information, or maybe some ammunition or one of them bottles of whiskey Booth's carrying back there, we might avoid a fight out here in the open and find out where them robbers went."

Another of the scalphunters kicked his horse up closer. "Y'all been smelling that smoke? It's coming from over yonder behind them."

Pletz always relied on his men for information he couldn't glean himself. His sight was going, though he hadn't told his men, and relied on Schaefer to see into the distance. The man who spoke was Manfred Marsh, who had a nose like a bird dog.

"Not too strong, is it?" Pletz's question was designed to make them think he'd been smelling the smoke.

"No, it ain't. Oak, if I's to bet." Marsh pointed with a crooked finger broken in a fight when he was a kid. "From that way. I 'spect them Indians fired something."

Pletz shifted direction and pointed his horse's nose directly at the mounted warriors heading in their direction. "I make out a bunch of 'em."

Schaefer nodded. "About the same number as us, but that other bunch coming in from the right is gonna tear us a new one. We're gonna have to form a skirmish line."

Pletz's head jerked in the direction Schaefer

was pointing to see if they were charging or riding in for a palaver. Pletz kept his paint walking at a steady pace toward the Comanche war party, already demonstrating that he wasn't afraid of them.

His men watched as he evaluated their situation, ready to do anything he commanded. Usually Pletz was set on charging in, no matter what the odds, but this was something new. He never minded a fight, and relished taking lives, but it was always when the odds and timing were in his favor.

"Nope." Pletz surprised him by digging out a white rag and tying it onto the muzzle of his rifle. "I'm not of a mind to fight today. We're gonna talk."

"That's money on the hoof! We kill a bunch of 'em at a distance, and they'll turn and run." The big Sharps .50 rifles a few of the men were carrying could reach up to a mile in the hands of skilled marksmen. It was that massive firepower that changed the course of the Red River wars several years earlier when the buffalo hunters who defended Adobe Walls picked off the attackers at a great distance, breaking the back of Quanah Parker's attack on the hide camp.

"It is, but let's talk a little bit. We can always kill 'em if things go sour." Pletz looked over his shoulder. "I want to talk, I said. You boys spread out a little, but not so's they think we're about to fight, and stay on them horses, and hide all that hair you're carrying in the open. No reason to aggravate 'em right from the start."

Schaefer shook his head. "I never thought you'd turn from a fight, Deitrich. This'll be two times you've ducked your head today."

The German studied his friend for a long moment. "Not running from nothin'. I'm heading *toward* it and have an idea. We're gonna come out smelling like roses when we win from all angles."

CHAPTER 30

Bullets cut the hot morning air around them, followed by the rattle of gunshots. The Ranger stepped quickly to the cottonwood and took a knee behind the trunk, which was so large it would take two men to wrap their arms around its circumference. The battered rifle they'd picked up from the fallen brave tucked against his cheek, Malachai readied himself to face the four painted Comanches bearing down on them, guiding their mounts with their knees.

Though the dark bank of blue-black clouds rushing in was still some distance away, the north wind took that moment to arrive, pushing through with what would have been a refreshing blast of clean air. Instead, it hit them with a physical blow that waved the grass and bent the cottonwood limbs.

Pushed from behind, Comanche hair flew and their horses seemed to be blown by the wind like mythical beasts from a fairy tale. The feathers adorning their clothes and woven into their hair took on a life of their own, once again flying free and colorful as the warriors whooped and charged.

Malachai held his fire until they were close, for he had no idea how many rounds were in the rifle. Garry had time to put down the buckets and drag one of the dead warriors on top of the other. Dropping behind the human barricade, he readied his pistol.

One potbellied warrior guiding his pony with both knees drew back his bowstring and sent an arrow at Garry. The wind caught it and the deadly missile changed course, missing its target and slithering and skipping through the grass. Seconds later, he sent a second arrow at him. This time the wind lifted the projectile and it stuck in the ground well beyond the intended target.

He was nocking a third when another charging Comanche riding only a few feet away shouted and raised a lance. Some braves preferred the old weapon that forced them close and indicated bravery when they killed an opponent.

Two other warriors with guns fired again. One chunk of lead gouged a chunk of dark, papery bark from the cottonwood above Malachai's head. He squeezed the trigger and missed with the strange rifle. Cursing the unfamiliar weapon, he jacked the lever and loaded another round.

They closed in, and war cries filled the air as a second set of hooves arrived, along with a shrill whoop from Garry. In the war, Malachai was familiar with the rebel yell, a yodeling shriek that originated in the ranks of Confederate country boys. Malachai's shout was a single version of that battle cry, and it came again.

Startled by something they weren't expecting,

the attackers charging their position wheeled their horses to circle around and out of range. With that immediate threat gone, Malachai whirled to take on the new danger coming from his left, thinking the first charge was a feint by a small group of warriors and the main body of attackers was coming in from a different direction.

He almost shot before realizing one of the riders bearing down on their position was a white woman dressed in town clothes that rose and flapped in the north wind like clean linen on a clothesline. She was bracketed by two cowboys firing their pistols as fast as they could cock them and pull the triggers.

Garry jumped up and waved. "Here!"

The mounted trio charged up as Garry and Malachai met them. One of the new riders pointed at the Comanches. His sleeve was bloody and tied tight with a scarf. "They're running."

"Just retreating for now." Malachai drew a long breath and studied the woman, wondering at the unlikely association of two cowboys and a woman in a town dress. "Comanches don't like to fight unless they have the advantage. Y'all surprised them and changed that. They'll have to regroup and think about it. You better get down and water them horses quick while we have the chance. We need to finish up and get inside the station."

The man who sat tallest in the saddle pointed.

"Them Indians are heading over that little rise. We got time."

"I hope you're right." Despite his long drink a few minutes earlier, Malachai's mouth was dry as cotton. "Would you keep an eye for us?"

The tall one nodded from his vantage point in the saddle and loaded fresh shells into his revolver. "Be glad to."

From their elevated position, the riders had a good view of the station and burned-out coach. The redheaded woman covered her mouth in surprise as she took in the scene. "They've burned out the station! What are we going to do now?"

"Drink!" Malachai helped her down as the wounded man dropped to the ground with a grimace. "Hurry."

In seconds, three horses and four people were sucking up water as fast as they could swallow. When the wounded cowboy on the ground finished, he rose and spoke to the tall one still on horseback. "Still clear, Daniel?"

"As far as I can see."

"They've been sneaking in that grass like rat'lers." Malachai wiped his mouth dry, leaving a clear smear through the soot on his face. He reloaded now that Daniel was their lookout. He pointed at the scarf around the shorter man's left bicep. "Looks like y'all already tangled with 'em."

The wounded man and Daniel exchanged glances. Daniel nodded in his direction. "Nate there took a bullet all right."

Nate grinned. "I been hurt worse in a schoolyard fight. Y'all are covered in soot. Them Indians burn you out?"

Malachai noted that none of them carried rifles. He was hoping for more rounds to go in the Indian's Winchester. "They'd already fired the station when we arrived, but yeah, it's been pretty rough. We had to fort up inside and look like this because we moved some of the timbers out of the way. It's a small price to pay to still be breathing."

Malachai barely heard Nate's comment, watching the woman's eyes as they talked. "You're not much dressed for riding, ma'am. Looks like y'all had to leave in a hurry from wherever you were."

"Traveling." Daniel spoke for her. He took a few breaths and drained the canteen. "And now this."

The Ranger noted the lack of information coming from the new arrivals. They'd offered nothing, and their vague answers were essential repeats from what he and Garry were saying.

"Boys." The front of his shirt wet from drinking, Garry toed one of the two lard buckets. "Y'all pitch down them canteens and I'll fill 'em up. We got thirsty people back there and need to get back undercover again before them Comanches come back and kill us all."

The conversation over for the moment, Garry filled the containers and handed one up to Daniel and the other to Nate, who'd just gotten back in the saddle.

Instead of waiting for the woman to mount up, Malachai swung up on her horse and reached down a hand. "Name's Malachai. Texas Ranger. Get up here."

Frowning, she paused.

"We don't have time to talk." He moved his foot from the stirrup, and she mounted up behind him in an unladylike fashion, wincing when she settled in behind the cantle.

Garry passed up one of the buckets. "Y'all take and carry the water and I'll walk, with that rifle, Malachai."

As the woman adjusted her seat behind him, the Ranger passed it down. "Careful. The sights might be off."

They struck off for the station as the wind pushed them from the side, replacing the hot day with cooler air.

CHAPTER 31

As if trying to inflict as much pain and heat as possible on the Llano before the norther blew in, the sun beat down on fighting men who approached each other with the wariness of predators meeting unexpectedly.

The horses under the Comanches looked to be as wild as their masters as a breeze kicked up out of nowhere. Thick, long manes flew in the wind as the warriors' hair did the same, both decorated with paint, feathers, and beads, catching notice of the professional scalphunters who looked on the trophies with greed in their eyes.

In direct contrast to the scalphunters' long, greasy hair, matted beards, and filthy clothing, the war party was lean, though dusty. Feathers, buffalo-hide shields, lances, rifles, and pistols in or near to hand, they were stripped-down fighting men. Most of them were naked to the waist and wore leather leggings and fitted moccasins. All looked tough as the bois d'arc wood they used to make their bows. The paint on their faces and animals added to their ferocity.

Pletz's men spread out, weapons ready but resting easy as the Comanche war party slowed and walked their horses. To let them know he was in charge, Pletz nudged his paint a length ahead of the others and stopped.

The warrior he assumed was the leader rode in the middle and slightly ahead. They stopped and waited for the band of white men to come to them, or prepare to fight. Intending to show strength by not approaching any further, Pletz reined up and waited.

He studied the men who ruled the plains from just south of the land claimed by the Cheyennes and Arapahos, to the Apache territory to the west, and all the way down into Mexico. They still raided to the more settled central part of Texas, but the massive influx of white men was quickly changing their hold on that part of the country.

Facing each other across the prairie as enemies had gathered for centuries, none of them showed fear or nervousness. Somewhere behind them and out of sight, and likely watched over by younger warriors learning their trade, was whatever they'd stolen, for they had no other ponies or plunder with them.

The second band coming in at an angle rode up hard and fast, then reined in at the same distance, throwing up dirt clods and grass to prove their insolence and bravery. They were younger than the ones squaring off with Pletz, full of piss and vinegar and looking for blood. One shook his lance and whooped, hoping to force a reaction and a fight.

The experienced scalphunters waited, hands near their weapons, seeming almost to be bored with the whole situation.

Pletz watched them from twenty yards away and finally broke his silence. "I've killed a passel of you heathens."

Not a one of the warriors changed expression. Maintaining eye contact, Pletz spoke to Schaefer. "None of them speak a word of English."

"That might not hold true for them younger ones over there."

"They look ready to fight?"

"Not so's I can tell. They're watching that bignose feller there in the middle."

"I 'spect he's the leader." Pletz made the sign for peace, though he was itching to kill the leader and take that thick head of hair that was greased back and decorated with beads and feathers woven into small braids hanging down to his shoulders.

The muscular Comanche did the same, sweeping the palm of his hand flat to the ground from side to side. The black war paint on his face and a brace of revolvers at his waist was unsettling to Pletz, who wasn't used to such a polished look worn by his adversaries.

The Comanche asked a long question in their language, but Pletz shrugged. He made a big show of not understanding, and spat to the side to prove he wasn't afraid. Fearful men had dry mouths and couldn't muster enough saliva to spit even though they had a chew in.

He turned to his men. "Everyone laugh to make them think I'm saying something funny so's they won't think we're afraid; then get Sandoval up here."

A long chuckle ripped throughout their party, and a couple held up their hands, palm outward. A sign of peace.

The man shot by Cap Whitlatch the night before, Herman Sandoval, was the only one who could speak Comanche. Born in Mexico, he had a gift for languages and spoke half a dozen fluently. He'd been captured south of the Red River by the Penateka branch when he was a kid and had escaped after a couple of years as a slave. The man had no use for Indians and would often point to the scars on his back where he'd been beaten as a captive.

Arm hanging lip at his side, Sandoval rode up beside Pletz and used his good hand to wipe away the bloody mucus caught in his ragged mustache. He wiped it on an already wet spot on the thigh of his pants. Expressionless, he drew a long breath and addressed Pletz in German. "I know this sonofabitch. Name's Broken Nose. We should just shoot him now."

The muscular warrior stuck a finger inside one big nostril and made a comment the others thought funny. They talked for a moment and then laughed.

"Says you ride like Buffalo Hump, but we all stink like a rotting coyote."

"He's trying to start a fight, as if he needs a reason." Pletz spat again, this time in the leader's direction as a show of disrespect. "Tell him we ain't interested in it right now."

Sandoval signed that they didn't want to fight, but to talk. Broken Nose responded with a wide variety of hand and arm gestures. It was a language created by the plains tribes who spoke different dialects. When the white man arrived, they quickly learned to hand talk as a way to trade with the various tribes.

"He recognized his name when I said it in English, but I don't believe he understands real talking." Sandoval continued to speak German. "They're making fun of my bloody nose too."

One warrior beside Broken Nose made a comment, and the others agreed. A ripple of comments went through the older band. The younger fighters on Pletz's right agreed.

"They don't know I understand what they're saying." Sandoval spoke softly. "When that snake of a leader tells them, they're gonna open up on us."

Pulling his attention away from Broken Nose, Pletz turned to look at Sandoval as if they weren't facing death. "Just what'n hell's the matter with your nose anyway?"

"Don't know." Sandoval shrugged. "Hurts like hell after I got hit with that shotgun. What are you planning to do with this bunch?"

"That's up to them murderin' bastards. Use sign to tell them I want to join up and find some people who wronged us. Tell them we'll help kill them all and they can have everything they own, except for the money they have on them. They can even have the woman. Dangle her in front of them. All we want is the money."

Puzzled by the German language and the hard-looking men who showed no fear, Broken Nose studied the scalphunters. He sniffed the air and said something loud in Comanche.

Pletz grinned. "I don't need a translation for that. He may act tough, but he's scared of us. We don't look like who they're used to butchering."

The wind increased, blowing across the surrounding grass that rippled and ducked in waves. It was the leading edge of the coming storm that was still a good distance away.

Sandoval looked back and forth between Broken Nose and Pletz. Their use of German allowed them to talk without being understood, making each of them more comfortable with the situation. "We're gonna make that kind of deal with them savages?"

"We are. Then when all of us get together,

they'll find them because they're better trackers. If we're lucky, they'll cut sign of that posse and we'll let 'em do most of the dirty work and wipe them out. That'll fire 'em all up and when we find them two bank robbers, they'll kill *them* and be more interested in the woman than us. While they're concentrating on her, we're gonna wipe them out and take their hair and get in out of the cold. We'll all win." Pletz barked a laugh.

Sandoval made the signs and when he reached the part about the woman, they showed considerable interest. One of the warriors had something to say, and Broken Nose listened. He nodded and cocked his head to consider the band of men. He signed for a long while.

Sandoval wiped his nose and added to the bloody wet spot on his pants as Broken Nose's hands and arms moved with dizzying speed. "He says we don't look like buffalo hunters."

"Did you tell them we were?"

"No."

"Then tell him we look like ourselves. Better yet, tell 'em we've been out west, killing Apaches. That'll make 'em happy."

Sandoval addressed them in Spanish. Broken Nose frowned for a moment, then shrugged and signed he didn't understand that language, either. One of them spoke Comanche to Broken Nose and signed at the same time so the band of white men could understand.

"He says he smells death on us," Sandoval translated.

"We smell it on *them*. Tell them it's an honorable death smell."

"That squatty sonofabitch next to Broken Nose wants to kill us all right now. He's talking it up, and the others are listening. Says we've been killing their friends, whatever that means. The mention of killing Apaches is stirring them up, and I'm not sure it's in a good way."

The Comanche leader asked a question, but before Sandoval could answer, he sneezed and the Comanches laughed. It was a good joke to see the funny expressions on the Mexican who spoke a strange language.

The squatty warrior nudged his horse forward, and several of the others started to follow. Concerned, Pletz let one hand rest on the butt of his pistol at the same time Sandoval sneezed again, harder. He shivered with the effort, as if a possum had run across his grave, and sneezed a third time so hard it seemed he'd torn something inside. This time a piece of buckshot shot from his nostril into his hand.

Shocked, Sandoval held out the chunk of lead so Pletz could see it. "I'll be damned. One of them shotgun pellets went right up my nose last night."

The German immediately saw the significance of that moment. "Hold it up between your fingers so they can see; then pitch it to Broken Nose there."

The Comanches were stunned at the sight of a man who could produce lead from his nose. Sandoval acted as if he were going to pitch it, to tell Broken Nose to get ready. The man readied himself, and Sandoval lobbed it across the space between them. Broken Nose caught the pellet in one hand. He looked at it in wonder and showed it to the others.

More than one of the warriors' faces expressed concern. So much that two of them backed their horses up, and a ripple of conversation washed across the band.

While the scalphunters sat and watched, Broken Nose weighed the pellet in his palm and passed it around. Each took the warped pellet in their palm and examined its weight and shape. To a man, their attitudes changed. Superstition took over, and Broken Nose spoke to his men in Penateka while Sandoval softly translated it into German.

"He says we have great magic, to shoot bullets from our noses. Says they respect that and will ride with us back where they just came from. They left some warriors back there in a fight and think we'll make great allies. They must have some folks pinned down. Says we can have the white man's greed, and they will take everything else."

The younger warrior who wanted to wipe out

the scalphunters listened for a moment and shook his head.

"That one's still gonna try and kill you when he can." Sandoval translated some more. "He at least wants your hair, because of the way you talk, he says."

Angry words flew back and forth until Broken Nose cut off their argument with a chop of his hand. The rest nodded and waited to see what would happen next.

"He can try," Pletz said in German, then nodded and gave them a grin that they misinterpreted for temporary friendship. "But I intend to have his hair in this bag too, before this is all over."

CHAPTER 32

"I want to kill them now." Huupi-evah, whose name meant Tall Water, stood head and shoulders above the others. He was Broken Nose's interpreter and spoke Apache and some English, in addition to his own language. Two white handprints decorated his chest, as if someone had reached out and pushed him.

The Comanche leader, Broken Nose, hated white men more than the Mexicans south of the Rio Grande. He was a youngster when a small band of men, women, and children saw that Quanah Parker was getting close to giving up and surrendering to the white soldiers. His father and several others took their families to the mountains there to raid and kill as their ancestors had done for decades.

"We will kill these dogs soon." They rode well to the side of the stinking white men to avoid the smell, and to keep an eye on them. Their alliance was balanced on a razor's edge of murder and gore, and Broken Nose was confident their leader who spoke the grating tongue was as treacherous as a rattler. "But we will kill them when their numbers are down."

It had been a hard time since the days of Comanche glory when they ruled the plains.

Broken Nose longed to go back to the times when his people followed the buffalo and raided across the land, terrifying anyone in their path.

Tall Water absently signed that he was annoyed. "We've already ridden away from this place. I don't see why we have to go back to such bad medicine. The young ones found us after we left them, so we should look for shelter and wait this weather out. We will all freeze in the open, if it's as bad as it looks coming toward us."

Surrounded by his older warriors, and still annoyed with the younger bunch who wouldn't give up on killing those in the adobe walls after they'd lost so many of their people, Broken Nose agreed with him.

"We will follow them like wolves and pick up the leavings when those in the walls have killed as many as they can. It will be a good joke on them. White people killing whites. Then we will finish them off and stay inside that building beside a fire." He'd been fighting the Mexicans in the mountains for years, and knew when it was time to quit and hide.

This time Broken Nose wasn't intent on hiding from anything on two legs, but from the storm that was bearing down on them. He knew the dangers of being caught in the open, and they weren't prepared for such weather.

He'd intended to lead them down to the protection of a canyon he'd been in as a boy.

There, the deep cut created by a river sometimes narrowed before opening in valleys chopped into pieces by ravines and hills. On either side of the canyon, high bluffs provided protection from both the weather and attackers.

But the young men were intent on showing their bravery and refused to listen. They held back until it was too late, and their run to beat the storm to the canyon would have been almost futile. When they came across the band of bearded, heavily armed white men, Broken Nose realized they'd have to fight, and maybe lose more warriors. That setback would take more of the time they didn't have, making their arrival at the canyon even later.

Thinking quick, he had an idea. For the first time in his life, Broken Nose intended to do something other than fight white men. He would befriend them, then use them as a screen to absorb the defenders' bullets until his warriors could get close enough to kill them all. Once the white people in the station were dead, they'd fall upon those buffalo hunters and get their revenge for all the animals they'd slaughtered, and for the starvation of their people.

He was surprised when the bearded leader of the band raised his hand as a signal that he also wanted to talk. Despite his distasteful, guttural language, the man proposed his own similar idea about killing the people who had inflicted so much damage to his war party. Though Broken Nose wanted to quickly take him up on it, he had to make it seem as if he was being convinced.

Tall Water flicked a finger toward a pair of hunters who rode a short distance from the group. "I saw their eyes. The white one who is friends with the man who can speak to us and shoot bullets from his nose. I think he would like to run."

"The one who had this in his head?" Broken Nose still had the buckshot pellet in his hand. He'd been worrying it under his fingers for some time, thinking it had to be good medicine and planning to weave it into his hair, or onto some article of clothing.

"No, the other who is to his leader as I am to you. Him and the buffalo soldier looked like they wanted to run. They are planning something. I can see it in their eyes."

"I saw them too. I think they are afraid of us and wanted to leave."

"Should we send some men after them if they go? They can catch them quick and shoot arrows into them and be back before we get to the station." Unaware of what the stage stop was called, Tall Water made the sign for a building.

"Let them go. I want as many warriors as possible here when we kill these hairy, stinking men." Broken Nose touched the butt of a revolver stuck in his waist. "I want to shoot these bullets into that man who makes my ears hurt with his mouth."

"His breath smells like when we squat," Tall Water agreed. "Even in the wind. I'm not sure you want his scalp to hang in your lodge."

"I might leave it flying in this wind when this is over, so it can be scrubbed clean by the air."

Broken Nose was getting chilled when they came into view of the station and both parties stopped to take in the scene. He knew his men were feeling the same, but they wouldn't show it to the whites. They'd ride tall and proud with their bare chests in the cold, though a couple of them had turned the buffalo shields strapped to their arms around so they would break the cutting wind.

Broken Nose and Tall Water rode forward and stopped close to Hairy Mouth, who turned and uttered something in his dreadful language.

Not understanding, they waited for the transation from his friend who pulled a buffalo cape up over his shoulders and neck. He spoke to Broken Nose in Spanish. "Pletz says we need to get after it. He's cold and wants a fire."

"Pletz." Broken Nose tried to pronounce the name, but mangled it. He laughed at Tall Water's translation and flicked a hand toward the station. "Then go. The day is getting away from us."

CHAPTER 33

The heat increased as the sun rose higher in the white sky, promising another blistering day. It was still, and there was no breeze at all, making it seem even more scorching than it really was. Feeling the rays on our skin, it reminded me of walking closer and closer to a hot fire.

I had the feeling that by sundown, we'd be in some weather. The blue line thickened in the north, and grew like a long, blue-black bruise against the much lighter sky. Such behavior told me we were in for a rough storm and we'd need shelter when it blew in.

As we rode, grasshoppers flew up from around the horses' legs and rattled away on dry, papery wings. Instead of hanging on at the tops of the grass, they'd already burrowed down near the soil in preparation for the coming weather. From time to time, one would come up and land on one of us. As we all knew, every tenth one headed for our faces, especially the shade under our hats. An occasional curse flew from someone's lips when the annoying insects struck them in the eye.

Some of the men flicked them off when they landed, but a couple of the guys grabbed them and either threw them at someone else for fun, or simply pulled their heads off and dropped the kicking bodies on the ground.

Gil tilted his hat to block the sun. "So here we are chasing outlaws when we oughta be taking Wilford Haynes in, like your old man sent us to do."

"They have Calpurnia," I said. As far as I was concerned, there was no choice in the matter. The right thing was to go after them. "It's as simple as that. I can't sit by and let someone steal a woman. It ain't right. We'll get her back and haul old Wilford back home in due time."

The posse was scattered behind us, and the last time I'd looked, a couple already seemed to be wishing they were somewhere else. Gil wasn't complaining; he just liked to talk things through. It had been our way since we were kids, and he hadn't changed a bit.

I usually didn't mind hearing him, because it helped pass the time.

"Besides, even if they didn't take that little ol' gal, I can't abide a thief. These folks had money in the bank, and most times it's *all* they had. They lose that, and more'n one will go under."

"Well, a town pays someone to be the law, and I'd expect them to have a man in authority to ride with us." Gil rode beside me, stirrup to stirrup. "Now take Stup for example. Someone coulda pinned a badge on that old boy and they'd have an official lawman worth his salt."

Stup had already proved his worth. He had us wait just outside of town while he loped out and made a wide arc toward the east, figuring that was the way they'd gone. Before long, he cut three sets of tracks and rode back to get us. Assuming they were the outlaws, we trailed them.

Some of the men with us wanted to ride hard and fast to catch them, but Stup explained that we'd soon be afoot out in the open if we did that. Riding horses into the ground was something only stupid white people would do. He said we'd just follow along at an easy lope at times, and catch up with them with fresh horses. He said to let them push their horses until they could run no more, and then we'd gather 'em all up and be done with it.

I kept an eye on the horizon. "For all we know, they offered him the job at some point and he turned them down. Not everyone's cut out to be a lawman. It's a dangerous business, and we're lucky the two of us are good at it. Besides, he's with us right now and that's enough for me."

Gil sighed. "You're the damnedest, most hard-headed guy I've ever known."

"That's why you're here alive and kicking right now, I reckon."

It was my stubbornness that made me agree to take Gil back for trial from up in the Indian Territories. I could have left him in that jail for the Gluck brothers to drag out and string up, but

I couldn't stand by for that to happen. He hadn't been tried, and there was no way a jury would be fair in that small town, intimidated by the rough, backwoods family that tried to run Gil up a tree.

The marshal in that town, Kanoska, had to get him out of his jail, so he pressed me to take Gil during a hard storm and clear out, with the promise that I'd get him down to Fredericksburg to stand trial. I've never crawfished on a promise, and though it was a hard journey south through hostile country to turn him in, he was still alive and kicking, despite losing an arm in the process.

He knew I was right and didn't like it. Instead, he changed tactics. "You know if we get to trading shots with them bank robbers, some of these old boys'll cut and run. Hiding behind barrels or around corners and shooting with others in town is one thing, but a fight in the open, or from ambush, tends to make some people nervous."

"It makes me nervous too." I was afraid he was right. "I hope that won't happen."

Gil was working himself up into more of a frazzle than usual. Maybe it was the coming weather. "What about Comanches?"

"What about 'em?"

"You think this bunch can stand up to them?"

"They'll have to, if they want to keep their hair. We get into it with some war party, they'll have to man up."

"That's just what I was saying. Fighting

Comanches out in the open's dangerous business, and it's a sure sight that somebody's gonna get shot with something."

"That's a fact." I considered the situation. "I'm still wondering where this bunch came from. After Quanah Parker surrendered most of them that was with him, I'd expect Indian fighting would all be over, and here we are again with raiding parties all around us.

"Stup said he cut some Comanche sign too, that's fresh. They've moved in here since we hit Angel Fire, and I don't intend to run into a bunch of fighters alone when we have all these guns to depend on."

"I heard someone back in town say these came up from Mexico where they'd been hiding out, raiding down there." Gil chewed his bottom lip as he always did when he was thinking. "How about you let Stup lead this bunch, and we break off and find that road we came in on. I'd bet those two and Calpurnia're headed out on it right now. Maybe to that station we passed on the way into town. It's about a day's ride to the stop. The two of us can make better time and catch them before they leave."

"They might be headed there, but following the road is the long way. We're cutting across in that direction, and it'll save several hours, and the horses." A grasshopper landed on my neck and I slapped it off.

"I'd bet they're out away from where people are. That's what I'd do if I was on the run with stolen bank money in my saddlebags."

"We're liable to come up on three bodies stuck to the ground by arrows out here, then."

Gil nodded as if I'd made some serious statement that required consideration. "There's that possibility."

I got some relief when Bright loped up to join us. His big hat was cocked to the side and tilted down on his forehead to break some of the sun. It gave him a rakish look that I figured would work for women seeing him ride into town. "Me and some of the boys have been talking. I have a better idea than to ride off here like this."

I sighed. Now I had to listen to him after Gil bent my ear on the same subject. "What's that?"

"I say we take the stage road. Split up into two or three parties and run alongside. Those guys probably stayed on the road to make time, then split off."

"I was just saying that very thing." Gil nodded, showing he was glad someone else was thinking the same way. "Just told Cap that was my thought too."

I was getting tired of being second-guessed about everything. "What if they did it the other way?"

He frowned, thinking.

"Look, Bright, none of y'all have to follow us.

This ain't no official town posse. I just gathered a bunch of men together because someone needed to do *something*. Take and go wherever you want. You nor anyone else behind us owes me a thing. We don't have a sure trail to follow, so do what you want."

He looked a little sad. I didn't believe he'd been expecting such a quick answer, and I mightn't have had one ready if me and Gil hadn't already been discussing the same thing. "I was just thinking's all."

I looked up to see Stup coming at us from an angle. He'd been gone for a while on the scout. He didn't want to have a lot to do with the posse. I could already tell he preferred to ride alone, but like a good point man, he came back from time to time to check in and tell us what he'd found.

We kept on at our pace, and he swung in to ride close to me, crowding Bright to the side. Some of the others tried to get in a little tighter to hear what he had to say, but he reined up a little to push them back. His roan didn't like it either, and fought the halter a little to give itself some room. A couple of men grumbled, but none of the others were tough enough to tangle with him.

Gil knew he wanted to talk and moved over.

Stup settled in between us. "All of a sudden I've cut a lot of sign." He pointed. "Ran across a bunch of unshod ponies, and a couple with shoes among them."

"Comanches."

"That's what I figure. Two or three groups, but the part I like the least is a bunch of shod animals coming straight from town and they all blended in together. Over yonder a ways." He pointed.

"What does that mean?"

"Means that a bunch of men from town caught up with Indian ponies. Wasn't no fight neither. They stopped to palaver, and then they all headed southeast together."

I felt a prickle on the back of my neck, and it wasn't an insect or grasshopper. "Pletz and his men."

"That's what I figger."

"What's out that way?" I knew what he'd say, but I wanted to hear it from Stup himself.

"The Moynahan way station is all I know." He shifted in the saddle to see Bright, then turned back around. "Also, I found a set of tracks for three horses."

"Is that good, or bad?"

"Good right now. They're making a beeline that way, toward the stage stop. One's missing a shoe and favoring that hoof. I'll allow he'll go lame pretty soon. The others need some tending themselves. It doesn't look like they've seen a farrier in a good long while."

"Have the Comanches crossed them yet?"

"Not as far as I followed. Didn't want to get too far ahead of y'all and have to come find you."

"We have to find them before the Comanches do."

"That's what I'm thinking." Stup waved a hand to the north. "And we either have to do it before that weather rolls in, or find a place to hole up. That's gonna be a rough one."

As if to punctuate his comment, a wall of wind struck us, snatching off a couple of hats and sending those members of the posse scrambling after them.

CHAPTER 34

The north wind blew the stage's remaining embers back to life, filling the station with smoke. The flames were small, and burned with bright heat, as the Ranger and his female passenger loped up to the door.

Seeing they weren't under fire from Comanche guns, Buck and Doc stepped outside. McGinty remained within the walls, peering around the charred doorframe at the new arrivals. Doc reached up for the water cans as Malachai took the woman's arm and helped her to the ground.

Once she was off, he swung down and Buck took the reins. He glanced down at the horse's hooves. "This old boy's in trouble."

"Aren't we all." The Ranger watched the other two dismount. "Y'all, this here's Daniel and his shot-up friend, Nate. And miss, you never gave your name."

"Calpurnia." She paused when Amanda stepped into the open. Her mouth opened and closed for a moment before she found the words. "I—I didn't expect a woman here."

"I was on the stage, with the others."

Daniel peered past her into the station. "Is there room for the horses inside?"

"We'll make room." Garry carried the lard

cans inside. "Y'all come in and get you a drink."

Throwing a quick look over her shoulder at the almost consumed stagecoach and the four horses dead in their traces, Calpurnia started to go inside and stopped at the sight of her boss. "McGinty!"

Malachai watched as the bank owner frowned. An unspoken conversation passed between them as McGinty swallowed. "What're you doing here, Calpurnia? Who's watching the bank?"

Daniel and Nate paused, intent on the exchange. Calpurnia swallowed and cut her eyes toward the Ranger. "It's been robbed."

McGinty's mouth fell open. He appeared to be looking for the words to say and finally squeaked out, "What'd they take?"

"Everything that was left."

Doc, who hadn't spoken up to that point, lowered the can of water from his lips and wiped his mouth. "What was left?"

"Banking business," McGinty snapped.

Buck grinned at their predicament. "Like that money in your grip there, and what's out there on the stage?"

All eyes lowered to the cloth satchel at McGinty's feet. He squared his shoulders and set his jaw. "Yep."

The Ranger saw Daniel and Nate exchange glances as the women did the same.

Something was up.

Before the conversation could continue, an

unseen coyote yipped outside, followed by another. Malachai took charge. "Those of you who haven't drank, do it. A couple of you get them horses somewhere back there and tied up. I don't want them breaking loose and running around in here when the shooting starts."

He paused and addressed Daniel. "Do y'all have any food with you?"

"No." Daniel waved a hand at his horse. "But we have some cartridges and I bet two extra rifles will come in handy."

"Had to leave fast?" The Ranger's eyebrow went up. "You'll have to tell me why y'all are out here when it's safer in town."

Doc stepped over to Nate. "Let me take a look at that arm, son. I don't have any medicine left, but I can take out a bullet if it's still in there. Don't want you to get a fever from it."

Daniel rested a hand on the walnut butt of his pistol, as if it was a natural rest. "How many Comanches you figure are out there?"

Garry turned from the window, blinking at the smoke filling the station. "More'n there was the first time. Y'all look."

The Ranger peered through the open window to see a band of Comanches out of rifle range, talking with a rough-looking group of white men.

CHAPTER 35

The ruins of the Moynahan stage stop were well out of rifle range as Pletz and his men put their backs to the wind. A couple of hours earlier, it had been hot and humid. Now the icy north wind brought fresh air scrubbed through evergreens far away. He reached back and pulled his scarf up to block the wind on his neck.

A couple of his other men were already digging ragged and stained coats from their bedrolls. More than one had thick cured hides they threw over their shoulders as the German studied the ruins. A stage was almost completely consumed by fire and dead horses on their sides and still in their traces were stiffening up, legs jutting out like branches.

It was all the work of the Comanches beside them. It had been several years since the tribe had mounted so many men in a war party, and many said, with the surrender of Quanah Parker, the half-white principal chief of the Comanches, they were all "civilized."

This bunch had appeared from nowhere and surprised everyone.

The big German had heard of holdout Comanches raiding up north of Angel Fire before they circled back around to the south. Colonel

Mackenzie said they'd all formally surrendered in Fort Sill by 1875, but like the Apaches in Arizona and New Mexico, no chief had command of all the tribes until Quanah Parker came along. For the past eight years, this new bunch had been raiding off and on, suddenly showing up and killing farmers, ranchers, and travelers before disappearing once again in the grasslands.

He'd heard that a couple of bands of the Nednhi Apaches were also down there as well, and the formerly bitter enemies were beginning to get along in order to survive. The Comanches were adapting, and that was how Pletz's band came to be riding with them.

It was the army's official stance that the Red River Indian wars were over, but no one told Broken Nose and his men. That was why their death toll on the white man was so high. Everyone assumed the plains were wide open and acted accordingly.

Once down in Mexico, Pletz heard of a large band of Comanches who were staying low in the mountains, along with renegade groups of Apaches. Hiding down there was easier, because civilization was slower to arrive in the isolated valleys south of the Rio Grande. Little news got out when they raided Mexican villages, and when it did, most shrugged the stories off as fanciful tales, or legends told around the campfires and hearths to scare each other in the night.

Now Pletz was convinced they were surrounded by that same throwback group who was going as extinct as the scalphunters themselves. This was a one-time association, though. He was more interested in the money inside than joining up with the raiders, though Sandoval had signed that they had the same feelings about encroaching settlers and the huge numbers of people passing through.

Cutting his eyes toward the warriors, the big-bearded German mentally tallied up what so much hair could bring down in Mexico. No longer interested in dealing with the Texas government, he'd carry those scalps down into the Sierra Madres and sell them to government officials who would be ecstatic to hear their generations-old adversaries were finally eliminated.

He'd take Broken Nose's head with them, as further proof. They'd likely make him mayor for killing the man who'd terrified them down there for years.

Broken Nose made a sign and spoke in Comanche to his men. Since Pletz couldn't understand them, he watched Sandoval's expression. If it went to shock, Pletz would draw the pistol in his sash and put a bullet in the side of Broken Nose's head right off. With the death of their leader, the others might react slower, giving his men time to massacre them, though if that happened they'd have to kill all the station's defenders themselves to get the bank money.

Sandoval asked a question in Spanish and Broken Nose nodded. They spoke for several minutes as Pletz picked out parts of their conversation. He almost grinned when the Comanches spoke in their language, still not knowing Sandoval was fluent.

It was an unusual saga of communication in the dropping temperatures as three distinct languages flew in the wind while two types of wet weather fell. Rain as cold as snow was mixed with sleet that rattled on everything around them. The sleet quit, returning to rain, but anyone who grew up in that part of Texas knew it was going to deteriorate further.

Sandoval grunted and turned to address Pletz in German. "One of those bucks who was here before we showed up says three more people joined them. Two men and a woman. All on horseback. He's concerned, because those extra guns worry him. Says they've lost several men already and he wants to find a warm hole somewhere to wait out the storm. Says those inside have it better, since the walls are gonna stop some of the cold."

Pletz hacked up a wad of mucus and spat. "That'd be them bank robbers and that little gal they took with them. Ain't that a fine joke, us riding up on them like that while that stupid posse and Whitlatch wander around out there looking for them?"

A cold trickle of rain ran down Pletz's cheek, as if emphasizing what his man said. A hard gust of wind threatened to snatch the hats from their heads, and he glanced up as the line of dark, leaden clouds raced southward.

"He's right about them having better cover, though. What's old wolf there say he wants to do?"

"Broken Nose's asking what *you* want."

"His blood."

"Yeah, but that's not the answer I want to give him right now."

Pletz shrugged. "Let's make a run at them before this storm gets worse. Maybe we can wipe 'em all out and squeeze in them walls together."

Sandoval laughed, knowing Pletz's idea. He spoke the words to Broken Nose, and the warriors around him let out whoops of joy. Broken Nose waved in one direction, then back to the other. His mounted warriors yipped in joy and split up.

Broken Nose flicked a hand at Pletz, then the station, along with a long string of questions.

Sandoval nodded. "He wants to know if you'll have the honor of leading them down there."

"He wants to use me for cover."

"That's what *I* think."

Pletz studied the situation and weighed the odds, scratching at something crawling on the back of his neck, trying to burrow deeper from the cold. He watched the mounted Comanches swing around to rush in from two sides. Knowing that most of the defenders' firepower would be directed at the Indians, he made a face that said, who cares.

For the next minute, a quick conversation full of translations flew back and forth between Broken Nose and Sandoval, until the Comanche leader flicked his hand at the station.

Sandoval shrugged and continued talking with Pletz in German. "This dog turd's done talking. He's not used to being questioned and told one of his men he's about ready to lift our hair and do it all himself."

"That'll be after the fight." With that, Pletz put his plan into place. "Let's go!"

Surprising Broken Nose by his fast decision, he spurred his mount across the whipping grass and charged the makeshift fort as those inside opened up on the advancing men and horses. Most of the sound was carried away by the wind, and the rattle of gunfire reaching his ear was soft pops.

CHAPTER 36

The skies lowered as dark gray clouds descended on the burned-out stage station. Malachai took charge as he looked out at the men gathered some distance away. "They'll be coming in a minute. Garry, you and Buck at that window. Daniel, you on the one facing front on the opposite side, and Nate, you work past the horses there and cover that side window."

They'd made room at the far end of the enclosure, moving a number of charred timbers out of the way. Rubble from the fallen roof added to their troubles, but they soon pushed and stacked enough to the side to make an opening three stalls wide. It was adequate to give the horses some protection from the bullets and arrows that were sure to find their way inside.

The gelding favoring his bad leg wasn't having it. He wanted outside, and all the strange odors and soot had him on edge. Malachai watched the nervous horse and decided it would soon be supper if they were under siege for very long. He didn't expect the fight to last that long, though, because the norther had arrived with a vengeance. Cold wind blew through the open door and windows, along with a rain so icy it stung when the drops struck flesh.

The men accepted Malachai's authority and moved into position. Malachai pointed to what he thought was the safest place in the building. "Doc, you come back here with the ladies. I'll need you to reload."

Amanda squared her shoulders. "I can shoot. Probably better than most men." Calpurnia nodded in agreement, as if she knew.

"Didn't say you couldn't, but the truth is, we're here on the front. If many of us fall, it'll be up to y'all to continue the fight. Doc as well."

Each woman held a pistol, and Doc had a small revolver behind his belt.

McGinty hesitated, unsure of what to do. Buck's voice caused his head to snap around. "Hey, banker. You come stand close behind us. We might need you to reload, too."

"I can fight."

The corner of Buck's mouth curved upward. "Not hardly."

"Why do you say that?"

"Because you're the kind of man who'll run, or sell out everyone to save your own hide."

"You can't talk to me like that!"

"I just did."

McGinty grabbed the butt of his revolver. "I'll kill you."

"No you won't." Buck's calm voice stopped him cold. "You pull that hogleg, I'll put holes in you before it gets level."

Doc stepped forward. "Boys, we don't need to be shooting one another right now. There's plenty of time for you two to do this, if you're still alive."

"Doc's right." Malachai walked between them on his way to the door. "They're gonna kill enough of us as it is, without y'all doing it for them. Save your ammunition for what's coming."

"Like right now!" Garry took careful aim with the rifle they'd taken from the dead Comanche. Instead of firing, he angled the weapon a little lower as he followed a racing target and pulled the trigger. The warrior grabbed his leg and yanked on his horse's halter, twisting the roan to the side.

Garry aimed again. "Now I got it figured out." He squeezed the trigger and the Comanche fell.

The north wind brought their attackers' whoops and cries into the station loud and clear. The men facing into the wind found themselves getting wet as light rain angled inside.

"Easy, boys!" Malachai held his cocked revolver ready. He felt a prickle on the back of his neck at the sight of so many people spread out and charging with the intent to murder everyone inside. "Let 'em get a little closer."

McGinty gasped behind him. Malachai whirled, half expecting to find someone already in their midst. Instead, McGinty's mouth opened and closed like a fish as he stared outside. "There's white men riding with them."

"Comancheros, I reckon." Buck spoke without turning around.

"I know one of those men."

This time Buck turned, his pistol pointed at McGinty. "What do you mean by that?"

"No, it's not like that. He had . . . has . . . money in my bank."

Garry turned around, his face pale with fear and concern. "What is this?! McGinty, you in with them?"

"No!"

"Not the time!" The Ranger aimed and fired the charging attackers as Daniel and Nate did the same.

The horses snorted and stomped, frightened of the rifles and pistols going off so close. They were work horses, meant for riding only, and weren't used to such sounds and the fear that radiated off the people around them. Calpurnia rushed to grab their bridles, stroking the nearest one and talking softly. The rest of them chose targets and fired, ducking as bullets whizzed back in return.

Outside, men fell.

Wounded horses screamed as they threw their riders.

Comanches whooped.

Buck fired, then again. "The Comancheros are slowing up, letting the Indians come in first!"

Malachai moved from window to door, and

back to a different window, choosing his shots well. Buck's hat flew off, a hole in the crown.

"Whoo wee!" Garry shouted. "Them two out there are fighting amongst themselves. That Comanchero just shot one of the Indians in the back and now he's taking his scalp!"

Frightened by all the noise, the three horses stamped their feet, yanking and pulling at the reins tied to fallen timbers. Black dust and soot rose from under their hooves and was picked up by the wind flowing inside.

Amanda rushed to join Calpurnia as Doc stepped forward at the same time an arrow sizzled inside. It struck the back wall where he'd been standing and exploded into splinters.

The roar of gunfire in the enclosed space pounded their ears, so loud they had to shout to be heard. The lame gelding Calpurnia had been riding was closest to them all and screamed when a bullet struck it in the side. She was holding the reins and the animal reared in pain, yanking her off her feet.

Wild eyed, it slung her around and she lost her hold, slamming into the back wall hard enough to stun her. Seeking escape, the lame gelding planted his feet wide and leaped to the side, trying to find a way out. Finding no escape there, it whirled and almost climbed over one of the other horses.

Out of its mind with fear, it spun and kicked,

catching Nate in the back of one leg. He shouted in pain and fell, scrambling to get out of the way of those hooves that were flashing above his head.

Doc darted forward, grabbed the bridle, and at the same time stuck the muzzle of his revolver against the side of the gelding's head. No one heard that soft pop in the chaos of gunfire, but the horse dropped where he stood.

With the two windows at the far end uncovered, Daniel was firing fast and steady. Nate was down for the moment, and a wiry Comanche stuck one arm through the window and shot twice before his pistol was empty. Putting a hand on each side of the bare opening, he jumped through and yanked a war club from his belt.

Daniel whirled and pulled the trigger on his empty pistol. With a cry of joy, the warrior swung the club at his head. Daniel fell back, and the Comanche tripped over Nate, who overcame his pain enough to stick his pistol against the man's lower abdomen and fire.

The brave staggered and fell when Doc ran up and shot the man from only two feet away, killing him. "Have to get close. I'm not much of a shot."

He knelt to tend Nate's fresh wound as the gunfire outside lessened enough to be able to hear the rain and sleet falling into the roofless way station.

There was no idle talk.

The interior was filled with harsh, shuddered breathing as the rattle of hot shell casings fell to the ground.

The Ranger slapped the empties from his revolver and took stock. "This must have been how those ol' boys at the Alamo felt."

CHAPTER 37

We felt the coming storm in the air. The wind had been blowing hard and fast, rippling the grass and trying to take our hats for some time; then it went still for a few minutes. Off over our left shoulders, the line of ominous clouds thickened and turned almost black.

Gil looked back and seemed to shrink into himself. "Oh, hell."

Stup loped up beside me and jerked a thumb. "This is fixin' to get bad. It's coming up the worst norther I believe I've ever seen."

I was glad there was a coat rolled up in my bedroll, along with an extra pair of pants. I reined up and faced the posse. "Boys, get ready for some weather."

The posse members dismounted, except for four men who'd hung back to talk. With a long turkey neck and big ears that were folded down under his hat, one spoke up for the others. "Cap, we appreciate you taking this on and all, but the four of us here don't intend to freeze to death out here in the cold prairie. We're fixin' to head back to town."

Stup took his blanket off the back of his saddle and unrolled it to reveal a thick leather coat. He gave it a good shaking. "It's gonna be just as cold going that way as it is in this direction, Phillips."

"Yeah," Phillips agreed. "But y'all don't know how far you're gonna have to keep going in this weather, and we're bound to get to town faster, where there'll be stoves and plenty of firewood." He paused. "And my own bed."

Dammit!

The man was right, and I was so pigheaded to keep after those men who had Calpurnia, I'd not thought that far ahead. "You have a point."

Phillips looked hopeful. "Then you don't mind if we go."

"I never forced anyone to join up in the first place."

"Well, we wanted to do what's right, and we'd keep on, but I've seen northers like this and there'll be a couple of feet of snow on the ground by morning." He looked sad. "Two of the boys didn't bring coats for this. It was so warm they didn't think they needed them."

"How do you know there'll be that much snow?"

"I don't, but it's already dropped about twenty degrees in half an hour. One time I saw the bottom fall out and it went from about eighty to ten degrees overnight. We woke up to a sheet of ice that didn't melt for days. I said it might snow, but ice is even worse."

Gil came over and leaned in with me and Stup. "He's making sense."

"I know it, and it galls me to death, but this is gonna get bad and we can't make it out here in the open. Stup, how far is it to the stage station?"

He scrunched up his face in thought, adding a few deeper wrinkles to those that were usually in evidence. "Best I can tell, just a few miles. Five or ten. We've come a long way and the road wanders a wide route. We've taken a shortcut, but I'm not sure how far."

"I can't completely give up right now." I noticed dark droplets of rain on my saddle and realized it was showering. "Let's head for the station and wait out the storm. I for sure have no intention of going all the way back to town."

"That works for me." Stup set his wide-brimmed hat against the wind and made a face when heavier drops of icy rain started falling. "At least we'll be doing something instead of standing around here jawing at one another in the rain."

I turned to the four townies still on their horses. "Y'all can go back if you want to. We're heading for the stage station."

Gil struggled into his coat. He still had problems with using only one arm, but he managed. Once he had it on, his fingers quickly found the buttons and closed it up. "You four not going with us for sure?"

"Nope." Phillips had also been digging out his coat, as had the rest of the posse. The one he shrugged into was more for chilly weather than cold, and the light material flew in the wind. "We'll see y'all back in town."

Stup's eyes flashed. "Y'all are damned stupid to peel off on your own. You're gonna get lost in this and freeze to death. Especially you two without coats. Stay with us, and we'll manage to get something over your shoulders."

"I know this territory." Phillips dug in his heels.

"Which way is north, then?"

My stomach fell when the man had to think about it for a moment. He finally pointed into the wind. "That way."

"You had to think of it. It'll be easy to miss town, you know."

"We'll watch for the road. If we reach it, we'll know we're off, but it'll be easy to find it."

"How'll you know which way? You might come out to the north and head out into nowhere. You die for sure, then."

A man with a thin mustache finally joined in as he pulled on an old blue campaign jacket from the War between the States. "We'll let the storm push us a little south; then we'll come in from that way."

"That's the stupidest idea I've ever heard," Gil said.

Thin Mustache's eyes flashed. "Watch how you speak to me, buddy. Phillips was one of the first people to settle here after Angel Fire started growing from a buffalo camp. He'll recognize where we are, and besides, what you're doing'll be the same thing, and you don't even know for sure how far we've gone, so that means you don't have any firm idea where the stage stop might be."

In a way, he was right, but I wasn't giving up on them. In my opinion, it'd be safer if we all stayed together. "I have a mind our way's shorter, but I've never been one to turn back on a job, nor quit one neither."

"Your choice," Phillips said, turning up the collar on a red striped coat.

I was done with them. "We all choose our own roads." Sticking a boot in the stirrup, I swung back aboard. Somehow it seemed colder five feet off the ground.

Thin Mustache wasn't giving up, as if convincing the rest of us was going to make them right. "Ours is faster." He jutted his chin up twice, as if to punctuate his words.

"We'll see. Good luck."

They wheeled their mounts and took off back the way we came in a lope. Gil drew a long breath. "If they're planning to follow any tracks we left, they'll be sorely disappointed."

"It's easy to get lost, even on a cloudy day in mild weather." Stup watched them disappear into the rain. "They'll have hell looking for prints. We'd better get going."

Gil nodded. "Which way?"

Stup laughed. "With the north wind over my left shoulder. Like them fellers, I intend to cut the road pretty soon and find that station. At least I know we haven't passed it yet."

The light rain was soon mixed with sleet. Minutes later, it was a hard rain before it turned to rattling sleet. Though the day had been warm and the ground still retained some heat, the scouring wind quickly chilled everything down.

Sleet fell at an alarming rate, but melted at first when it hit the ground. However, the volume was such that the cold wind soon chilled the water that quickly dropped in temperature until the ground turned white.

Gil pulled his scarf up over the lower half of his face, pulled his hat down, and raised the collar of his coat. "I hate cold weather."

CHAPTER 38

Two hours after the scalphunters joined up with the Comanches, Schaefer let his mount drift back from Pletz's side, angled over to Leroy Booth, and whispered what he'd heard between Pletz and Sandoval. The buffalo soldier's eyes flicked around the bands of professional murderers, and he made a quick decision.

With a nod of his head, he agreed and stayed close to Schaefer. By the time they reached the stage stop, the icy wind and stinging rain was upon them. While Pletz and Sandoval discussed their plans with the Comanche leader, they pulled up at a distance to evaluate the stage.

"I've had enough of this." Schaefer spoke low, though he knew the wind would pluck the words away from the others. "When Pletz charges and the shooting starts, I'm heading due west."

"What's out there?"

"Fewer guns and no Indians who outnumber us and want blood. One of them young bucks kept staring at us back there, and I swear he knows what we're planning to do."

"No matter what the plan is"—Booth studied the halfway destroyed building—"we still need shelter."

"The stagecoach road is right there. I say we hightail it as fast as these horses can run and follow it back to town."

"How far is that?"

"I don't know, but we can make damned good time at a run and put some distance between us. As long as we're moving, the horses'll be fine. If it gets cold enough, we can spread our blankets over them for a little more warmth. We lope for a while so they can rest, and then run some more. They'll make it back to Angel Fire."

Booth looked down at his horse and flicked his fingers through the gelding's mane. "This has been a good 'un. I'd hate to run him to death."

"We get to town, we can have our pick."

"What if we don't make it?"

"We will."

"Dammit, I done told you colored folks can't take the cold like y'all can. You think there's a place we can dig in until this passes?"

"We crossed a few arroyos and ravines out there. We're sure to run across another. If you think we can't make it, we'll drop down and find a bluff or a bank with some overhang. We'll build a fire and wait out the storm."

Schaefer saw Booth studying on the idea, considering how much he hated to be out in the dropping temperatures as opposed to getting shot by the people in the station, or the Comanches. "It could last for a couple of days, at least."

"Dammit, Booth. Okay, we run these horses as fast as they can until this falling weather gets so bad we have to stop. We find some kind of shelter, build a fire and warm up and let them rest, and then take off again. Think about it. Once we get to town there'll be a warm stove and plenty to eat and drink."

"We still don't have hard money. How're we gonna get them things without it? You know that!"

"Who says we don't?" Schaefer grinned at the expression on Booth's face. "I have five twenty-dollar gold pieces squirreled away in my boot. You don't think I tell everything to Pletz, do you?"

Booth's eyes narrowed. "Where'd you get that kind of money?"

"One of them Mexicans back there in that last village tried to buy his life. Told me where the town had money stashed, and said they'd stolen it from a rich traveler one of 'em found dead in the desert outside of town. He paid me to kill him. Ain't that a laugh!"

Schaefer's and Booth's good spirits evaporated as Sandoval moved back up beside Pletz to translate and get a read on their situation. They talked; then the Comanches talked amongst themselves.

The two scalphunters watched the exchange but, like the other men in their party, positioned themselves so they wouldn't be surrounded by the Indians. They didn't have the numbers, but firepower was on their side, and if the shooting started in amongst them, the white men would lay waste to those close by.

At the same time, the Comanches tried a similar tack, edging their mounts to face the bearded men who glowered at them from under their hats and thick eyebrows. Some of the warriors watched the signing closely, while others kept an eye on the men they thought of as buffalo hunters.

Schaefer studied the stage station down below and realized those inside would use the coming storm to their advantage. They needed the protection of the walls to turn the attack, and the weather as well. Buffalo guns in the hands of the scalphunters would make little difference. They couldn't set up a shooting stand at a distance, because the rain that might soon turn to sleet would obscure the building.

The only way to win was from a charge, and none of the whites were inclined to ride into the muzzles of well-maintained rifles. Accurate fire and plenty of ammunition would make all the difference. They preferred to have surprise on their side, riding quickly into an Indian or Mexican village to slaughter women, children, and old people, and shoot down those few men who showed fight.

A village was completely different than a war party, and none of them had the stomach for a standup fight. They'd proved that the night before when that Whitlatch feller and his one-armed buddy backed them down from the Occidental high ground.

Schaefer knew it was time to go when one of the Comanche leaders let loose a war whoop, followed by shouts from the bearded scalphunters. Pletz kicked his horse into a run, but Schaefer saw he was holding his mount back, letting the younger, more violence-driven warriors take the lead. Their enthusiasm soon overwhelmed the more cautious white men who held back as the defenders' guns opened up.

Those inside picked their shots, and four men went down, two Comanche warriors and two of Pletz's men. One of the scalphunters hit the ground hard and rolled behind a dying, kicking horse for cover. Throwing a Winchester over the barricade of flesh, he took aim and fired. Several rounds immediately sought him out, and he jerked and twisted sideways when one round caught him in the forehead.

Schaefer recognized the dead man as Martin O'Toole and took off west, hoping no one would see what he was doing and, if they did, they'd maybe think that he and Booth planned to circle around. With that, he cut past Booth and motioned for him to follow.

The former buffalo soldier took one look at the attack and fell in behind his old friend. Leaning over their saddle horns and riding hard, Schaefer and Booth fled the scene. Fifty yards away, they looked over their shoulders to see if their maneuver sparked any concern, but the attack on the station was full on and no one was watching.

Icy rain mixed with sleet pellets rattled off their hat brims and immediately found a way down their shirts, despite the scarves and turned-up collars. Once they were a couple of miles away and soaked to the skin from the melting ice, they slowed their mounts to a walk to let the animals get their wind back. The ground became white as the horses walked at a steady pace, and soon the sleet changed to snow, and the grass was white.

"You reckon anybody's after us?" Booth looked over his shoulder.

Schaefer didn't bother turning around. "Nah. They're all busy fighting and dying. They won't miss us for a good long while, at least until they kill everyone inside; then they'll have to deal with them damned Comanches. They'll think we're dead and laying out there for sure. If this snow keeps up, they'll think our bodies are covered. Maybe they think that if any of them Indians get away, they'll have taken us with them. No matter what, we're going to come out smelling like lilies when this is all over."

Schaefer had ridden with Pletz for years, but he knew the ending they were all in for. This way, he had a chance. He saw nothing but death in that unholy alliance back there, and when he overheard Sandoval tell Pletz the Comanches were talking about how they'd ambush them after using the scalphunters as human shields, he knew this was the only decision.

The attack would either be quickly over, or a long, drawn-out battle for the shelter. Fallen men would remain where they lay until it was over and the victors had time to take stock of their survivors, be it defenders or attackers, and would likely submit to the weather before looking for their comrades.

It would give them at least a day, maybe a two-day head start to reach Angel Fire and rest up, outfit, before heading to the Arizona mines.

"Keep going or try and hole up?" Schaefer asked.

Booth grumbled and adjusted a pair of thick leather gloves higher on his wrists. "Let's make some more miles and see if this gets any worse. I'd rather wait this out in that warm saloon than camp out here in the open."

They kicked their mounts into a lope and headed for Angel Fire.

CHAPTER 39

Wet grass cools faster than the warm ground, and the rainwater soon coated the plains in ice. As the sleet passed, snow came down and stuck to the ice, pushing the tall stems downward. The wind still beat us up and our horses' hooves crunched through the brittle prairie with a muffled sound of shattering crystals.

Beside me, the white fluff had built up on Gil's back, drifting against the cantle and catching on everything that would hold it. Even our hats were drifted with snow that wouldn't quit falling. It landed on the horses and melted quickly from their body heat, but I was concerned that if it kept up, we'd be in trouble.

Bright Bolton rode up. "Hey, Cap."

"I know. It's cold and everyone wants to turn back."

"That's right. I've been talking to Shorty and the boys, and we have an idea."

"What's that?"

"We all need to head for a place we know might still be standing to warm up. It's only a few miles that way, and we can wait out this storm."

Once again my decision to push on had blinded me of everything around me. I'd almost forgotten Bright and the cowboys, and the idea of asking for shelter at their ranch hadn't occurred to me one whit.

"What's out this way? I wouldn't expect there to be folks who'll take us in."

"There was a family who was trying to make a go of it in an abandoned ranch, but when the Comanches started raiding, the man showed good sense and took them back to Fort Griffin."

The fort, only recently decommissioned, had held command over the Texas plains. Though the cavalry was officially gone, there was still a company or two in the area, and when the Indian troubles arose again, settlers flocked to the safety of numbers.

"The old house I'm talking about was built by a guy named Al Bradshaw who gave up and went back where he came from. It has a big sod barn that'll hold all the horses. We use the place as a line shack now, and there's plenty of room. For all we know, them outlaws took Calpurnia there to hole up."

I looked around to see that what was left of the posse was miserable, riding heads down. There was no fire left in any of them, and we were all in danger of freezing to death.

We were following the tracks of Stup's horse, and I perked up at the sound of gunfire. It had to be close, because the north wind should have blown most of the sound away. "Is that the direction of the ranch house?"

"No." Bright pointed at an angle. "It's over there."

Stup appeared in the swirling flakes, riding fast. "The station's ahead. Comanches and Comancheros are attacking!"

"How many?" Gil's fingers flicked up and down his coat, unbuttoning it to free up his guns. Heads snapped up around us, both the ranch hands and townspeople finally showing some spark.

"A lot. It's a mess up there, and people inside are shooting back. There's people riding everywhere. I saw a couple who weren't interested in fighting, though, heading west. Maybe back toward town. They were riding hard and didn't see me for the snow, and I was standing still. Travelers, maybe."

We were between a rock and a hard place. We needed to join in with the defenders, but we had no idea what we were getting into. As far as I could see, there was no choice.

I pulled my shotgun free of the scabbard and loosened my coat. "Let's hit 'em hard and fast and get inside."

"I ain't no cavalryman!" one of the posse members shouted.

"None of us are." My face flushed with heat. That was no time to argue. "We need to help them folks and at the same time get in out of this weather."

Stup nodded short. "I bet them Comanches are thinking the same thing about getting inside.

They may be heathens, but they're just as cold as we are."

I adjusted myself in the saddle, feeling some of the melted snow soak through my pants. "I'm riding in hard and fast. Y'all stay with me!"

Spurring the steeldust into a lope, I started for the station. I didn't want to run her fast, in case she might slip and go down. Neither of us could afford that. Whether they wanted to or not, the posse thundered along behind.

Stup rode up to my left, and Gil was on the right. That was good, because his bad side was toward me and it was easier for him to shoot to the right. The gunfire grew louder, despite the wind. We didn't need to see where we were going, because the battle sounds increased.

The station came into view, and I was shocked to see most of the roof was gone. The blackened remains of a burned stage or wagon was stark against the white snow, and several splashes of red marked where fresh bodies fell. Horses were down, and men using them for cover fired at the stage stop.

Flashes inside showed that more than one person was fighting back. I saw the best place to push through. A Comanche buck yelped when he heard us coming and rose. He charged us with a revolver in hand and pulled the trigger. The muzzle flash was bright, but the round missed us all.

Stup proved to be an experienced Indian fighter. He raced toward the warrior and fired his pistol. The first round missed, but the second caught the brave in the midsection. He doubled over and Stup rode past without slowing.

Two white men taking cover behind a dead horse spun at the sound of hooves and shooting behind them. I knew in an instant they were some of the scalphunters from back in town. Not expecting anyone to come roaring in from behind them, they fumbled with their rifles.

Both managed to get a shot off and I heard a shout behind me. The Spencer barked, and a load of buckshot caught one of them left of his crotch. The shot spread out enough that I saw his dark clothes puff from the impact of the .32 caliber pellets. He dropped his rifle to clutch his business, face white with pain and horror.

I didn't have time to shuck another round into the shotgun, but Gil's pistol barked twice. He had the buckskin's reins in his mouth, making up for his lost arm, and the second man was down as we ran past. Shots came from behind us as the others found targets and popped off shots at them.

We split their forces in two and I saw a Comanche running at us from the right. I couldn't shoot because of Gil, but he fired and missed. The warrior threw a heavy war club that struck Gil in the thigh. He grunted from the pain and thumb-cocked his pistol again. This time the warrior was close enough that Gil's shot caught him in the chest. The man's forward momentum carried him another step, and he slid on the snow underneath Gil's buckskin.

A slug punched through the shoulder of my coat close enough that I felt the heat on my skin. The steeldust mare slid to a stop between the destroyed stage and the doorless building. I was off in a second, like when I was roping calves back on the VR ranch.

Two white men on horseback charged us, looking like bears in the saddle. I dropped to one knee. Shouldering the twelve-gauge, I cut them both down with two loads of buckshot. A hand darted out of the door.

"Reins!"

I handed them to the stranger inside and swung around to cover the rest as they rushed in. Gil landed beside me and fired from only feet away. A shape fell back, and Gil yelped and staggered. Droplets of blood flew as someone inside grabbed him by the shoulders and yanked my old partner through the door. The buckskin went inside next, followed by Stup's roan of his own accord.

For a minute, the area around me was pure frenzy with men shooting, cursing, and dropping to the ground. Somehow they managed to get inside, one after the other, along with their horses. Soon it was just me and Stup still outside, both on one knee and throwing lead at those who realized it was better not to charge in.

A huge roar blasted from a distance, and the *thunk* of a big slug against the adobe behind us told me someone out there had a Sharps. I wished we'd had one of them photographers with us, to maybe get a photograph of the two of us rolling backward into the door like acrobats to find a dark world full of bloody, blackened people and snorting horses.

CHAPTER 40

The snow fell hard, obscuring the stage stop and sapping all the energy that Pletz once possessed. His nose felt as if it were frozen, a bitter reminder of growing up in Germany where the winters seemed to last for years.

Accurate fire from the defenders inside was cutting down the attackers like wheat before a scythe, and within minutes of the first rush, he was finished.

A man like him didn't want a protracted fight. It was hit, slaughter, and run, and if the job turned into work, he wanted nothing to do with it.

The younger Comanche warriors pressed hard for the honor of killing those inside. The moment they were ready to attack, the men who grew up on readying themselves to fight wanted to be first. Because of their enthusiasm, Pletz held back and let the defenders mow them down. It would deplete their ammunition and prove to be less work for him and his men when it came time to collect their trophies.

He almost thought they'd overrun the station until a group of mounted men arrived with guns blazing. At first he thought they were cavalry until he got a good look at the clothes they wore and realized they were a mix of townies and cowboys.

It was that damned posse, led by Whitlatch and his one-armed friend.

Instead of spreading out in a skirmish line, they made a beeline for the station and shot their way in. With almost practiced ease, the men cut through the surrounding line of his scalphunters and Broken Nose's Comanches, and disappeared into the station's open door like bees into a hollow tree, changing his plan.

Infuriated that his plan was torn to shreds by the added firepower of the posse, Pletz looked around for Schaefer. The man had been at his side for years, but he was nowhere to be found. The number of men he rode with had dwindled. Bodies lay everywhere and would soon be covered in the falling snow, along with a dozen dead or dying horses.

Schaefer was likely one of those mounds under the falling snow.

The second man that stuck close by was Booth. His absence proved he was down too.

Pletz was well out of range from the guns in the station and walked his mount as if it wasn't snowing. His men weren't idiots, or Comanche warriors. They didn't press attacks, and when Sandoval saw him alone, he rode up.

His face was red from the cold. "What now, boss? This has gone to hell."

"Gather ze others." When he was down or tired, Pletz's German accent returned with a vengeance.

"Some of the boys are down."

Pletz couldn't have cared any less. "Get what's left."

Sandoval pointed to several shapes moving at a distance. "That's Broken Nose and his men. They've pulled back to regroup."

"They're cold and we're freezing too. This has to be over and done with. Like I said, get the boys."

"Then what?"

"We collect our wages here and get back to town."

"Wages?"

Pletz pointed at a Comanche body lying nearby. A spray of blood showed where a bullet caught the brave in an artery and he had bled out. Drawing his knife, Pletz dismounted and scalped the dead man. Shaking the flap of skin and hair to remove any blood, he remounted and stuffed it into the sack holding other scalps. "When we're all together, we finish the job with Broken Nose and his men."

"We're still going to freeze to death."

"We'll cross that bridge when we come to it."

CHAPTER 41

The inside of the station was a madhouse. Gunsmoke filled the air, along with the odor of manure, blood, and voided bowels from the dead men. The steaming horses were packed in so tight they had no room, and both them and those already there were stumbling over downed timbers and the body of a stiffening gelding. One roan stepped on a body tucked against the wall, then pawed it a couple more times as if wondering why the person wasn't reacting.

It was an oddly horrifying thing to see a horse step on a person with no reaction from the human. The cold, stiff body lying beside two others barely moved.

From the moment we were inside, I knew the whole thing was a death trap, dark and gloomy under a thick layer of clouds. At least we were out of the worst part of the wind, for the moment. Brass shell casings were everywhere, and tension was thick and almost cloying. There was a lull in the shooting, and I made a decision that would either haunt me for the rest of my life, or kill us all.

Both the defenders who were already there and my posse were looking at me as if expecting some kind of announcement or speech. After the greetings and relieved backslapping from both groups, we fell into an awkward silence. I had nothing to tell them, other than we needed to gather everyone up and leave, despite the falling weather.

I hadn't expected so many people. I immediately recognized Calpurnia, but instead of rushing over to welcome us who'd come to save her, she remained with another woman with a calm demeanor, something else I wouldn't expect in such a situation. We'd been after three, two outlaws and a woman. Now we had a whole crowd to deal with, and two of them were bank robbers.

To a person, the men took positions to watch outside, whether it was through glassless windows or the gaping, open doorway. They talked quietly among themselves, giving me time to gather my thoughts.

For the moment, I ignored the others to get a grip on our situation. "We can't stay here. Gil, we have to do what they're not expecting out there."

"What's that gonna be?"

I noticed his right hand was bloody, as well as the right side of his face and his shoulder. "You hit?"

"Yep. Shot took off my earlobe. Every time I go anywhere with you, I get some piece of me shot off, or cut off." He moved his hand to find a good chunk of his ear was missing. "Before long, I'll just be a head left on a pillow that you can come in and talk to from time to time. I hope you'll bring a little whiskey with you, as a courtesy."

"You'll live. You're lucky it wasn't three inches over. Then you wouldn't be able to talk at all, which might not be a bad thing, come to think of it."

A potbellied white-haired man beckoned from the shadows of the back wall. "Come over here, feller, and let me look at that."

"You can see it from there."

"I'm a doctor, and I might be able to do something for you, though I doubt it. I can stop the bleeding, though."

Gil picked his way across the littered floor, and the doctor squinted at his wound. I looked around at a sea of faces—some I knew, which was the posse—but the rest were defenders. Those who were already there were smudged with soot and gunpowder. They passed around canteens and buckets full of water as everyone settled down.

Bright and his cowboys were close by. Stup came close and we leaned in together. His jaw was set, grim and determined. "Those people out there have to take this station, or they're gonna die, Comanches or the scalphunters who've taken up with them."

I agreed. "That means none of 'em are gonna stop, so we have to mount up here in the next minute and hightail it for Bright's ranch house."

"Why's that?"

"Because it'll benefit us all. They want this place more than all of us inside, I reckon. Once we're gone, they'll settle in. We'll wait out the storm at the ranch house."

Stup nodded. "Makes more sense than anything else around here."

"Bright." I raised my voice to make sure the cowboy heard. "How far'd you say?"

Calpurnia was near the two men I recognized as the bank robbers. I decided to hold that information in abeyance for a few minutes. Bright had her in his arms, though she didn't look to be enjoying his embrace.

He turned his head to answer. "Fifteen miles or so."

A high-pitched voice I didn't recognize caused a stir among those who'd been there when we arrived. They were all filthy, tired, and to a person every one of them looked as if they could eat a three-day-old dead skunk. "Fifteen miles! In this weather? We'll all die out there!"

Despite the dim light, I found the speaker in his suit and derby hat. Derby hats were common, but this guy looked like an oily city slicker, despite his smudged face and clothes. "Who're you?"

"McGinty. Joseph McGinty."

"He's the banker who started all this mess," Bright said.

McGinty's eyes flicked from me, to Bright, to a

hard-looking man with a big hat and thick white mustache I hadn't yet noticed. A Colt jutted out from the holster on his left side. His jaw was set, and I knew for a fact he'd been in charge before we rolled in.

Ignoring McGinty, I turned to him. "You ramrodding this outfit?"

"I was until y'all rode in. Might still be. Name's Malachai Holman. I was on the stage when we pulled in."

A black-haired woman spoke up. "He's a Texas Ranger."

I considered her comment. "And you are?"

"Amanda. We were on the stage together."

I'd seen the blackened remains of the stage outside. "Well, Malachai, ol' Bright here says there's a better place than this with a roof and a barn. I think if we ride through that bunch out there, they won't chase us because of the weather."

"It's a ranch house halfway between here and town." Bright held one of Calpurnia's arms. "There's food, water, and plenty of cut wood. Feed for the horses, too."

I saw the look in the other man's eyes and knew he liked the idea. "If the Comanches haven't burned it down."

"There is that."

The Ranger's lips pursed in thought under his big mustache. "Them out there'll think we're just running, and they need shelter the same as us."

"That's what I'm thinking. If I'm right they won't chase us. They'll move in here and wait out the storm instead. I read an old book about war once by a Chinaman who says people in battle need to give one another a back door when things get bad. It's an easier way to win. We're all in a fix, and I think every one of us needs a way out."

"You *think?*" McGinty's voice was incredulous.

The Ranger seemed to be done with that snake in a derby. "Do you have a better idea, banker?"

His eyes fell. "This is all a mess."

"It sure is." Glancing around, I saw a cowboy watching out the open window for the next attack. He looked like a solid man, so I left him alone. The doctor was dabbing at Gil's ear with a piece of stringy cloth, while another man with soot on his face and arms kept a lookout at the other end of the building, hemmed in by the horses packed against one another.

I still had the Spencer in the crook of my arm, but the Russian .44 was in hand. I didn't remember drawing it, but that didn't matter. Everyone held a weapon, or had one close by. I used the pistol to casually point at the two outlaws who stood off to the side, not necessarily aiming it, but kinda indicating what I was talking about with the barrel.

One of them was wounded in the left arm, and blood stained his shirt and pants. The arm hung limp, so it was either broken, or hurting pretty bad.

"You two there. I know y'all. Saw you in the Occidental back in town, so make sure you point them pistols at the floor, or outside. Boys, those two behind Calpurnia are the men who robbed the bank—"

"Robbed my bank?!" McGinty's voice rose in indignation.

Guns rose around me, as if the outlaws were about to draw down on everyone.

"Easy, boys." I was already tired of that little barking pest who kept yipping at me. "We're all in this together right now, so I don't want anyone to start acting stupid. I ain't concerned with a bank robbery right this minute, only getting out of this mess alive. I just wanted the posse to know who we were associating with, since that's the reason we're all in this situation in the first place."

"You said they stole my money! Put 'em in cuffs!" McGinty shouted.

"Not right now."

"Who put *you* in charge?!"

"This posse"—I nodded the brim of my hat to point, and hefted the Russian—"and this pistol here."

"And me." That short comment came from Ranger Malachai, who looked like he wanted to lay the barrel of his Colt up against McGinty's head. "Buck, if McGinty there does anything stupid, shoot that sorry banker. I'm tired of listening to him."

"That'll be a pleasure, now that we have enough guns to take his place."

"You can't be serious," McGinty squawked.

"All of you listen." I was running out of patience. "Those people out there ain't gonna wait too much longer. They have to get in here before they freeze to death, and the only way to do that is to kill us all. To stop that kind of bloodshed, we have to go before this snow gets deep."

McGinty's mouth fell open. I almost grinned at an old Spanish saying that fit.

"*En boca cerrada, no entran moscas.*" Roughly translated, it meant, keep your mouth closed so flies can't get in.

McGinty shook his head. "So you expect us to just *ride* out into that blizzard and them savages."

Buck casually flicked his pistol, catching McGinty on the jaw. "It appears to me Mr. Whitlatch don't *expect* anything. He's the one giving orders."

The man's head snapped back and he recoiled. He used one hand to cover his face. "Hey, you can't just hit a man like that for speaking his mind. The Constitution says I can say what I want. You almost broke my jaw."

Holding the bloody cloth against his ear, Gil shook his head. "Buck, you didn't hit him hard enough. Break that jaw, and he'll shut up." He started forward. "Here, I'll do it."

McGinty's eyes went wild and scared. He held up a hand to stop Gil.

The black-haired woman named Amanda stepped forward. "Y'all need to stop this. Mr. Whitlatch, do you think we can make it out of here?"

"We will, or we won't. We'll die for sure if we stay here, though."

The Ranger rested his hand on the pistol stuck butt forward in the holster. "Daniel and Nate, y'all didn't mention you were bank robbers when you rode in, so listen to me good. If either one of you even make a face I don't like, I'm gonna put a slug in you."

Nate shrugged and winced when his wounded arm moved. "It didn't come up in conversation."

"Do what I say."

They nodded as one.

"Then let's go. Some of us'll have to ride double. We're shy a few horses."

"And one's lame." The other cowboy at the far window spoke up. "Saw it limping when y'all came in."

I didn't know one person from the other, and trying to remember names was the least of my worries.

"Garry's right." Buck chimed in. "It belonged to Calpurnia, and he won't make a mile."

"Leave it." I noted the bodies lying in the back. "We'll have to leave *them,* too."

A pained look crossed Garry's face. "That's my brother. His name is . . . was . . . Larry."

"I'm sorry, but he's dead and you're not. I figure your mama'd rather have one than none, so get ready to ride."

The wind was still blowing snow that was coming down at a heavy rate and drifted in the station's doors and windows. Our hats and shoulders were already thick with the white fluff accumulating on everything that didn't move.

My cheekbones stung from the cold, and everywhere a flake of ice touched skin, it felt like someone was driving needles into me. I figured we had little time left before those outside tried to push their way in once again, and I needed to get everyone convinced that we had to move.

I'd learned long ago from my dad, who'd fought in the War between the States, that staying still would get you killed. Moving and fighting kept a man alive, and anything like honor in a fight or on a battlefield of any kind was misplaced. Nothing is fair when you're fighting for your life.

"This is gonna be slow as molasses, because we have to mount up outside. Those of y'all who know how to fight and shoot, use the horses for cover while everyone sorts this out."

"They might ride off and leave us!" McGinty held his jaw and flinched as Buck made a fist.

"We move fast." The Ranger nodded. "Doc, Garry. Figure out who you're riding with before we get outside." He shrugged at all of us new arrivals. "We were on the stage, and they killed all the horses."

Buck turned his attention back outside for a moment. "Storm's getting worse. Are we gonna die out there, or in here?"

The Ranger pointed at Amanda. "You get on back with me."

She nodded and gathered her skirts as if ready to run.

A sharp voice belonging to the outlaw Daniel Morgan stopped her. "Hey, Ranger, you didn't have a horse until *we* showed up. That's mine you're talking about."

The Ranger stayed where he was, turning only his head to address Daniel. "You're a bank robber and a thief, and so is your shot-up partner there. Y'all probably stole them horses, anyway. I don't want to hear any more from you."

"You're not taking my horse! I'll need it to get out of here!" Daniel raised his Colt toward the Ranger, who drew his revolver and shot him in the chest so fast it took everyone by surprise. The place was packed, and the bullet fairly brushed past two people before it struck the outlaw. Daniel took two steps back on rubbery legs and collapsed against the wall where he lay still.

Already cocked again, the Ranger's pistol

swung toward the man's partner, and everyone shrank back to get out of the line of fire. Nate raised his good arm. "I have no argument with you."

"You'll do as I say, and that goes for this deputy, too." He nodded toward me. "His word is law."

"I will."

"That makes things a little easier." Bright picked up the dead man's pistol and unbuckled his gun belt. He took Calpurnia's arm, marking his territory.

The rest of the posse was ready to go, and they readied themselves for my order. I took one last look around, hoping I hadn't missed anything. "Don't leave anyone behind if a horse goes down. They'll die at the hands of those savages out there."

I'd seen death and violence all my life, but the ease in which that Ranger shot the outlaw took me aback. I vowed not to cross him, if possible.

He was already moving. "You boys tighten your cinches. We need to get."

I took the steeldust mare's reins and, taking a deep breath, led her through the door. Beyond me was the remains of the stage, and four humps covered with snow that was the team. There was nothing to hide behind, so I led her a few feet away and waited, expecting to be shot at any time in the dim light despite the heavy windblown snow.

Stuffing the shotgun into the scabbard, I faced away from the station and shouldered the Winchester in hands that felt like two chunks of ice. The only movement was swirling snow, and my stomach fell. Second-guessing myself had always been a problem, and I had the terrible feeling that we were making a mistake.

But there was no backing out at that point.

The others followed me out. Hooves muffled by the snow thumped soft and quiet. Soft, muffled curses and curt comments came to my ears. Leather creaked as everyone mounted, and still no one shot at us.

There was little conversation, and what there was reached me in whispered instructions as the horseless riders mounted behind the others.

Rifle in hand, I swung into the saddle just as a shape rushed out the door and knelt beside the stage. McGinty put down a cloth satchel and dug with both hands into the snow and ashes.

I kept my voice low. "Banker, what the hell are you doing?"

"I had real gold on this stage."

"It don't matter. We have to go."

"I can't leave money behind."

Impatient hooves thudded against the ground.

One of the posse members urged his horse forward. "Get on if you're riding with me."

"Just a minute."

"We don't have a minute!"

I saw McGinty stuffing something into his pockets. "You're riding double, you idiot. That horse can't carry the two of you and a satchel *and* gold! Leave that grip!"

"No!" McGinty picked it up. His eyes flicked across the whole of us. "It's full of cash."

The man on horseback waiting for McGinty grunted at the same time the report of a shot reached us. He fell sideways off his horse as another gunshot cut through the falling snow and wind. I rode the mare right on top of McGinty, knocking him to the ground.

"Get on that horse now, or we're leaving you!"

Stup rode up beside me and fired three times with his pistol in the direction the shots came from. "Let's git!"

Scattered gunfire and soft flashes came from all around as we kicked our horses into a run and left the station behind.

CHAPTER 42

Stunned at their losses, Broken Nose sent word for his men to regroup well out of range from the station. His medicine that he thought was so strong was broken. Chilled to the bone, he longed for the comfort of those walls several hundred yards away, although he could barely make out its shape through the snow.

Tall Water rode up. "What do we do?"

"Live through this storm, after we kill these demons who have damaged our spirit."

"Good! When?"

"Now."

"How? They're scattered like our people."

"That's best. Collect as many as you can and fall on them like newborn buffalo calves."

The warrior yelped and kicked his mount in the ribs.

One of Pletz's men named Harry Sands loped up beside him. His beard was covered with snow. "Sandoval said we're gathering here."

"Yep, get the rest."

He rode off and returned minutes with Thomas Graham, who had a Sharps rifle resting in the crook of his arm. "I saw people moving down there, but I believe I missed."

The moment he spoke, a flurry of shots rang out, but the falling snow prevented them from seeing who was doing the shooting. None of the rounds came near.

Sandoval rejoined them. "I passed the word." He pointed at an equal number of Comanches walking their horses toward them. "What do you think *they* want?"

Pletz noted the warriors. "Us."

An indistinct string of mounted men poured from the vicinity of the stage station. Sandoval drew his breath to shout when the close-by warriors raised their weapons.

Still holding the Sharps in his arm, Graham angled his body and pulled the trigger. The nearest Comanche brave flew backward over his horse's rear. The huge bullet blew a massive hole in his stomach and took out his spine.

One of the warriors with a rifle killed Harry Sands with a direct shot through the heart, and their little piece of the world erupted in muzzle flashes that reflected in the falling snow. Pletz saw the flakes freeze in the bursts of gunfire, and the remaining three braves fell bleeding into the snow.

From around them, scattered shots told how the story was repeated in a number of locations. Pletz waved with the pistol in his hand. "Sweep that way and kill everything that's not with us; then head for that station! It's empty now!"

CHAPTER 43

I was shocked that there were so few shots fired at us, though all around us small skirmishes rose and fell. With no way of knowing what was going on, we dug in our spurs and followed Bright as he led the way through the blowing snow.

Without landmarks, I wondered if he knew where he was going, but he seemed to be following a ghost trail. Maybe it was a map in his mind, or he'd gone that way so many times it was second nature. We followed the stage road for a short while, until he angled off. I squinted through the blizzard, looking for a trail or some kind of marker, but there was nothing but grass bending over under the weight of snow.

It wasn't deep out in the open yet, and that was a blessing. The wind blew much of it off the ground, where it drifted against small, thick tufts of grass, or collected enough for unknown reasons into sweeping drifts that for a while were of little impedance. The cold cut right through our clothes, which seemed to do little to stop the chill.

A heavy feeling of dread fell over me when I realized we'd have to ride in such conditions for the next few hours. I wanted more than anything to get in out of the wind, my mind racing to find a different solution, but there was none. We were all going to be miserable until we found that house that I wasn't sure existed.

We were strung out in Bright's tracks, each rider terrified that he'd get lost in the vastness of the storm. I glanced over my shoulder to see Gil riding directly behind me with his head down against the wind. Behind him was Stup, followed by the Ranger and Amanda. Beyond that was nothing but indistinct shapes following the tracks we made.

Once we were away from the station, there was no more shooting at us. At least I was right about that part. The Comanches wanted no part of a running gun battle in such weather. The small skirmishes were swallowed in the distance, and I wondered what had happened, finally deciding that the two factions had had a falling-out.

It was a given, though, that the winners would hole up in the station and wait out the storm. No one would be following us, because the snow and wind would quickly wipe out our tracks. I only hoped Bright knew where he was going.

CHAPTER 44

"Throw them damned bodies outside." Pletz tied his horse to a blackened timber angling downward from the back corner of the station. There was no roof, but at least the walls broke the freezing wind, and it felt downright comfortable inside the enclosure.

Graham and a skinny runt of a man named Bishop grabbed the first stiff corpse and carried it outside as the remnants of his gang led their horses inside. They unceremoniously pitched the body onto the stagecoach's ashes like it was a plank and went back for another. The others busied themselves with dragging out the remaining remains and hurrying back.

Favoring his wounded arm, Sandoval called to Graham. "Bring your flint and steel over here and light a fire in this fireplace. It looks like it'll still work. I'll knock some firewood together."

Experienced survivalists, they were always prepared. The roof supports and timbers hadn't completely burned when the station went up, so they had enough wood for a while. Much of it was thrown to the rear of the station by those who'd just left. Using a small hatchet from his gear bags, Graham set upon some of the timbers, chopping the blackened pieces into manageable lengths.

All told, there were seven men left, and to Pletz, that was more than enough. "Cable, you and Brantley take first watch. I doubt them sonsabitches that're left out there have any more fight in 'em, but there might be one or two with a little spirit."

Nodding, the two scalphunters split up, Cable taking the doorway and Brantley covering the window at the far end of the station. Their breath made white clouds in the air.

The horses also breathed fire, and steam rose above them as their body heat melted the snow. Packed together, they generated their own weather, and a soft white cloud of vapor formed over them.

Sandoval toed a lard can and, when he felt weight, pried off the lid. "Looky here. Water!"

They gathered around the container like animals, drinking deep until it was almost empty. By that time, the fire was burning hot and the sounds of chopping and breaking wood filled the interior as they broke up everything that would burn.

The snow and ice in front of the fireplace melted as far as the heat could reach, and Pletz squatted directly in front of the hearth. He flicked his fingers. "You got them stretchers?"

Graham opened one of his saddlebags and took out several small willow rings about twelve inches in diameter. He pitched them in front of the German and brought out a stained bag.

In minutes Pletz threaded a fresh Comanche scalp onto one of the rings and propped it some distance from the fire to dry.

Even though they'd been fighting for their lives out in the storm, his men had fresh scalps, because you don't leave money behind. After Pletz finished his task, they took turns stretching the hair that had been blowing in the wind only an hour earlier.

Sandoval chewed on the stem of an unlit pipe he took from his shirt. "There's only seven of us left."

Pletz had the premium spot in front of the fire that was finally warming the sod-and-adobe fireplace. He didn't bother to move when a couple of the others squeezed in to take off the chill. "How many horses did we wind up with?"

"One for each of us."

"I'd hoped for more."

"Wind and shooting scattered the rest."

"Lots of money disappeared with those ponies."

Sandoval puffed as if drawing smoke. "Lots of men too. I fear we'll miss Schaefer and Booth in the future."

"We'll miss the horses more."

"They rode with us a long time and were faithful to you."

"That's all I ask." Pletz stuck a forefinger in his mouth and worried at something caught between his teeth. "Schaefer had quite a few scalps in his bag. I reckon it's buried under the snow out there now."

Sandoval studied the growing fire. He pitched another chunk into the flames. "I hope they were dead when they hit the ground."

"I hear freezing to death is peaceful."

"Cold too."

Pletz reached into a pocket and produced a small packet of tobacco. He handed it to Sandoval, then dug back into those pockets and found a plug of tobacco. He bit off a chew and tucked it away. "Your arm still serviceable?"

"Not completely."

"Good thing you're proficient with a pistol, if the fight resumes."

"I figured those wretched savages out there were finished."

"They will be by the time this storm blows out."

"So then we're going back after the banker and his money?"

"I don't see why not. Then I am going to Tucson or Tombstone where it is warm and live out my life there."

Near the far window, horses shifted with a clatter of hooves. A soft curse came from the watchman on that end. Intent on the life-giving warmth coming from the soot-covered fireplace, the scalphunters fed the flames and ignored a thump and clatter of metal underfoot.

"Howard! You better find your feet over there or them horses'll step on you." Sandoval gave a soft chuckle over Brantley's clumsiness and winced at the pain in his injured arm. He spoke to Pletz. "Considering where you're from, you should be used to this cold."

"This is the reason I came to this land, but then I learned how warm it is supposed to be there. Now this godforsaken country has this weather that changes on a whim."

"It has been this way all my life." The horses at the far end shuffled and snorted. Steam continued to rise from their bodies. Sandoval glanced in that direction and through the mist saw Brantley's floppy hat move between them, settling the animals down.

Behind them, someone coughed. The other five huddled in front of the fireplace were fixed on the coals. One of the men behind them shoved forward, knocking against those who reacted with the violence of rough men. Like ripples in a pond, they shoved back, only to find frigid bodies smelling of smoke and grease falling among them with knives, war axes, and pistols.

"Savages!"

Packed so tight in front of the fire, they had little room to respond to the warriors streaming inside. One wore Brantley's bloody hat and swung with a war club, striking Sandoval in the back and knocking him forward.

Sitting cross-legged, Pletz struggled to gain his feet, grabbing at the pistol in his sash. A knife flashed over his shoulder and grazed his chest. Sticking the muzzle of his Colt against cold skin, he pulled the trigger and the warrior gasped and fell.

   By then, screams of the attacking Comanches pouring through the door and windows and cries of pain and horror filled the air as the compressed cluster of fighting men fought hand to hand in a melee of flashing weapons and the soft pops of gunfire muffled against bodies so close that more than one man's clothing sparked and flickered with fire.

   It was a slaughter on both sides as firearms ran out of ammunition and the final struggle was reduced to cutting edges, blunt tools, bare hands, and in Pletz's case, teeth buried in a dead man's throat.

CHAPTER 45

Head down so my hat blocked as much wind as possible, my mind was beginning to grow as dark and cold as the world closing in around us. It had been hours of frozen hell and I'd just about given up hope. My feet and hands were numb, as well as my nose and cheeks. The scarf I'd tied over my hat did little to protect my ears. Like the rest of the men, we'd drawn in on ourselves to preserve as much body heat as possible.

I was worried about Callie and Amanda. They were as unprepared as the rest of us, and wore only what they were given by the men who were generous enough to endure the weather with less than they started with.

Bright's voice sounded strange, as if he barely had enough air to shout. "We made it!"

He was as good as his word, and I looked up. Snow reflected what little light there was, and before us was the silhouette of a small, low barn that appeared to be part of the landscape. Beyond was the shadow of a similarly squatty house.

In front of me, Bright stopped at the barn and stuck out his arm so Calpurnia could dismount from behind him first. She had less snow on her clothes, and I realized that his body broke the wind us single riders had endured, and their combined body warmth must have helped a little.

Stiff, tired, sleepy, and cold, she almost fell when her feet hit the ground. When she was steady, he dropped off and used the heel of his hand to knock loose a rectangular chunk of wood held in place by one nail that held the twin barn doors together.

Twisting it vertically, he pulled at one of them. It wouldn't budge, held in place by ice and drifted snow. He yanked at it so hard the top part was bending out by the time I joined him. Knowing life-giving shelter was at hand, others crowded in, using their feet to kick away the ice and break the door free.

I was afraid the whole thing would snap in two, but several more grunting yanks and kicks later, we pushed it open and a string of ice-coated, nearly frozen horses and people poured inside the dark interior.

Just to get in out of the wind was a relief, and the barn almost felt warm.

"Thank God!" Stup tied his horse to a tether ring on a well-chewed support post and leaned against his saddle. "My feet are damn near froze off."

Someone had enough feeling in their hands to strike a lucifer and light a lantern. The globe briefly fogged on the inside from the heat until the wick caught and the interior of the chimney warmed before glowing bright. Doc twisted the knob on the burner to raise the wick and provide even more light.

The interior came into definition as soft chuckles and conversation showed the first signs of life I'd seen in the posse since we left the station hours earlier. I looked around and right off saw something wasn't right. It took a moment to figure out what was bothering me.

Our numbers were way down.

"Stup. Bright. We've lost a lot of men."

The relief we all felt vanished as the men looked around to find half of our number was gone. The liveryman, Jeter, was there, as well as two of Bright's men. Those we'd picked up at the stage stop were all accounted for, except for the wounded outlaw, Nate. I'd been concerned about him, since the man was facing a hanging judge sometime in the future and might have been dangerous. Instead, he was gone as the wind.

I went back to the door and stepped outside. Holding my hat, I saw our tracks already filling with snow and tried calling, but the wind whipped my words away as they left my mouth. The steeldust mare and I were too exhausted to go back out. It would have been the death of us both, so I went back inside.

"It's just us." The pit of my stomach was dark and empty, and it wasn't because I hadn't eaten. It was the loss of so many lives that threatened to draw me down in a dark place.

The Ranger looked deep into my eyes, looking for something more, but I had nothing else to give. He nodded as if I'd made some significant statement and went back to unsaddling his horse.

"They'll follow the tracks, if they fell behind. It's the only thing they can do, and we're so frozen that we can't go back out looking. We need to rely on their spirit to make it through."

For the next several minutes we tended the horses before thinking about ourselves. It was second nature to men who knew those animals made the difference between our lives and death. Bright removed the top on a barrel of grain, and Jeter filled the feed bins with hay, doubling the horses in the stalls, and leaving the rest in the hall half again the width of a wagon running down the middle.

Bright went to the door more than once to look outside, only to come back with a grim look on his face. He wouldn't let Callie help with the saddle and said something the wind took away. She shook her head and drifted over to speak with Amanda, who was standing close to McGinty. I couldn't hear what they were saying, but their heads were together in soft conversation.

There was little talk from the rest of us as our lips and faces thawed there out of the wind. Our breath, as well as that of the horses, fogged the air. Finishing with the steeldust mare, I helped Gil with his saddle. We left the blankets on, but shook them a few times to let their backs air out.

The wind moaned outside, and Bright opened a rough wooden box knocked together with old planks, taking out two coils of rope. "While y'all are finishing up in here, I'll tie one end of this to a snub post out there, and the other to the house. That way no one'll get lost going from the house to the barn. Come on when you're done."

It was an old trick cowboys and ranchers had been using for years.

Since me and Gil were among the first to enter the barn, we finished and followed Bright back out into the wind. He looped one end of the rope around the frozen post and played it out as we crossed the distance to the house.

The door wasn't locked or secured in any way. It opened inward, so it was easy to push it open into the dark interior. All the windows were shuttered.

"I can't see a thing." I felt around for a table.

Bright's voice came from my left. "Over there."

"I'll need more than that."

"To your right."

Holding his hand out, Gil passed me, and I heard a table scuff on the wood floor as he bumped into it. He snapped a lucifer to light with his thumbnail and lit a lamp as Bright pulled the slack from the rope and knotted it to a porch post. While I struck a fire that had already been laid in the fireplace, the others drifted in, one by one, slapping their hats against their legs to knock off the snow and ice.

Bright pointed. "There's a barrel of water out there. I doubt it's had time to freeze solid."

"I got it." One of Bright's cowboys named Timms set his hat and went back outside. There was a flurry of activity as we settled in. As promised, the ranch house was equipped with everything we needed to survive the storm. It was the way of that part of the world, to lay in supplies and leave them available for travelers in need.

I was thankful that the last visitors there before us were good people and that the Comanches hadn't raided and fired the house.

The fireplace smoked for a moment until the air in the chimney warmed from the small flames; then it drew well and the fire caught. I vaguely wondered who'd taken the trouble to haul wood to the house and lay it back for just such an occasion.

Making a mental note to thank the owner of the Panther Creek ranch, Mr. Scott Halpin, for his thoughtfulness, I rose and checked out the house that was made up of the one big room we were in and a pair of adjoining rooms with bunks on the left side of the doorway.

The Ranger named Malachai Holman and Amanda were the last to come inside. Seeing the fire, he took her by the arm and waved a hand.

"You get close and tend that fire, would you?"

She tilted her head in question. "Why me?"

"Because your clothes are thinner than what we're wearing and I figured it'd give you a chance to warm up faster." He shrugged. "You can do whatever you want. I just thought I'd give you a chance to melt some of the ice in your hair."

He was right. Without hats, she and Calpurnia had suffered more than the men even with a couple of our scarves over their heads to preserve the heat and cover their ears. Our clothing was thick, and in the case of McGinty's suit, made of wool. The rest of us had layered up from our saddlebags.

Amanda took off the scarf and gave it a shake. Holding both hands out to the little fire, she rubbed them together. "I like your idea."

We all wanted to huddle in front of the flames, but the fire wouldn't produce heat for some time. Instead of laughing in relief, our mood was subdued with the absence of so many people out there behind us.

Proving his worth, Bright opened a couple of cabinets above a plank counter. Inside were large tin cans and a number of jars filled with food. "We got canned goods in here, some corn, carrots, and potatoes." He held up two lard tins after prying off the top. "And looky here!"

The one he'd opened was something dark

sealed with a layer of grease or lard. "Somebody put up dried meat. With as many as we are, I say we get a pot of stew started over that fire."

McGinty put down his grip and saddlebags in one corner. "Calpurnia, why don't you get that started."

Her eyes flashed. "I don't work for you anymore, McGinty."

"You'll do as I say, woman."

I was done with that little weasel, but Gil beat me to it. He stepped between them, pushing past a couple of the townspeople and stopping so close the brim of his hat bumped the one on McGinty's derby. "You listen to me, feller. You're about to get your ass beat by a one-armed man if you don't shut your mouth."

McGinty's mouth opened and closed. "She's just a woman and she's nothing to you."

Full of fury, Bright came out of nowhere and grabbed McGinty by the shirt front, driving him against the wall. "You're talking to my woman!"

Shocked by the attack, the banker tried to push back as Gil stepped to the side for Bright to have at it. The cowboy who worked hard all his life was more than a match for the soft businessman who stuttered. "You can't—"

"I can blow your head off if you don't stay away from her."

"Don't do that." Gil had a soft grin on his lips. "You shoot this fool and it'll leave a mess on the wall and floor and we're gonna be in here for a while."

I was done with the fighting. "That is *enough!* Bright, turn him loose."

"Make me."

The Ranger chuckled. "That'll be easy, son. We have one boss in this outfit, and it's the deputy here."

Bright's men had scattered, but they paused, looking back and forth between us. I wasn't worried. They were cowboys, hardworking men who blew off steam once in a while when they came into town, but they weren't gunslingers.

They were more likely to wade in with fists and boots, but I didn't expect anything to happen. We were all too tired, too cold, and that little pissing contest was over. Just to be sure, I stepped over against the wall so there wouldn't be anyone behind me.

"Bright. He won't be ordering her around anymore. Until we get back to town, I'm in charge."

"Hey, looky here." Stup's voice cut through the tension. He'd opened a small wooden keg under the small lone table against the wall. "There's two bottles of whiskey squirreled away in here. How about we have a drink while this place warms up?"

McGinty held my look for a long moment before he lowered his gaze. "Fine."

"We can make that popskull last a little longer

if we drink it with a little water." Gil picked up his saddlebags and dug out his cup. "How about a little splash here?"

"Where is that water?" Calpurnia asked. "We can't make stew without it."

"Timms went after it." Bright looked around. "He must be having trouble getting the lid off the barrel out there. Probably froze over."

"I'll check." Gil pulled his hat low and threw a look at McGinty. "I need to cool off anyhow."

He went out, letting in a river of cold air filled with flakes. The door closed behind him and everyone relaxed. The house was quickly heating up with the growing fire and all the people inside. We should have been a small army, but with the loss of so many men, I felt I'd failed somehow.

Jeter came in from the barn. Since his profession was stabling and managing horses, he'd remained behind to tend the last of them. He glanced around at the bustling activity in the house and shivered at the warmth.

"That rope idea's a dilly. Saw that trick up in Wyoming a few years ago." He had an armload of split firewood and dropped it beside the fireplace, pitching one stick into the fire. "I was tickled to see wood stacked in the barn and some outside the house here. Better'n burning buffalo chips. Say, what's Gil doing poking around out there? He's gonna get himself lost if he gets away from the house."

Bright frowned. "He's looking for Timms, who went out for water. He come back to the barn?"

"Haven't seen him. Looking for water where?"

"Barrel outside."

His eyes went flat. He put his hat back on. "I'll go help."

Three people outside in a whiteout looking for one barrel of water was a concern.

CHAPTER 46

The only sound was the wind doing its best to push the station down. Picking drying blood from his beard and mustache, Pletz fed more wood into the fire. Around him was a sea of cooling, stiffening bodies that had long ceased to bleed.

He'd spent the last few minutes collecting what he needed, or wanted, from the bodies of both his men and the Comanches. Layered in the clothing of dead men, he was finally getting warm.

Leaving them to lie where they'd fallen, he squatted in front of the blaze with his back to the open door with no fear of further attack. There were no survivors outside in such a storm, and the only thing left to hurt him was the cold.

One of the three horses left alive snorted and stomped its feet. Missed gunfire had killed or wounded the others, and Pletz had dispatched those with a war ax that he pitched into the fire when he was finished.

He drank the last of the water in the lard can and chuckled to himself, studying the pile of scalps lying nearby, and the treasures and meager possessions of those men who'd ridden with him. Once the storm was past, he was free to leave and start over.

With the deaths of all those Comanches around

him, he wasn't worried about being alone and running into another war party. He would simply drift on to another town, sell the scalps, and find a new line of work.

The fire had enough coals underneath to provide plenty of heat that warmed him from the front. As was life, his back was cold, and he turned for a few minutes to bake that side. Facing the door, he looked out into the darkness and wondered at life.

Here he was, a survivor once again. Food, water, and horses made him a rich man, and he reveled in his success. There was a world of opportunity out there, and Pletz had every intention of taking advantage of whatever came his way. He pulled a piece of something from his beard and dropped it onto the ground, realizing as it fell from his fingertips that the chunk was dried blood that wasn't his.

Turning back around, he gave in to exhaustion and sat there, feeling the warmth on his face. His eyes closed and he dozed.

A burst of heat woke him up, and Pletz blinked at the fresh wood catching in the fireplace. Looking to his left, he saw the Comanche leader, Broken Nose, sitting cross-legged, almost knee to knee beside him.

Pletz marveled at this new development as they shared the life-giving warmth without a word.

What an exciting world.

CHAPTER 47

The ranch house was warm and smelling of woodsmoke, wet clothes, unwashed people, and coal oil fumes from three lamps by the time Gil and Jeter came back inside. There had been a soft hum of discussion and activity until they closed the door and everyone realized there were only two men.

Gil crossed to the table and set a bucket of ice water down. He turned to find all of us waiting. "Timms is out there, dead. We wouldn't'a found him if we'd waited any longer, the way the snow's drifting."

Jeter stopped the first question. "We don't know what killed him. It wasn't Indians; no tracks and there ain't no blood."

"We turned him over and checked." Gil shook ice from his clothes. "He wasn't wounded nowhere that we could find. I thought he'd bled out from a hole he didn't know about. You remember, Cap, when Tate Shepherd was shot by his brother by accident when his pistol went off?" He turned to the others. "They were so surprised that he didn't realize he'd been hit until he'd almost bled to death inside. Never saw anything like it."

The old doctor was beside the fire, warming

his backside. "Could have been anything. The cold might've got to him, or a heart attack." He wrapped a blanket around his shoulders. "One of you boys take me out there and I'll look at him."

Jeter shrugged. "I'll do it. I ain't good and warmed up yet anyhow."

They went outside while Calpurnia poured half of the water into a huge pot hanging on an iron swivel that she swung back over the flames. It was an odd feeling to watch something so common while we were in a fight to survive from more than one direction.

She shook her head. "Everything must have been too much for his heart, poor man."

"What'd he do for a living?" Gil asked.

"He was a shoemaker."

"He didn't have any business out in this. Some people shouldn't take on tasks that're too much for them."

Calpurnia turned to the men and wiggled her fingers in a *gimme* motion. "I know y'all have jerky and maybe a piece of bacon. With what was in the cabinets, and I'm glad we got here before those jars froze and burst, we'll have enough stew for everyone. I saw that one dead horse back in the station too. Someone cut a hunk off his flank, so bring it out, too. Those two jars of meat won't go very far with this crew."

Without a grumble or cross word, they rummaged through saddlebags and possibles bags for whatever they had. Amanda went around collecting what a few held out while one by one the others brought their offerings to Calpurnia. Garry had the chunk of horseflesh and handed it over.

"Me and Larry've been hungry before." The mention of his dead brother's name took some of the life from his own face. "I don't intend to ever be hungry again."

We'd all lost men in the last few hours, but Timms dying so unexpectedly once we were all in a relatively safe place quieted us all and put a damper on our excitement. The survivors around me were a marvel to have lived through the attack back at the station, the long, cold ride that took the others, and the deadly storm that still whistled around the eaves.

Garry took one of the whiskey bottles and poured a little into his cup, then added water. He held it up in a small salute, and I had a mind he was saying goodbye to his brother. I felt that one in my chest. We'd been surrounded by death for so long, but only that one person had lost a family member.

One by one the men took their turns, repeating the process of making a drink and settling back to gather themselves. The two women had other ideas for the water. There were a couple of stiff, filthy rags left behind by the previous occupants of the house, and the ladies used some of the water to rinse the rags out and wash their faces. Calpurnia's original beauty was again visible, but Amanda's soft face was revealed for the first time.

Gil took his turn. "At least we don't have to use hard money for a drink here, like the Occidental."

Several of the others chuckled, though the mood was still somber.

The Ranger and I stood together on the opposite side of the room, watching. Buck, the cowboy who'd been at the stage station when we arrived, joined us. "That don't sound right, a man just dropping dead like that for no reason."

"I've heard stranger things." I watched Gil offer to share his drink with Amanda, who declined with a smile. "Most of us don't have coats, and all he had was that blanket and a couple of shirts, so the cold might've got him. Lots of men die when they lose their body heat. That might've been what happened to them others out there."

The Ranger crossed his arms, watching the men settle in. There were only a couple of chairs and a bunk where we were. There were two small rooms without doors, containing two bunks each, on the left side of the little house. Other than sticking their heads in to look around, everyone stayed in the big room with the fireplace.

He tilted his wet hat back. "I've seen 'em die in the heat too. Just riding along and fell out. Dead an hour later."

I was thinking about all the people in that house that I was responsible for, in my mind. I didn't want the job, but I'd led the posse from town and so many of them were dead or dying out in that storm. Stumbling across the others at the stage stop added to my burden, even though the two outlaws we'd chased were dead and by all rights my job was done.

In my mind, it should have been, with everything handed over to the Ranger. I was a deputy in a small central Texas county, but his commission covered the entire state, and those with enough grit and determination often turned a blind eye to state borders. It was a puzzle that he seemed inclined to let me run things. It made me wonder, because I'd never seen a Texas Ranger who stepped aside for anyone or anything.

Again, he might have the same sense of responsibility as myself, and since I rode in with men who'd volunteered, maybe he decided to stand aside until I failed in some way. I'd talk with him about that later, when we were alone.

On the other hand, Buck, who was over against the wall, was a self-sufficient man. He looked to be the kind of loner who drifted with the wind and took care of his issues with either fists or a gun. I'd known men like that all my life, and respected those who walked the straight and narrow.

Unfortunately, there were way too many men

with that description who crossed the line, and those were the ones who needed to be behind bars, or swinging on a short rope from a tall tree limb.

The door opened again with another river of icy air. Doc and Jeter were back, their shoulders hunkered from the cold. Doc found us with his eyes and came over. "I have nothing else to add. He's dead without a bruise or mark on him. We tidied the body out in the barn, but there's something else y'all need to know."

"What's that?"

"There's already another body out there. There's so many of us in here that we've missed someone."

The Ranger's expression was flat, and I couldn't tell what he was thinking.

The same went for the rest of the men in that house as they pondered the strange death.

CHAPTER 48

It had been dark for several hours when Broken Nose finally moved. Digging into a bag hanging over his shoulder, he took out two pieces of jerky and handed one to Pletz. Without a word, the Comanche tore a piece free with his teeth and chewed.

He had an old blanket over his shoulders that Pletz recognized. It had once belonged to Sandoval, who lay nearby with a crushed skull. That meant the Comanche had been inside the walls for some time before joining him. He could have killed Pletz as he dozed.

Letting the dried meat soften in his cheek, Pletz grunted at the thought. He rose and kicked a broken table to pieces. Returning to the fireplace, he pitched a few pieces onto the coals and sat back down.

"Is this not odd?"

The Comanche looked at him and swept his hand from side to side.

"I do not know what that means, but I think you agree with me."

Broken Nose chewed.

Pletz held his hands toward the flames. "You fought a good fight, and you have more than enough grit to come in here to share this with me."

The warrior only blinked before looking back into the fire.

"Here we are, sitting in front of a pile of hair that your people wore, and you are not doing a thing about it."

Eyes closed, the warrior seemed to be dozing.

Pletz studied his profile, seeing the man's hooked nose and solid jaw. As if to tease him, the Comanche slowly lifted one hand and adjusted something woven into his braid. For the first time since he'd opened his eyes, Pletz saw it was a blackbird hanging behind the man's ear.

He wondered why it was a songbird. Feathers and other fetishes symbolized power. He'd heard of a Comanche who wore a small hawk in his hair, but a blackbird?

Broken Nose's eyes were still closed, and Pletz studied him in the flickering light. The Comanche wore a trade knife at his waist, and a pistol on his right-hand side was stuck through a belt in a cross draw. The man was a leftie.

He also had a rifle lying nearby.

None of that was any concern. Pletz wore several guns and knives, and all he had to do was grab the butt of a pistol in his sash, tilt it, and fire without drawing.

Oddly, right then he had no animosity toward

the man, or any desire to kill him. They were simply two men in a deadly storm, sharing a fire.

He wondered what the Comanche leader was thinking.

CHAPTER 49

"Jeter was the last one in," McGinty accused.

The little stable owner rested his hand on the pistol stuck in his belt. "Banker, you better think real hard about the next thing that comes out of your mouth."

"Don't shoot him yet, Jeter." I held out a hand. "You boys look around. Who's missing?"

One of Bright's cowboys spoke up. "Why, it's Montgomery Abrue. He was right next to me when we got in the barn."

"Who?"

"Abrue. Quiet little clerk in the A. F. Mercantile."

"How'd nobody miss him?"

"Just the way he lived." It was Calpurnia that spoke up. "Nobody ever really saw that little man. He seldom spoke a word, even when I went in with a list of supplies. It's no wonder we missed him."

I shook my head. "How can we overlook a man?"

"How can we lose all them others?" Buck shook his head across the room. "None of this is right."

"You didn't know who was riding with you." McGinty pointed an accusing finger at me. "All you do is set up there in front and issue orders, from what I've seen."

"I'm gonna shoot him now," Gil announced in a matter-of-fact voice. "Y'all get out of the way."

"If you don't, I will." Buck stepped away from where he was leaning on the wall.

"You men settle down." Doc's voice was firm for the first time since we'd joined them. "I'm tired of straightening dead men."

"Hang on." I turned to Doc. "Where was he?"

"Just laying in one of the stalls, up against the outside wall."

"Someone lay him there like that?"

"Can't say. I thought he'd dropped where he was and went to sleep. Wouldn't have bothered the man if it was warm; I'd've let him sleep, but it's too cold for him to be out there so I gave him a shake, but he was gone as Aunt Rodie's old gray goose."

"What killed him?"

"Can't say about that neither. Just dead."

"Maybe there was somebody in that barn when we showed up?" Buck asked. "We went in so fast nobody looked."

"Can't see how," the Ranger said. "We had to force the door, and I didn't see any tracks in the snow. Anyone who was here first would've been in the house beside a fire, instead of an old cold barn."

I looked around and saw that several of the

men had positioned themselves to keep an eye on everyone else. It seemed as if guns were more prominent, and my attention drifted over to the wall where my Spencer and Winchester leaned way out of reach.

"Someone's murdering us!" Shorty, who rode with Bright, said what everyone else was thinking. I hadn't thought much of Shorty since our fight in the street, and it seemed that the cold had taken some of the swelling from his face.

"There's a killer in this room," Doc agreed. "And I'd suggest none of y'all turn your back on anyone until this deputy finds out who it is."

CHAPTER 50

"So why are you sitting here?"

Broken Nose opened his eyes and watched the flames. Recognizing the words as some kind of question, he spoke in Comanche. His words flowed soft and steady, almost musical to Pletz's ears. As he spoke, his hands rose and swept in the hand signs of Plains Indians.

Once he pointed at Pletz, then made a fist and tapped his own chest.

When he finished, he glanced over at the German then back to the fire.

Wishing he hadn't relied so much on Sandoval's interpretive skills and had learned at least a little of their language, Pletz nodded as if he understood. He kind of did, for that one motion with a fist seemed as if Broken Nose either said they were both strong warriors, or brothers.

Copying the other man's movements, he swept his palm flat. "I don't want to do anything but sit here. Killing you would be tiring."

"I do not want to fight. I just wish to sit here."

Stunned that the man spoke English, Pletz breathed through his mouth and wondered how long either of them had to live.

376

CHAPTER 51

A new scent added to what we'd already been smelling. Fear.

I looked over and saw the Ranger with his hand near his gun. Our gaze met for a moment before we turned our attention back to those around us. Eyeballs flicked around the room as Shorty's and Doc's statements soaked in.

"Gentlemen, we don't know how those men died, but y'all need to keep them hands away from your weapons." I hoped they were listening. "We don't need to lose our heads over this. Fear has a way of taking your common sense, so just settle down and enjoy your drinks."

Any other time I wouldn't add fuel to such a fire, but there was only enough whiskey for a drink or two each, and if anything else, the alcohol might just soothe all the frazzled nerves around me.

Doc sniffed, finally realizing there was whiskey. "Y'all have any more of that?"

Amanda held up a small metal cup. She'd washed her face with some of the water and looked completely different in the light. "This one's mine and I saved it for you."

Licking his lips like a kid seeing a peppermint stick, Doc crossed the room. "Bless you, young lady."

The corners of her eyes crinkled as she handed it over. Harvey, one of Bright's riders, changed his expression, and he stuck his nose into his own cup, thinking. I saw that face and wondered what it meant.

Across the room, leaning against the space between the two doors leading into the bunk rooms, Gil watched the proceedings. The pinned-up sleeve on his left arm was to the room, but I saw he'd drawn his pistol and was holding it against his leg, knowing that few people would pay much attention to anything except for his missing arm.

Harvey whispered to his buddy Shorty, who frowned in thought.

The house quieted, and the wind whistled through small holes and cracks in the walls. Two or three of the men stuck whatever came to hand in the spaces to preserve as much heat as possible.

Something was up between those two cowboys, and I wondered what it was. Beside me, the Ranger's eyebrow went up and I realized he was working on the same problem. Finally, Harvey walked over and whispered in Bright's ear.

He frowned and studied Amanda. He twisted his head, bumping hats, and whispered back.

I didn't like secrets, especially in such a situation. "Bright, you want to tell us what you two are whispering about?"

The room went silent. He and Harvey waited

for the other to speak. Harvey cleared his throat. "Well, I'm thinking I know Miss Amanda there."

Not knowing what to say, I waited for her. She seemed not to hear him for a moment, then sighed. Touching her high collar with slender fingers, she appeared to be increasingly uncomfortable. "I'm a schoolteacher. On my way to Dallas to take a job."

The men around us were silent. The tone of her voice wasn't quite right.

Buck grinned. "My teachers were all mean old maids, at least until I quit in the sixth grade."

The tension was broken and we laughed.

Doc sipped his whiskey. "At least y'all were taught by women. My teacher in grade school was a strange young man with a neck like a turkey who had nothing to do with the people and town, and barely tolerated any of us. When I got to medical school, they were all older than me. Miss, I'd've made a doctor when I was ten, if I'd had you at our old schoolhouse."

We all laughed, but Harvey and Shorty weren't through. Harvey tilted his hat back. "No, ma'am. I know you from somewhere else, but things have been so busy, and y'all's faces so dirty from all that soot from the fire, it's taken a good long while to figure it out."

"What does it matter?" McGinty asked from the corner where he'd holed up with his satchel and saddlebags.

"Because it's bothering me."

Shorty backed his friend. "Miss Amanda . . ." His face showed surprise. "Ah!"

She squared her shoulders. "All right!" She licked her lips. "I worked there in Angel Fire for a while at another job."

Calpurnia joined her. "It's no one's business but her own what she's done."

"What she's done is work above the Occidental." McGinty's statement was a shock.

I'd only been in town a few hours, but I knew there was only one job in the small rooms above the Occidental, and it was no secret what they did up there. "It doesn't matter. Let it go."

"It does to me," Bright said. "I recognized her the minute she washed her face. She's McGinty's favorite whore."

CHAPTER 52

Some of the wood Pletz put on the fire was cedar, likely scorched roof poles from a nearby creekbank. It crackled and threw sparks that went up the chimney and out onto the ground near their knees. "So you speak English."

Broken Nose made a hand sign to accompany his words. "I have learned some."

"Enough to understand what I was saying."

"Some. Enough to question prisoners, if we took them."

"You're pretty good at this language."

Broken Nose sighed. He put his fingers against his lips then against his head. "Be quiet. All your talking hurts my ears. I do not want it in my mouth, either. I just want to think about my brothers you have killed."

"And you want to do that beside me." Pletz's voice was full of irony.

"I want to do it beside the fire, alone. You *haaki*."

"What does that mean?"

"You smell like old dead things that should not be walking or talking. It does not matter. You are nothing but a spirit, anyway. Go *haabiikwa*. Lie down and be still until the spirit people come get you."

Not understanding, Pletz frowned. "You are being *philosophisch*."

Broken Nose frowned.

"I cannot think of the word . . . philosophical."

"That is another of your stupid white man words I do not understand. Be quiet. I want to think about when I was a boy and the Comanche was strong and we killed white people like flies."

"I've killed many white people."

Broken Nose cut him a look. "Was there honor in it?"

"There was money in it."

"You people. When all the buffalo and deer and grass and wind is gone along with the land, which will belong to others and not you fleas that swarm in here in my ears on this land, you will learn that you cannot eat money. You will pay for all of us with hunger in all our bellies."

"We all have debts to pay. You know more than you admit."

The Comanche tore off another piece of jerky. "Fill your mouth like this so you will stop talking."

CHAPTER 53

McGinty snorted. "Favorite? I have no favorite."

"Gentlemen." The Ranger pushed away from where he was standing. "That is enough of this kind of talk around women. Miss Calpurnia, is that stew ready yet?"

I picked up the only plate in the house. "Would you fill this for Miss Amanda?"

Calpurnia nodded and used a large wooden spoon to dip. She handed it to the woman who wouldn't raise her eyes. Doc moved and she joined him at the small table.

The tension was broken for the moment, and the others took turns eating. McGinty held back, watching us like a dog run under a porch. When he finally decided to move, his foot bumped the saddlebags nearby.

They didn't move an inch.

I saw that Gil noticed, and his eyes flicked from the floor to McGinty's face, then mine. Buck saw it too, and I addressed the banker. "You sure are protective of that stuff at your feet. You have any more food in there?"

"No. Just my stuff."

The Ranger crossed his arms. "What kind of stuff?"

The banker shrugged. "Personal items. There's

some bank money in the satchel that belongs to the people in town. I need to deposit it in Gainesville."

There sure were a lot of people in that big room looking at one another, and I felt the hair on the back of my neck prickle.

The Ranger stood there with his arms crossed. "McGinty, you and your bank seem to have been the root of all this trouble. I'd feel better if I knew what all you're carrying in them saddlebags and that satchel that's growing to you."

"Nothing that's any concern of y'all's."

"Open it up." Garry's voice cut the air. "All this started because somebody murdered everyone at the stage station and burned it down. Something's going on and I think it all has to do with you and that bank."

McGinty shook his head hard enough for his jowls to quiver. "No, that was Indians did that."

"Nope." The Ranger's eyes flashed. "Something else happened. There wasn't any Indian sign when we rolled up."

The banker swallowed. "Sure it was, and there's nothing going on y'all need to be interested in."

"There's a lot that interests me," I answered. "You'll go a long way by shaking out them bags."

McGinty reached for the pistol stuck under his coat and stopped when the Ranger's .44 was suddenly pointed at his forehead. "Dump 'em out."

After a moment's hesitation, McGinty knelt on one knee and fumbled with the straps holding the bags closed. He paused, then emptied one out. A lump of fused coins dropped onto the floor, along with a number of burned singles that rattled on the packed dirt floor.

A gasp went up at the sight of so much money. McGinty stayed there with his head down, and the Ranger spoke again.

"The other side, and then empty that grip."

McGinty sighed and opened the other bag. Another piece of melted metal dropped out. Without waiting, he flicked open the latches on his satchel and dumped out a pile of wrapped bundles.

The expression on his face changed when he saw that instead of thousands of dollars in currency, there was only cut newspaper. "What? Why, I—" He looked up and around, searching for an explanation.

Doc stepped forward and used the toe of his boot to nudge the metal and bundles. "Well, that ain't gold, and from the look on your face, you weren't expecting newspaper. What do you have to say now, banker?"

Instead of a fortune lying in a pile at the feet of men and women who seldom saw fifty dollars together at one time in their lives, there was nothing but junk.

McGinty stood. "This was supposed to be

money from the bank. It's y'all's money that's missing, that I was supposed to be carrying to the big bank in Gainesville." He spread his hands. "I know this looks bad, but bankers transfer money all the time. Of course I couldn't tell anyone I was moving so much cash, but this was supposed to be routine and now it looks like I've been robbed."

He was right, and I knew it was common for companies and banks to travel cash and gold, but the circumstances didn't ring true and the trash on the floor was a puzzle.

Still beside the bunk rooms, Gil stood there and watched the scene unfold. My attention was drawn from the drama on the floor, to those around me who were exchanging looks of wonder and shock.

The Ranger's face was blank, his lips almost invisible under the big mustache that took up so much real estate on his face. "Where's the money, McGinty, and when'd you gather that metal up?"

"Amanda and I were the last to leave the station. I knew right where it'd be after the wagon burned. It didn't take a couple of minutes to dig down and stuff it in the bags."

"You risked your life for that, that . . . junk metal?"

McGinty nodded like a child trying to please his dad. "I risked it for y'all's money. It's my job to take care of it after it's deposited. Then we hightailed it in your tracks, but I don't know where the real gold is. I promise."

I didn't care about the money, though in a roundabout way it was why me and the posse were there. We hadn't been chasing McGinty, though. It was the now dead outlaws we wanted and here we were, with the man we'd intended to give it back to once we returned.

The whole thing was so twisted that it made my head hurt.

"Wait a minute," Gil said. He'd been over there thinking. "Back in town your businesses only took gold or silver. So you're taking the cash to Gainesville, but shouldn't that hard stuff stay in town for people who need to buy stuff? Makes sense to me that you need to keep coins on hand to exchange."

"It's complicated." McGinty looked for the words. "This is all about a balance of coins and cash. In the banking business, we call it cash flow."

Money and business was never something I was good at, and they were talking about both. "Answer me this. I can see moving the cash, like Gil says, but the money that was supposed to be here belongs to the people back in town."

"It does." McGinty spread his hands. "And they can have it whenever they want . . ."

Calpurnia sighed in exasperation. "Tell them the truth, McGinty!"

Shocked, his mouth fell open. "I am."

"Then I will."

There was a light in her eyes I didn't like.

"You'll do no such of a thing."

"McGinty's been pulling the wool over y'all's eyes from the start." She flung a hand at him as if slapping water in his face. "He's moving cash and gold to his own account in Gainesville. He trades the cash for coins that aren't real. They're counterfeit. Fake. That's what's on the floor right there."

Bright pointed. "All that? It looks real to me."

"Those are the fake coins. People bring in real silver and gold, and cash there too. He trades real cash for counterfeit money, and that's what some of y'all have in your pockets right now. You're essentially giving him your money for something worthless, and he takes it in and deposits it as his own."

"But we're buying products with it from his own businesses."

"The whiskey is rotgut popskull. The food is essentially stolen from the government—"

McGinty started for her, but the Ranger cut him off with a hand to his chest. "Hold, sir. Keep going, Callie."

She swallowed. "Much of it's supposed to go to the army and the reservations for the Indians. Pennies on the dollar. He's been doing this for a long time and everything has been going in his pockets."

I was trying to put it all together and not having much luck.

"This was his last trip." She looked around, her eyes glassy. "Which is why we're all here."

Then it dawned on me. I was in a room full of snakes and innocent people, and there was no way to tell them apart.

CHAPTER 54

Snow fell through the open roof of the stage stop, settling on the two men sitting cross-legged in front of the fire. Beyond the range of the flames, snow whitened everything it touched.

Pletz fed the fire with a hand black with soot and dried blood.

Broken Nose watched without moving. "That is the hand of a warrior."

"It's just my hand."

"You do not have a tongue to tell stories, either. You would be a poor human around our council fires."

"It does what I require."

Pletz picked at a piece of jerky between his teeth with the sharp point of a knife. "So why are we sitting here together after we tried to kill one another today?"

"You are a warrior and we sit here as brothers."

"You're as far from a brother as you can get."

"Does your mouth move without your thoughts? I am hearing words that do not come from your mind or your heart."

"I'm trying to figure this out. You know what I am."

The Comanche's face had no expression. The nearby pile of scalps and the ones already on stretchers were answer enough.

"I know that you are an evil spirit."

"I'm human."

"*Mu buaru.*"

"I don't understand your words. What does that mean?"

"It means stop talking. You are not human, a *paauani* . . . foreigner. My people are the real humans. You are not real. All of you are like *anikuuara*, ants with no souls to be stepped on. My people will rise up and stomp on you with our feet until you are all gone."

Pletz laughed. He pointed beyond the walls. "You know how many blades of grass there are under all this snow?"

"I know."

"The country I come from is filled with as many people as these. There are other countries, as many as all the horses in your world. Each country has people who are as many as all the blades of grass in the prairie outside. You will never stomp us out."

Broken Nose frowned, trying to understand what he'd said. "I can kill *you*. That will be one less."

"You can try."

Both men started when a gruff voice came from the doorway behind them. "Told you we'd find them."

Shocked that someone was out in such a storm, Pletz whirled, reaching for the pistol in his sash, but Broken Nose remained where he was, staring in the glowing coals.

"Schaefer! Booth!"

Nearly frozen and looking like walking corpses, they pushed inside. Schaefer reached a stiff hand toward his weapon at the sight of the Comanche.

"Hold!" Pletz rose to his feet. "He's with me."

"He's an Indian."

"You'll not harm him."

Face white with frostbite, Booth pushed forward and knelt in front of the fire, reaching his hands so close to the flames Pletz thought they'd blister.

"Back up a little." Pletz laid a hand on his shoulder. "Them hands'll hurt bad enough when they start to thaw."

Schaefer brushed past the Comanche and took Pletz's place, dropping into a squat. "I've never seen anything like this storm. Lucky the wind's blowing so hard it swept some of the ground clear and we found the wagon ruts. Hell, I thought we were heading for town and we got turned around and wound up here."

Pletz cut his eyes toward the pair. "Where were you?"

Booth swallowed. "Got separated. Found this one and he was lost too."

"Lost so bad y'all couldn't hear all the shooting?"

"You know how this wind is." Schaefer slapped

Pletz on the shoulder while the Comanche settled back down again as if two more white men hadn't arrived. "And here we are with y'all, nice and cozy."

Pletz studied the coals. "For the want of a nail, a battle was lost."

Booth rubbed his hands together and extended them back toward the fire. "What does that mean?"

"A proverb written by a clergyman nearly three hundred years ago about war and actions that have grave consequences."

Schaefer ran his gaze up and down the stoic Indian. "It being just the two of you here, I'd guess the rest of the boys went under."

Pletz suddenly felt protective toward the silent Comanche. "All *his* people too."

CHAPTER 55

The north wind wailed around the stage containing nearly frozen men and horses.

"Does he do anything but sit there and stare into that damned fire?"

Pletz was so tired he had to translate Schaefer's words into German to understand them. He sighed. "It is the same thing we're doing."

"When you're hunting wolves, you don't crawl into the den with them." Booth's voice was soft, as if speaking low would prevent the Comanche from hearing.

Broken Nose spoke just as low in English. "Have you ever seen a water hole when it has not rained for many moons?"

Shocked that he used their language, Schaefer and Booth almost gasped.

"When the sun lowers, all animals come together to drink. Wolves, birds, buffalo, deer, and even lions. They lower their heads to what gives life and all feel safe at that time. It is the way of the Great Spirit. This fire is our watering hole. This is a sacred place—"

"One you burned down?"

Broken Nose shook his head at Schaefer's question. "No. This was done by white men who we then killed." He shrugged. "We do not know why these people made war on their brothers. But they killed them all, just as we tried to do with you. It was a pleasure to kill them, though."

He pointed. "One died trying to hide under that table. One tried to run, but we caught him outside by the horse pen. The third was fast, but we ran him down and my brothers shot arrows into him way out there." He pointed to the south, away from the road and station. "None of them died like warriors."

Booth cut his eyes at Broken Nose, then at Schaefer. Pletz saw the look in Booth's eyes and drew his knife, which was easier to reach than his revolver. "No."

It was a short swing to bury the blade in the buffalo soldier's chest to the hilt.

The big man fell backward with the gang's leader on top. He yanked the knife free and struck again and again as Booth struggled to hold his arms and prevent another lunge. Gasping and grunting, Pletz stabbed him repeatedly until the big man's body lay still.

Breathing hard, Pletz pushed himself upright to find Schaefer lying on his back, throat cut from ear to ear. Broken Nose was still sitting cross-legged, as if nothing had happened in the past minute, yet his hands were wet with blood and his leggings were streaked where he'd wiped his blade clean.

Cleaning his own knife on the leg of Booth's

wet pants, Pletz slipped it back into the sheath.

Face blank, Broken Nose settled himself under the blanket over his shoulders. "The water hole is sacred to our people and should not be disgraced."

CHAPTER 56

Doc sipped his whiskey and water, surveying the room. "I'm a medical doctor, not a banker, so someone's gonna have to explain all this to me."

"I've been studying on that." The Ranger's arms crossed over his chest, looking as if he was standing there relaxed, but his right hand was only an inch above the handle of his pistol. "I think I have it all figured out."

"I wish you'd explain it to me, then." I still didn't have a good grasp on what was going on, though the spark of an idea was glowing in my brain.

He nodded toward me. "You don't know what happened back in town before y'all got there, but some of us were in that coach when a man tried to knock us all out with some kind of poison. They knew McGinty had gold and cash on the stage and were working with others who killed the folks running the stop."

When I didn't interrupt with questions, he continued.

"I shot them who tried to rob the stage, but I've had a sneaking suspicion ever since then that there were others in on the thievery."

"How'd they find out I was carrying money?" McGinty wanted to know.

"Pillow talk, I'd suspect."

Half a dozen heads turned toward Amanda. That's when it dawned on me. Her face had been particularly dirty and I'd assumed it was from being in the ruins of a fire, but she'd hidden her looks back there and apparently hadn't come up with a reason not to wash up once Callie dipped a rag and cleaned her own face.

Only two men in the room had likely been customers, besides McGinty. They were the Panther Creek cowboys who'd come to town to blow off steam. Now they recognized her without the disguise of dirt and proper clothing.

Buck chewed his bottom lip. "She was in on knocking us out?"

"That's what I think," the Ranger said. "She was working with that drummer and the stage guard."

Stone faced, Amanda stared at the floor.

Everyone paused, considering what they'd heard. The wind outside wailed and moaned, and the fire collapsed in on itself, throwing out a burst of heat and sparks. Calpurnia shook her head and picked up another stick of wood. Adding it to the fire, she kept her back to the rest of us as if not seeing what was going on was safer in some way.

I couldn't stand still. I've always had to move in order to think. Prowling like a caged panther, I found myself in front of the fireplace, then didn't know where else to go. Buck held out his whiskey and I took a grateful sip. Only after I swallowed did I realize it might have been laced with poison just like in the coach.

He must've seen my expression, because he took the cup back and sipped again. "This is the good stuff."

I didn't know which way to turn. "Malachai, your name's Malachai, right?"

The Ranger grinned. "It is."

"In your opinion, Amanda here was set on robbing the stage."

"Was, and likely still is." He pursed his lips, thinking. "And the rest of you boys need to stand where you are while I think this through, because I suspect McGinty and Amanda aren't the only ones left who were in on this."

CHAPTER 57

The night passed slowly at the Moynahan station as the two men sat in peace beside the fire.

Broken Nose finally stirred. He reached for one of the stretched scalps and fed it to the fire. It sizzled as thick white smoke went up the chimney. The nauseating odor of burning hair filled their noses and they watched the skin turn black and curl.

Warm and almost loggy with fatigue, Pletz picked up one that hadn't been stretched and pitched it onto the coals. Again, the stomach-turning stench reached out to envelope the two men before dissipating.

"The white smoke is their spirits going free."

Pletz grunted at Broken Nose's statement. "Do you think that's true?"

"I think that is what you want me to say."

The exhausted German nodded as if those were the sagest words he'd ever heard.

Several minutes passed, and they alternated burning the scalps piled nearby. As if in a trance, Pletz stood and brought bags back to the fire. He dumped the belongings of his men onto the ground, and they took turns burning everything he shook out.

CHAPTER 58

The Ranger seemed not to know where to look, and I watched him. He stayed where he was. "I'll require you all to keep your hands away from your guns."

Garry peered into his drink. "You've already told us that."

"Emphasizing my point."

I kept quiet, letting the man with the big hat handle things.

"So, Amanda . . . what's your name, anyway?"

She licked her lips. "Luciana Giordano."

"That ain't Mexican."

She drew a long-suffering sigh. "It's Italian."

Stup took his hat off and scratched his head. "This is all confusing, but most of the men I've ever run into who've changed their names are running from something."

"I've been running from something all my life." Amanda rubbed her forehead. "Malachai, are you saying I'm a thief? I haven't ever stolen a thing, only done work that most women don't have to do."

"I'm voicing my thoughts, that's all. Trying to figure out what's going on here." The Ranger's eyes rested on Garry. "You lost a brother in all this. You have any thoughts?"

"None that I understand. Just the thought of accusing a woman of thievery is perplexing to me."

"It's happened a time or two." The Ranger still hadn't moved.

I realized that no one else had moved either. It was as if roots had grown from the soles of their boots and into the house's dirt floor. The tension in the room lessened, but it was still thick enough to feel between one's fingertips, like the oil we used to clean our guns.

The Ranger turned to Buck. "What do you think?"

"I think all this is a puzzle." He swallowed, thinking. He inclined his head toward me and Gil. "The only ones who might not be mixed up in all this is your posse."

"What there is left of it," I said.

"Which brings me to my next point." The Ranger jerked a thumb toward the door. "I'm thinking those boys we lost coming over there didn't get separated, and no one in his right mind would think Comanches snuck up in this weather and took 'em."

Calpurnia's voice broke. "We have a killer in here with us. Someone was picking them off as we rode in the storm."

"That is my belief."

I watched the Ranger as he spoke. He knew something none of us did, and I wondered how one learned such things other than from experience. Something was about to happen, and I wanted to be ready.

My shotgun was too far away, but not the Russian .44 I wore. "Gil, you and Stup listening to all this?"

My old friend swallowed. "Kinda hard not to."

"Mr. Ranger, I'm hearing a lot of talking that don't make much sense. So I'm asking you nice, would you get to it?"

The Texas Ranger's middle finger tapped the butt of his pistol, but I was the only one that saw. That action was the mark of a man who made a living with a gun, a nervous tic that might tell what he was going to do next.

He pursed his lips, thinking. "What I think is that Larry and Garry here heard from Amanda, or Luciana, that she wanted someone to help rob the stage."

Garry snatched the revolver from his holster, but the Ranger's gun was out and cocked before he'd even touched his Colt. Garry's face tightened, whether in anger or fear, I couldn't tell.

"Jeter, would you care to relieve that man of his weapon and tie his hands?"

The liveryman took the pistol from Garry's holster and looked around for something to tie him with. "I don't have anything in here. I saw some piggin' strings in the barn."

"Would you go get them?"

No one else noticed that he said "them," but I did, and so did Gil.

Jeter went out without his coat, he was so het up.

The Ranger's Colt didn't move at all, pointed at the man's face, and I saw death in his eyes. Trying to sort it all out, I addressed Malachai. "How'd you know?"

"I didn't. Just throwing rocks to see what would happen."

The others relaxed, and shoulders lowered in relief. However, the Ranger still held the pistol aimed between Garry's eyes. "I'd tie Luciana's hands, but it don't seem right to do that to a woman. But, little missy, you do anything I don't like, I'll lay the barrel of this six-shooter against the side of your head before you can blink, and believe me, that's something I've done before."

CHAPTER 59

Instead of receding, the storm increased in intensity around the Moynahan stage stop.

The enemies, one a German immigrant and the other a Comanche native, continued to share the fire. Pletz finally gave in to the demands of the day; his body weighed heavy, and he lay on his side, feet toward the fire, facing Broken Nose. "We had storms like this back in Germany."

"Is that far away, where you are from?"

"As far as you can walk in a year, if you could get across the great water that seems to have no shore."

The Indian considered the implications of the comment. "I saw a storm like this when I was a child. It lasted so long that wolves came to our lodges, looking for food."

Pletz rose on one elbow. "You talk English better than . . . you understand it."

"I do."

"You were joking me when I thought you didn't know what I was saying."

"We are learning how to fight you, and one way is to speak your language, but I am afraid it is too late. Your kind wash over us like the flash floods down a ravine."

Chuckling down deep in his chest, Pletz rested

his head in the crook of his arm. "You don't speak German, do you?"

"What is that?"

"The language I speak, the one my friend Sandoval used when we were talking out on the plains."

"No. It is an ugly language. You should learn to speak Spanish. It is a better tongue."

"Maybe I will. It'll be easier to communicate once I'm down there."

Despite the danger of being so close to a sworn enemy, Pletz dozed off. When he awoke from the cold, the fire was down to ash coals and the Comanche was gone. Throwing another piece of wood on the fire, Pletz went back to sleep.

CHAPTER 60

"This is a bit awkward and tiresome," Stup said.

Though I was half expecting for him not to return for a number of reasons, Jeter was back and covered with snow. He held up a handful of piggin' strings as if they were a limp bouquet of flowers. "I got 'em."

"Tie Garry's hands." The Ranger's voice seemed tired. "Behind him."

A man familiar with rope and knots, Jeter had him secured in just a few seconds. "What do you want me to do now?"

The Ranger swung the pistol from him to McGinty. "Now him."

The banker looked up in shock. "For what?!"

"For bank robbery."

"I done told you what I was doing!"

"We heard you, but your lips are lying. Mr. Jeter, if you would."

"Be glad to." He walked around behind McGinty, nudging the satchel and saddlebags out of the way with the toe of his boot. Pushing the banker forward to get some room, he tied his hands behind his back.

Bright and his cowboys hadn't said a word, or made a move. They stood as tight as a covey of quail in a snowstorm, not knowing what to do, or who to believe.

The Ranger lowered his weapon. "That takes care of that. Now, that wounded feller, the brother of the one I killed, he was the last of this bunch of robbers."

"He was one of the bank robbers," Jeter pitched in.

"Yes, and it saves me the trouble of taking him in. So now, Mr. Jeter, we have one more to tie up—"

"No you don't!" Buck slapped leather, snatching his pistol in a flash. It all happened so quick I was frozen in shock.

Guns rose.

Two lances of fire split the air, and the man I thought was a solid cowboy fell back, landing against the wall. He fired again, the bullet flying only inches above the floor to bury itself in the outside wall on the opposite side.

My own gun was in my hand, and Gil's was out also. The cowboys around Bright threw up their hands, lest they get mistaken for robbers and thieves, but despite being tied up, Garry lunged forward.

"You sonofabitch!"

The Ranger shot him too. The distance was so short that it was nearly impossible to miss his heart. With his hands behind his back, Garry groaned from the impact and sounded like a thrown calf when his limp body hit the floor.

Lying with his head against the wall, Buck tried to raise his pistol, but the Ranger stepped close in two strides and kicked it out of his hand. "You stupid fool!"

Buck's mouth moved as he tried to speak, but the bullet must have punched through a lung. Blood welled in his mouth, running out both sides, and he lay there, drowning in the red wetness that up until then had kept him alive.

He raised a hand to the Ranger. "He's not . . ." Breath failed him as he tried to point with a crooked finger, and died.

The Ranger glanced over at Garry's body. "Now I'm sure of it."

CHAPTER 61

Gunsmoke hung in the air, and for the life of me I don't know how we all breathed because all the air had sucked out of the room in the aftermath of the shooting.

Calpurnia and the woman I still thought of as Amanda were backed as far away as possible, eyes wide with fear and shock.

Gil walked up beside me. The Colt was still in his hand, pointed at the floor. "What'n hell just happened?"

"Best I can tell, the Ranger there's doing his job."

"That is correct, sir. Buck there was in on the stage robbery from the start. I suspected it all along."

Shaking my head, I holstered my pistol. "Did you have any proof? What made him act like that?"

"Criminals always fear getting caught. Sometimes you have to set a trap, either physically or verbally. That's what I did, letting him think I knew he was in on it." He grinned from under his white mustache, and for the first time I saw how bright his teeth were. "But the truth is, I was only talking and let him have enough rope to hang himself."

Gil shook his head. "But how do you know none of these others are in cahoots with them, or each other?"

He shrugged. "I don't."

CHAPTER 62

Bright's boys shrugged into their outer clothes to drag the bodies outside, saying they were taking them to the barn. I watched them, working out in my mind what I'd seen.

Watching them attend to the aftermath of the shooting, the Ranger shucked out the empty hulls from his revolver. He shoved out fresh shells from his belt loop with the end of a finger and slid them into the cylinder. Sliding the Colt back into its holster, he watched Shorty and Harvey wrestle Buck's limp, muscular corpse up. Bright held the door for them and they carried him outside.

Shorty, the quiet cowboy who rode with the Panther Creek boys, helped Bright carry Garry's body outside. The Ranger watched them leave without expression. "I'll go out with these guys. Would you watch McGinty and Amanda while I'm out there?"

"Sure."

He nodded and went out into the cold.

The house suddenly felt completely empty, though there were still several of us still inside. For the first time since I'd known Gil, we didn't have much to say, each of us deep in thought.

"Calpurnia." McGinty's voice startled me.

Stirring the stew, she turned back toward him. "What?"

"You know I put that money back for the two of us."

Her eyes flicked to the flowery carpet satchel she'd carried in. "I know no such of a thing."

"I did. We can have it. I earned it by building that town."

Amanda laughed. "Don't fall for it, honey. That's the same thing he told me in my room above the Occidental."

Jeter's face reddened in the flickering light from lamps and the fireplace. "I oughta put a gag in your mouth, banker. You've stolen from us in ways none of us know. If it wasn't for you, Angel Fire would be a fine town by now."

"*I've* made it what it is."

"That's not true, and you know it."

Their schoolyard argument was too much. "Jeter, I'd appreciate it if you'd just let him sit there and be quiet. He's gonna talk and twist things around any way he can to get untied, and right now I think the Ranger's done us all a favor."

Calpurnia shrugged. "I never believed a thing McGinty ever said."

"Neither did I!" Amanda said.

They laughed like women doing the wash alone, and I stood there looking at the blood puddled on the floor. Their laughs were hollow, though, and they trailed off into silence.

Callie's colorful grip looked to be about the same size as McGinty's bag, and something stirred in the back of my mind.

CHAPTER 63

"I hope that's all of 'em." Gil walked back to the fire.

Amanda was kneeling there, staring into the flames. Calpurnia went over to one corner of the house and, using a thick-bladed knife, scraped at the hard-packed dirt floor. She scooped up handfuls of dirt and carried them over to the congealing pools of blood. She scattered some on one puddle, and the remainder on the other.

"Can't stand looking at that."

For the first time since I'd laid eyes on McGinty, he was quiet, sitting cross-legged and watching Calpurnia work.

Stup rose from where he was sitting. "Boys, if y'all don't mind, I believe I'm gonna go in there and lay down on one of them bunks. This old man's plumb wore out."

"I'll be doing the same thing before long," I told him.

He went inside the rearmost room and I heard the bunk creak when Stup sat down to take his boots off.

The wind must have gotten its shoulder against the house, because the constant wail around the eaves and corners increased as the house groaned and shook. That gust was so strong both Gil and

I looked up at the pole roof to see if it would stay in place.

Doc circled the room, picking up the cups and containers set down by those outside and poured the contents into his own. He took a sip and smacked his lips, swinging the container toward the door. "That is why I drink. I've seen so much and the only thing that'll quiet the demons is demon rum." He laughed. "I tried opium, as I told the others in the stage, but it wasn't my friend."

He grinned at us and drained the cup before the rest of them returned and raised a ruckus. "*Whiskey* is my friend."

Jeter chuckled. "How long were you in Angel Fire, Doc?"

"Only a day. I'm on my way back east."

"From where?"

"Ah, uh, Den . . . Tombstone."

I watched him recover, wondering just how much whiskey he'd scrounged. Since we hadn't eaten much, it must've gone straight to his head. It was quiet, and the smell of gunsmoke had already dissipated. It almost felt homey, despite our situation.

The guys were taking a long time out there, dealing with the bodies. When I thought I'd have to go look for them, I moved over to the door. Noticing that my Spencer was sliding to the side from where it was propped against the wall and about to fall, I picked it up.

Gil took a seat on a sawn stump brought in to use as a chair. "Would you hand me that rifle? I don't like it being so far away."

I picked it up as well and carried it over to him at the same time the door opened and the Ranger came inside. He slammed it and used an elbow to make sure it stayed closed. "Damn, it's cold out there."

Doc set down his cup. "Did you get 'er done?"

"I did." The Ranger took off his hat and shook off the snow, holding it at waist level.

"Good deal." Doc picked up his bag and opened it up.

Callie watched me cross the room, and her eyes flicked from me to her bag. Tired of all the suspense, I kicked at the bundled newspaper at McGinty's feet. Without thinking about what would happen, I knelt beside Callie's grip and flicked the thumb lock.

She rose with a start. "Hey! That's mine!"

What I found inside was no surprise. Lifting the bag with both hands, I dumped out piles of real currency banded together with bank strips.

Amanda rose from in front of the fire. She went to McGinty's corner and picked up his empty satchel. His eyes flicked up to her, and clarity flashed into my mind.

"No!" I leveled the shotgun at the same time Gil reached for his own Colt.

CHAPTER 64

Doc was the first to pull a little pocket gun from his Gladstone doctor's bag, but the most dangerous snake in the den was the Ranger. His own Colt appeared from behind the hat, cocked in his hand and aimed at me, and I cut him down with the Spencer.

Calpurnia screamed a warning that came way too late.

Smoke and flame billowed in the room as the Ranger pulled the trigger, only an eyeblink behind my shot. The slug hit the Spencer, which flew from my hands. The deformed chunk of lead whizzed away past my right shoulder and struck the wall.

I fell backward in surprise, seeing all eight buckshot pellets catch him in the chest and stomach. Off balance from both the bullet's impact and the sudden gunfight that came out of nowhere, I stumbled back.

Gil shot across me, his bullet missing my chest by the breadth of a hand. I felt the hot wind of it pass and Doc grunted, spinning from the slug's impact. He staggered sideways, but grabbed the table to steady himself.

He was a tough old cuss. The little pistol in Doc's hand rose a second time, but I caught that from the corner of my eye as Amanda whirled with her own revolver taken from McGinty's bag. She extended her arm as far as possible, and the bore of her pistol was huge and dark.

My hand was almost numb from the bullet's impact on the shotgun's magazine, and I grabbed for the Russian pistol. Fingers feeling dead and useless around the butt of the .44, I saw she was the more immediate threat, but she fired too fast, the slug going God knows where.

A streak of bright fire came from the bunk room as Stup shot out the door and behind me. The bullet plucked at Doc's shirt, and he staggered sideways.

The smooth handle of my Colt was finally in my hand, and Jeter shot Amanda the same time as my tingling finger pulled the trigger. His bullet hit the woman and spun her around. My own shot caught her in the back as she turned, the impact knocking her on top of McGinty, who squalled like a terrified baby.

Gil's next shot was right on top of that one, and Doc grabbed his chest and fell back. Stup came rolling out of the bunk room and caught sight of the Ranger on the floor, still trying to raise his pistol. He couldn't shoot, because I was in the way emptying the Russian into Malachai Holman until the impersonator's revolver finally dropped to the ground.

There was so much gunsmoke in the air, I thought something was on fire.

McGinty shoved Amanda's body off and used his heels to push himself into the corner, looking at her and the Ranger in terror.

Doc lay on his side, his back to us. I crept forward and turned the old man over. His eyes were already empty and starting to glaze in death.

Jeter couldn't move from where he stood. "What the hell just happened?"

Instead of answering, I went over to the Ranger, who was somehow still sucking air despite all the holes we'd put in him. I knelt and took the pistol from his hand.

Determined, he reached a bloody hand into the opposite side of his coat, but I caught his wrist. It was like holding a baby's arm, and I used my other hand to reach in and take out a small Smith & Wesson pocket revolver with a yellowed ivory handle.

His head was against the door. I pulled him away so the others could come back in. "What's this all about, Malachai?"

Eyeballs loose in their sockets, he tried to focus on me. "Money, son." His voice came through a liquid gurgle in his throat.

"You're not a Ranger, are you?"

"Naw." Malachai's breath was shallow and the word came out soft, low, and wet.

Stup's voice came over my shoulder. "Doc's dead."

"I am too." Malachai swallowed.

Sweating from nerves and the suddenly warm room, I remembered why they'd been outside. "The others on the stage in on this with you?"

He tried to laugh, the mark of a man tougher than me. "Almost." He wheezed for a moment. "Funny. The drummer. He was . . . alone. Wanted the money for himself." The Ranger's eyes were already looking into hell.

A red rage washed over me, and I almost shot McGinty for what he'd done, and for making me do the things I'd done.

I heard empty hulls drop to the ground as Gil reloaded his pistol.

Jeter knelt beside me. "You killed the others? Those Panther Creek boys out there?"

The Ranger's nod was almost imperceptible.

"Hell ain't hot enough for you, and eternity ain't long enough." Jeter rose and Stup joined him, and they rushed outside.

I watched the light fade from the Ranger's eyes.

CHAPTER 65

The sun rose over an icy, white world.

I opened door and squinted at the brightness. Water was already dripping off the ranch house roof. Settling my coat against the chill, I tightened the scarf around my neck and followed Jeter to the barn.

The horses snorted and shuffled as we forced the door open and light poured into the interior. It was almost warm from the big animals' bodies.

"This is going to be a hard thing," Jeter said.

I intentionally avoided looking at the corpses laid out against the wall. "It'll be harder when we get back to town and tell them we've left bodies strung out between here and there."

"Though no fault of your own."

"They won't see it that way."

In true Texas weather, it was warm enough by the time we reached town that most of the snow was gone, except what was on the north slopes of ravines, or in the shade of brush and the few trees growing along water courses that ran with melt.

Following a wide game trail, we rode back to town without issue. I was in the lead, followed by McGinty with his hands tied behind him. Calpurnia and Gil followed. Her hands weren't tied, but there was no danger of our female bank robber getting away.

Jeter had the worst job. He brought up the rear, leading a string of ponies bearing the bodies of my posse and all those in on robbing McGinty and the stage.

People stopped on the streets of Angel Fire when we arrived, riding single file, leading a string of horses muddy to the hocks and loaded with dead people. A crowd gathered.

Head down, my hat brim kept me from meeting the townspeople's eyes. They pointed and whispered as we passed, following us down the middle of the boggy street. With the exception of Callie, we were the pitiful remains of the posse that took off after the bank robbers.

Two men I recognized as those who turned back met us, their attention on the bodies. One was Phillips and the other I thought of as Thin Mustache, who still wore his Union cavalry jacket.

They stepped forward, as if they were town officials. I gave Phillips a nod. "Good to see y'all made it."

"Two of us did. You were right, it was a hard trip, but y'all didn't do so well neither."

Thin Mustache pointed and started to ask a question, but I held up a hand to stop him. "I'm not going to tell everything that happened. You can ask Jeter while I go in the marshal's office and write it all down. Phillips, I'd like for you to take McGinty down to that jail and put him in with Haynes."

"What's he tied up for?"

"Bank robbery, theft, stealing, counterfeiting—"

"And just generally being an ass." Gil's voice cut me off.

Trying not to grin, I tilted my hat back. "He's under arrest, just like Callie there. Just put him in with Haynes, like I said." I stopped to address Thin Mustache. "I'd appreciate it if you'd have someone escort Callie to her room at the boardinghouse and make sure she stays there until we get a judge here."

He scowled. "It's a boardinghouse. Not a jail. If she's under arrest, she can just leave."

I waved a hand. "Other than here in town, there's nowhere for her to go. I think it'll be all right. Phillips, I'll be along directly to speak with both McGinty and Haynes."

"He ain't there no more."

"Where is he?"

"About six feet under the ground. Buried him not long after y'all left."

"What killed him?"

"J. W. Gipson, most likely."

"I thought he quit."

"He did, but he kept checking on him. Went in right after y'all left and saw Haynes laying on his bunk like he was asleep."

"Starve to death, or freeze?"

"Neither. Town doctor says it was natural causes."

I thought of Doc hanging over a horse back there. "Would you go get the undertaker for me? I have work for him."

Phillips nodded. "There ain't enough bodies hanging over those horses. Where are the rest of our people that rode out with you?"

"That dead man in black back there and a couple of them others killed them somewhere between the stage stop and an old abandoned ranch. That's where we holed up in the storm, but him and the others murdered your friends and those Panther Creek boys under cover of the storm. Some of 'em are scattered between that ranch and the Moynahan station that's burned out."

Shaking his head, Phillips led McGinty's horse down the street. Thin Mustache left to go find the undertaker.

Gil looked up at Callie. "I'll carry you down to your room at the boardinghouse."

She shrugged. "I don't care what you do, other than hang McGinty."

"Nobody's gonna be hung until they get a trial," I said.

A voice came from the crowd gathered around us. "Who says? I have a rope and there's a hoist over there in front of the livery that'll work just fine to get his feet off the ground."

"I say so."

"And just who are you?"

I almost grinned. "The man with a badge, for one thing. For right now, I represent the law, and you'll do as I say until there's a new marshal."

I swung down and tied the steeldust mare to the hitching post.

That's when I saw Pletz riding down the middle of the street all by himself.

CHAPTER 66

The scalphunter looked even filthier than the last time I saw him, if that was possible. I reached for the Spencer shotgun and remembered it was broken from one of the Ranger's last gunshots.

Sliding the Henry from its scabbard, I pushed past the crowd that parted like I was on fire. Pletz saw me and reined up in the middle of the street. "Hold it!"

Gil's voice came from behind me. "Right here, Cap."

"I don't want no truck with you!" Pletz called. "I just need food and I'll go."

"You'll step down and be under arrest."

"I will not." He turned his horse so that it was between us and dismounted, acting as if he were loosening the girth. "I've done no wrong in this town."

Holding the Henry ready to fire, I stopped and waited. "You broke the law when you stole that whiskey before we left town."

"I paid for it with hair!"

"The barkeep said they don't take hard cash, nor hair. I have to do my duty. You'll ride with me to stand trial in Fredericksburg where there's a judge. It'll be him or the jury to assign guilt or innocence on that charge."

He fiddled with something on the off side of the horse that I couldn't see. "Leave me be. I'll beat that. You have nothing else to bother me with."

"I do, for murder!"

"I've killed no one."

"You joined the Comanches. Murdered white people in the process. You'll stand before a judge for that as well."

An audible gasp came from behind and around me.

"That's what *you* say." Pletz talked to me over his saddle.

I was getting tired of arguing in the middle of the cold street. "Show yourself!"

"The Comanche slaughtered my men. I am the lone survivor and intend to go about my business when I leave town."

"You'll do none of that."

"You have no authority here!"

"I do. Give yourself up! Come out from behind that horse." I saw only his hat and legs as he remained behind the animal. "Come out now, or suffer the consequences."

A rifle appeared over the saddle and the muzzle swung at me. "Leave me be!"

"No!"

Something startled the horse. Maybe it was my shout, or he spooked it in some way, but it jumped, throwing off Pletz's shot, which whizzed past overhead. Voices shouted in alarm behind me.

Dropping to one knee in the churned mud, I aimed carefully at one of his legs and squeezed the trigger. The man's shin folded from the impact of the .44 and he went down hard, losing the reins. The horse crow-hopped and took off in my direction, running with its head to the side so it wouldn't step on the reins.

Lying on his side, Pletz levered another round into his rifle and twisted around to fire again. The slug whizzed down the street, and I levered another shell into the Henry's magazine and aimed again.

"Stop this!"

He worked his lever again and I squeezed off another shot, as if finishing a wounded deer lying on the ground. The round took him in the chest and his shirt puffed from the impact. He grunted and folded in the middle, curling like a screwworm in hot ashes, still trying to draw a bead on me.

Tired, frustrated, and madder'n hell that I was in such a position, I shot him again and he stilled.

I jacked another shell in the chamber and a hand fell on my shoulder. Gil's soft voice came through the red fog that blinded me. "Cap. He's dead. It's over."

A shriek came from behind, and I turned to see Jeter and Stup kneeling beside Calpurnia's still body. Pletz's shot missed me but found flesh, and Callie was dead with a hole in her heart.

I rose, numb.

Gil took the rifle from my hands as people gathered around her limp body. "There's nothing we can do for her. Let this town take care of its own." He slid the rifle into its scabbard on the mare, beside Callie's carpetbag full of the town's money.

I stood there, suddenly exhausted and wanting nothing more than to sit down somewhere and have a drink. Gil collected the steeldust mare's reins along with those of his buckskin and pulled me off the street.

I followed like a dog on a rope. "Where are we going?"

"Down to the Occidental. Your report can wait, and everyone here has a job to do. Let's go get that drink and then we can get on with life."

I looked around at the fresh blood on the ground, Callie's body now covered by someone's coat, and a line of corpses hanging over the backs of horses. Stup took charge, ordering everyday people to help clean up the mess we'd left on the street.

Jeter watched us walk away, and raised a hand to wave as I allowed my old friend to lead me away from all the death in the streets of Angel Fire and into the dim interior of the only saloon in town.

Center Point Large Print
600 Brooks Road / PO Box 1
Thorndike, ME 04986-0001 USA

(207) 568-3717

US & Canada:
1 800 929-9108
www.centerpointlargeprint.com